★

Four sets of eyes stayed glued to the balloon, which had lost more than twenty-five hundred feet in altitude by now. Sam divided his attention between the radio and the road, while I watched all of them.

"Why's she coming down so fast?" asked Justin, hunched beside me in the bed of the racing pickup. "That doesn't look normal. She usually waits till we get right below her."

It didn't look normal to me either; the balloon's shape was now elongated into a long, inverted teardrop. It still held air, but there was something decidedly strange about Rachael's maneuver.

Justin and I held on for dear life, unable to keep the balloon in sight because of the wind in our faces. I caught one glimpse of her just above the treetops, still at least a mile away. What the hell was going on? I chafed at the fact that I was stuck here in the back, not knowing what was happening. Had the killer managed to get to Rachael after all? Had he engineered some malfunction in her fuel system or burners? Where was she now? The balloon had completely disappeared behind the trees and buildings.

★

connie shelton

BALLOONS
can be
MURDER

W🌐RLDWIDE®

TORONTO • NEW YORK • LONDON
AMSTERDAM • PARIS • SYDNEY • HAMBURG
STOCKHOLM • ATHENS • TOKYO • MILAN
MADRID • WARSAW • BUDAPEST • AUCKLAND

For Dan, always

BALLOONS CAN BE MURDER

A Worldwide Mystery/October 2006

First published by Big Earth Publishing.

ISBN-13: 978-0-373-26580-0
ISBN-10:   0-373-26580-8

Printed in U.S.A.

Acknowledgments

My thanks and appreciation go, as always, to Dan for your help and encouragement and for being my first reader. Special thanks also to Derek Lawrence and Susan Hill Newton at Intrigue Press. Your suggestions really improved the book and your encouragement helped me finish it. There are a ton of people who were involved in the ballooning community in Albuquerque during the 1970s and 80s, without whom I would have never had the experiences of flying and of setting a world record. It was a unique time in my life. Carol Rymer Davis, you were a big inspiration to me.

Acknowledgment

ONE

RACHAEL FAIRFIELD FILLED a doorway with quiet authority. At least that's the attitude I picked up as I glanced up from my position behind the reception desk, where I'd been going over expense reports with our part-time receptionist, Sally Bertrand.

The visitor's slender build and sleek hairstyle stood out against a brilliant blue October sky in the open portal, as Sally and I stared. Something about the firm set of her shoulders, maybe, or the grip on her leather handbag. Perhaps it was the tailored business suit that surely hadn't come off the rack.

"Is Ron Parker in?" she inquired in a clear voice, one I could equally imagine making closing arguments to a jury or briefing a roomful of pilots before their mission over enemy territory.

In a quick overview, I judged her to be about my age, early thirties, a professional of some sort, accustomed to her own authority. Her highlighted blond style was the every-hair-in-place type; vivid blue eyes and shapely lips brightened a thin face that might have otherwise been gaunt.

Sally glanced at her appointment book, buzzed Ron on the intercom to inform him that his nine thirty had arrived, and nudged me discreetly in the thigh as her eyes shot toward the conference room.

I took the hint and ushered Ms. Fairfield toward the room

that had once served as a dining room in our old Victorian. Above, I could hear Ron's chair roll across the hardwood floor in his office, followed by his footsteps on the stairs. He never remembered to step to one side on the fourth step from the bottom, so it was easy to know that he would enter the conference room three seconds later. He did.

"Ron? Rachael Fairfield," our client said.

"Ron Parker." He shook her hand and tilted his head toward me. "My sister and partner, Charlie."

He waved her toward the chairs that surrounded the rectangular mahogany table and she chose one facing the double doors. Ron took the head of the table and I sat opposite Rachael.

"From what you told me on the phone, I think we're going to want Charlie in on this," Ron said. "Do you mind?"

She gave a small shrug of agreement.

"Rachael has received some threats," Ron explained, "something the police won't handle. Did you bring the notes?" he asked Rachael.

Out came a large plastic bag from her purse. Inside, two generic white envelopes lay at angles. She slid the packet across the table toward Ron. He glanced up at her before touching it. She tilted her head in consent and he picked up the bag.

"As I mentioned over the phone," she said, "I contacted the police as soon as I got the first one. To their credit, they sent someone out who asked some questions and took the letter to their lab to run fingerprint tests on it. Nothing showed up."

Ron removed one letter from its blank white envelope and smoothed it out. Generic white bond paper, the kind everyone who owns a computer uses by the ream. Cut-out magazine letters trailed across the page. Five words. YOU WILL NEVER MAKE IT.

"That was the first one. Two weeks ago. The other one came last Friday."

I picked up the page and turned it over a couple of times, noticing a few dabs of extra glue on the front.

Ron pulled a similar note from the second envelope. Its message was more sinister. YOU'LL DIE BEFORE YOU SUCCEED.

"You said you'd told the police about a suspect," Ron said.

"Yes. They basically brushed it off, I think. They made a few phone calls and said it came to nothing."

"Who's the suspect?" I asked.

Rachael shifted in her seat, and a flicker of something— uncertainty, insecurity?—flashed across her face. She tucked it away, though, and re-arranged her features. "I think they're from my father," she said quietly.

I must have sputtered because she glanced sharply at me. Ron picked up on my surprise as well.

"That first one—it's the exact phrase he used to use on me as a kid," she continued. "Those are his words."

"But—" I stopped short as I watched a child's vulnerability waver across her face.

She quickly covered it and went on. "I sent him to prison when I was fourteen. And he's out now."

TWO

THE ANNOUNCEMENT HUNG in the air for a very long minute. Ron was the first to recover.

"And the police didn't find this information pertinent?" he asked.

"They called the state prison and verified that he'd been released, then they said they'd located him in Clovis. He claimed he hadn't been in Albuquerque for the past two weeks."

I felt my blood pressure rise at the ridiculous assumption. "So, therefore, that's the truth," I said.

"As far as they're concerned," Rachael said. "They said I could get a restraining order." She rolled her eyes at the absurdity of trusting such a useless document. "They'd be happy to talk to me again if he actually does something, beyond shoving pieces of paper under my front gate, that is."

"What can we do for you?" Ron asked.

"As you know, I'm going to be in the public eye for the next couple of weeks. I was hoping you could protect me, be extra sets of eyes and ears to keep me safe."

"We're not really equipped to provide bodyguards," Ron said. "There's really only Charlie and me here."

"Can someone bring me up to speed here?" I asked. "What's the *public eye* stuff? Are you running for office?"

"Sorry. I thought you knew," she said. "I'm going for a hot air balloon world altitude record." She gave a little self-deprecating grin.

"Really." I felt my interest spark.

"The final weekend of Balloon Fiesta. I've applied for official FAI sanction for the women's world altitude record for an AX-7 balloon."

Some of that was Greek to me and she noticed.

"Fédération Aéronautique Internationale. It's the sanctioning body for aviation records, not the Guinness Book as most people think. The AX-7 part just refers to the size category of my balloon, *Lady Liberty*."

"Ah."

"The part about being in the public eye is really my brother's idea. He's launched a big publicity campaign around the record attempt." Her mouth gave a sideways twitch. "I could be just as happy to go out somewhere on an empty mesa and simply set my record."

I felt myself warming to her.

"We can't possibly hope to catch someone who's trying to harm you in a crowd of fifty thousand or more," Ron said again.

"I know it's not terribly practical," she said. "It would take the Secret Service to watch a crowd that size. I'm hoping you can watch him, my father, and keep him from getting to me."

I could see my brother wrestling with the idea. It sounded simple enough. Find one guy and dog his every move until he tried something, catch him with the evidence, and have the police haul him back to jail. And the money would be good. We hadn't exactly been crawling with cases the past couple of weeks, and this one could really help the bottom line.

"Let's get some background information," he said.

I found a yellow pad in the credenza drawer and tossed it toward him. He got Rachael's address, her father's last known whereabouts, and contact information for the brother who also lived in town.

"Grayson Fairfield is your brother?" he said. He glanced at me but I failed to pick up the meaning.

"My father was a banker in Clovis, twenty-some years ago," Rachael offered. "I don't know whether anyone who knows him would still be there." She also gave Ron the address of her childhood home. "It's sad, you know. At one time he had serious intentions of going into politics, maybe state-wide. Too bad he blew it."

I started to ask, but Ron seemed in a hurry.

"We'll get on it right away," he told her. "I can drive to Clovis this afternoon and see what I can learn there. Tell me again, when does the Fiesta start?"

"Saturday morning."

"Okay. We've got two and a half days. I should be able to get some leads on him before then."

Rachael wrote out a retainer check and passed it to Ron. "Oh, there's a pilot party on Friday night. I've got a spare ticket, if Charlie would like to go with me."

I reached for the heavy paper invitation. "Sure, I'd like that." I glanced at Ron and saw that he was nodding in agreement.

"Good idea," he said. "We should stick close to you until we get a feel for this whole thing."

After Rachael left, Ron dashed up to his office to tie up a few loose ends, then to go home and pack a small bag for a night or two in a motel at the far edge of the state. I called home to learn that Drake was also packing.

His helicopter service had grown in the past year, keeping him busy nearly all the time now, and this was another Forest Service job somewhere in the northern part of the state. If I wanted the chance to kiss my husband goodbye, I needed to get home right away. I left Sally to close up, called to Rusty our red-brown Lab who also helps hold down the office, and headed out back to my Jeep.

I FOUND DRAKE IN the garage, tossing gear into a pile near the door. He flashed me that smile that always melts my insides.

"What's up?" I asked.

"Cimarron Forest District called. They want to do a few preliminary game counts up in the Sangre de Cristos and keep an eye on the hunters." He set his flight helmet on top of the pile. "I could use your help if you can come along."

I felt my insides tense up. It had been over a year since the engine failure over the North Sea, but I still wasn't entirely comfortable at the stick.

He caught the resistance in my expression. "Hon, you've got—"

"I know, I know," I interrupted, knowing he'd launch into the you've-got-to-get-back-on-the-horse speech. I'd heard it. "I've tried but I'm just…"

"Fine." He turned back to the toolbox where he was sorting through wrenches.

My mouth opened but nothing came out. How could I convey the array of feelings? I'd been back at the controls several times. Being up in the air didn't bother me, sitting in the pilot's seat with Drake beside me felt fine. It was that idea of being alone, the only one in control of a million dollar piece of equipment. Whether it was over an ocean of water or a sea of trees, I didn't want the full responsibility.

"Hon, I—"

"Can you check to be sure the base station is on and ready?" he said.

"Um, sure." I escaped to the small bedroom he used as a home office, and checked the radio controls to be sure I'd hear his calls. Everything looked fine.

I caught myself staring at the wall calendar without seeing it, my mind an unfocused blur of images and memories.

Finally, I shook myself out of this state and wandered toward the kitchen. Pulling a couple of canned Cokes from the fridge, I packed Drake a little cooler full of snacks to take with him.

The connecting door to the garage opened and closed, and I worked up a cheerful expression before he walked into the kitchen.

He spotted the cooler. "Thanks for the provisions," he said. He picked it up. "So, what're you going to do while I'm gone?"

"We got a new case at the office this afternoon," I told him. I filled him in with the details, making it sound like I was really needed there or else I'd be going with him instead.

He set the cooler back on the table. "Sweetheart, please be careful," he said, lifting my chin, brushing my hair back and tucking it behind my ear.

"I will. You too."

The air still didn't feel right, but we'd vowed never to part on bad terms. We both knew that every flight could be the last. One day, one of us might not come home—it had almost been me, last September. We could not, would not, take the chance of leaving the other with a lifetime of regret.

I leaned into him and wrapped my arms around his middle. My throat tightened, but that was another thing I'd vowed, never to leave him with a last impression of me with tears. Keep it happy, Charlie. I sniffed and swallowed and relaxed my facial muscles as we pulled apart.

"How long will the job be?" I asked.

"Probably four or five days. Hard to say, though. The Cimarron guys are working on finding budget money for a few other projects, but it's not certain yet. I'll keep you posted." He picked up the cooler again. "Well, better get going."

By the time he got out to the airport, performed his preflight, and loaded the gear from home, he'd be pushing darkness as he flew into the northern mountains and landed at the remote ranger station. I refused to let myself think about it.

Rusty and I walked to Drake's pickup truck with him and we kissed through the open window. His normal ebullience as he left for a new job seemed subdued this time. The unresolved problem hung between us like a gauze curtain and we both knew it would have to come to a head soon. I squeezed his hand then waved to his rearview mirror as he pulled out of the driveway.

"Come on, kid," I said to Rusty as we turned back toward the house. "It's gonna be a long afternoon."

With Ron on the road to Clovis and Drake in flight, I'd need to be on hand for news as they each reported in. I spent the next two hours cleaning the house until every tabletop gleamed and the kitchen floor shone.

By the time I heard the squawk of Drake's incoming call, I'd begun to berate myself for not being more aggressive about flying, for not going along on the job with him. We spoke only briefly, just long enough for me to know that he'd made it safely and to get the name of the motel he planned to stay in. His tone had returned to normal and I relaxed.

I made a sandwich and settled onto the living room sofa with a movie on TV. Rusty watched me eat, his head following each time my hand went from the plate to my mouth. I finally flipped him the last of the bread crust and set the plate aside. By ten o'clock, when I still hadn't heard from Ron, I drifted toward the bedroom where I showered in my sparkling clean bathroom before crawling between my clean sheets. I fell into a sleep that consisted of sleepless bouts interspersed with restless dreams of hovering in flight over a roiling ocean.

THREE

I FOUND MYSELF ALREADY at my desk by seven thirty the next morning, keying payables into the computer and wondering how things were going in Clovis. By the time Sally arrived at nine, I'd finished the bills and taken care of a couple of letters that needed to be written.

"So, what's with the face?" she asked. She stood in the doorway of my upstairs office, coffee mug in hand, her shaggy blond hair more tousled than usual, her freckled cheeks showing high color.

"Shows, huh?" I hadn't bothered with makeup this morning, which surely didn't help. "I've got to resolve this... I don't know what it is, this feeling I have about the helicopter. It's making for some tension at home."

"Ah." She nodded and offered to refresh my coffee. Nice thing about Sally as a friend, as well as an employee, she made a good sounding board and didn't make many judgments.

She'd just set the steaming mug on my desk when the phone rang. She picked up my handset rather than running downstairs.

"Ron," she reported, handing me the receiver.

"So, what's up?" I asked.

"Well, I don't have William Fairfield in hand yet," he said. "He was here. Probably during the time Rachael's letters came, although I haven't found any positive proof of that yet. Talked to the new manager at the bank where Mr. Fairfield used to work. The woman's too young to have worked there twenty years ago, and she'd never heard of him. Said there's an older woman teller who might remember him, but it's her day off, so I either need to call her at home or wait until tomorrow. We'll see what works."

"So, not much luck, huh?"

"After I left the bank I went to the old neighborhood and quick-canvassed some neighbors. One was home and she knew the family. Lucky for me Mrs. Pinkley is the gossip of the whole neighborhood. The minute I mentioned Fairfield's name she said something about lightning striking twice and invited me in for coffee."

I fiddled with the phone cord while he cleared his throat and settled in to tell the story.

"I just let her go on. Through three cups of coffee. She started out with, 'Isn't it odd that I should ask about William Fairfield, he'd just been there last week. Hadn't seen him in years, yada, yada.'"

"Well, we knew about that," I said. "Was he in Clovis on the day the letter arrived under Rachael's front gate?"

"Probably. Like I said, no proof, but this lady's pretty sure he came around last Thursday."

"Uh-huh. And?"

"Remember how Rachael said something about how she sent her father to prison? I meant to question that but never got back to it."

"Yeah. Me too."

"She literally did. This neighbor told me that the Fairfield family was a mess. Father a well respected banker, had put his hat in the ring for the mayoral election. Apparently well to do, I mean this is still a real nice neighborhood here. But the couple wasn't close, and the mother took to the rounds of charity balls and society luncheons, and worked herself into a pretty good alcohol problem. William—Pinkley calls him Bill—wasn't going to let that slow down his campaign and they got into some pretty good verbal battles over it."

"And he harmed his wife?"

"Hold on, I'm getting to it. Linda Fairfield went off to some dry-out clinic out of state for awhile and seemed better when she came back. The trouble came when *the little girl,* meaning Rachael, reported that he was molesting her."

The line went quiet until I was able to take a breath again. "What?!"

"Exactly. Our friend Rachael apparently called the shots back then, too. At the age of thirteen she decided she'd had enough and called the cops. Well, you can imagine the stink that caused in a town this size. I just spent the last hour listening to what a scandal there was, how Bill's political aspirations went straight into the toilet, and how he was fired from the bank almost before the police car pulled away from his house with him neatly cuffed in the backseat."

"Whoa. So, what happened to Rachael and her brother?"

"*The boy* was already away at college. He must be about ten years older than Rachael. *The little girl* stayed home with her mother, whose drinking kicked right back into gear, about ten-fold. Must have been pretty bad."

"I'll say. Wow, what she must have gone through."

"Yeah. I got the whole blow-by-blow of the trial, in which Rachael was *the* witness. Guess she swung the jury with her combination of youth, innocence, and steadfast insistence on her story."

"So you think her idea that her father is now out of prison and out to get her is probably correct?"

"Someone wrecks your career, your political aspirations, your marriage, and your life, it's a pretty strong motivator don't you think?"

"What about the mother? Is she still in town?"

"Died. The neighbor didn't know many details about that, amazingly enough."

That seemed odd. My mind sorted and resorted the story. What a mess. What an ordeal for a kid.

"Look," he said, "I'm gonna try a quick check of the motels in town, see if I can find out for sure whether William was in town when that letter came."

"Even if he was, couldn't he have gotten someone else to slip an envelope under Rachael's gate? It'd give him the perfect alibi."

"Yeah, and we'll probably go on that theory next. For now, I'd like to know if he's still in Clovis. His parole officer has an Albuquerque address of record, so that's probably where we'll end up finding him."

But not without a lot of work. Not if he didn't want to be found.

"Maybe I'll give Rachael a call," I suggested. "See if she can help fill in any other details that might be pertinent."

"Good idea. Find reasons to stick close to her if you can. Until we know where William Fairfield is, I'm not going to assume she's safe. Meanwhile, I've just pulled into a gas station where I'm going to use the facilities before I bust. Then I'll track down the other bank teller and start checking the motels. I'll give a call when I head back that way."

We hung up and I brought up Rachael's customer record that I'd just set up on the computer an hour ago. Got her phone number and dialed it. She'd listed her home and office at the same west side address, saying her law clientele consisted of wealthy people for whom she drew up wills and trusts. She worked from home and kept appointments at their homes or offices. Luckily, I caught her and we decided to meet for lunch at eleven thirty.

In the meantime I tried some of the really obvious ways to find a person. Called Information for a new listing for William or Bill Fairfield —there was none); checked with his parole officer, a harried-sounding woman who said she had no phone number for him either. I knew Ron had already gotten an address so there was no point in bothering the lady for that. Without his Social Security number—I wasn't even sure he'd still have one after twenty years in prison —could they revoke it?)—I couldn't get a whole lot further into employment records or possible credit transactions.

I informed Rusty that he'd be staying in and lunching with Sally as I pulled on my jacket and headed downstairs. Rachael had suggested a lunch spot on the west side and I figured I better give myself thirty minutes to get there. As it turned out I was right on time.

Today she'd dressed casually, although no less elegantly. If jeans can be custom made to precisely fit, hers were. They hugged her slender hips without one spot that looked too loose or too tight. Her purple sweater was surely cashmere, and black leather boots added just the right touch. She stepped out of a Porsche convertible about two minutes after I'd pulled my Jeep to a halt.

She greeted me with a generous smile, much less reserved than yesterday. "I'm so glad you called. It's great to get out of the office for awhile. What a gorgeous day!"

I had to agree with that. We were enjoying a spell of that crisp October weather where the mornings are nippy and you can peel down to a T-shirt by afternoon. A few of the trees had turned, but most were still in the stage of brilliant green that precedes yellow, then gold, and finally rust.

"I take it that there've been no more notes," I said.

A tiny line creased her forehead but went away immediately. "So far, so good," she said. "Has Ron found him?"

"Not yet." We walked inside where a cutie with purple hair told us it would be about five minutes for a table.

"He's getting lots of information, though." To say the least.

Our table came up and we followed purple-hair to a back corner. The conversation didn't go beyond the usual chit-chat until after we'd been properly greeted by our server, Sean, who recited a list of specials that went by so fast I didn't get half of them. Once we'd ordered, received iced teas, and could be reasonably sure of peace for a few minutes, we got to the nitty gritty.

"Ron met the woman who lives next door to your old house," I told her.

"And no doubt got an earful if it was Mrs. Pinkley. Did she invite him in for coffee and bend his ear for a minimum of an hour?"

I chuckled. "Apparently so."

"She's a gossip at heart, but usually gets her facts straight. So now you know about the trial and why he went to prison."

I nodded.

"And undoubtedly she gave the version where my poor, long-suffering mother finally drank herself into oblivion and I abandoned her to my own selfish teenage doings while my loyal brother stayed by her side and watched her decline and eventual death. And you probably also got the part about how my brother blamed me because 'why couldn't I have just kept my mouth shut.'"

Sean came back then, arms laden with salads—Chinese chicken for me and southwestern ranch for Rachael. He set them down and fussed a full minute over whether we needed anything else and to be sure and let him know and on and on until I was about ready to choke him. When he finally left, I picked through the whirl in my mind.

"I don't actually know what all she said to Ron," I said.

"He didn't get that far into it with me. Only as far as your testifying at the trial." I took a generous bite of chicken and lettuce. "You must have been pretty young when your mother died."

"I was thirteen. I remember reading lots of fashion magazines and experimenting with makeup and hairstyles and being pretty full of myself. I don't know why. I didn't have many friends and certainly no boyfriends. The months around the time of Mom's death kind of blurred together with Dad's trial and my being questioned by a bunch of lawyers. I was sent to live with my Aunt Carolyn in Albuquerque, who kept me pretty well sheltered from the whole mess back in Clovis."

"Do you still stay in touch with her?"

"She died about five years ago. Alcohol. I didn't put this all together at the time, but now I can look back and remember that she used to buy cheap wine in big jugs, a new one every week or so. Mom was a little more upscale about it. She kept crystal decanters of brandy on a sideboard and discreetly refilled them so no one figured out how quickly the magic elixir disappeared."

She reached for a breadstick from the basket in the middle of the table. "I was young but I wasn't stupid. I'd watched Mom quietly drinking for years and I knew the pace picked up once she figured out what my dad was doing to me. Aunt Carolyn tried to protect me but I overheard conversations. I knew Mom went to some clinic, someplace where she was supposed to quit drinking. And then all at once she was dead. Aunt Carolyn came into my room one morning to tell me. That one scene is vivid. I wasn't really awake yet, kind of fuzzy and snuggled deep into the covers. Aunt Carolyn had big, thick quilts and I loved to burrow into them. She came into the room and opened the curtains. It was bright outside and I squinted my eyes shut. She said, 'Honey, your mother's died.' And I just kept my eyes squeezed shut tight, like it wouldn't really be true if I didn't look at her. She patted my arm and sat beside me on the bed for awhile. Then she just tucked the quilts around me and left me alone. A few days later we went to the funeral and I remember looking all around for my dad, but he wasn't there. Thinking back now, he must have been in jail but I didn't figure that out then. People whispered about it, saying Mom had killed herself. At the time I took the comments literally and thought maybe I was the reason. Looking back now, I guess they could have meant that she simply drank herself to death. I don't know. I just kept my mouth shut and went back to live with Aunt Carolyn until I was old enough to leave for college."

The fact that the Fairfield's nosy neighbor hadn't remembered the details of this nagged at me, but I wasn't sure how to formulate a question to Rachael about that. I'd nearly finished my salad while she talked so I ripped up a breadstick while she worked on hers.

"So now, as they say, you know 'the rest of the story.'" She stabbed her fork into the pile of lettuce on her platter and came up with a wad that was far too large to stick into her mouth. She scooted most of it off and tried again, more gently.

I let a moment pass while I went for the last of my crispy chicken pieces and mandarin orange slices. Rachael chewed furiously for the first few bites, then slowed down.

"At some point you went back to Clovis and testified at your father's trial."

"Months later, I guess it was. Like I said, I don't have a very good sense of the time line. I probably should have kept a diary and poured my heart out. I could have used it to write a bestselling tell-all later on. Since I'm still being harassed about it." She laid her fork down with a clatter. "Sorry," she said. "Parts of this still rankle."

"Well I guess so. I can't blame you." I took a long sip of tea to let the conversation settle. "I don't really need the grizzly details unless you want to talk about them, you know. Only as far as any of this might have to do with these threatening notes."

"It's okay. Probably time I let some of it out, rather than keeping everything inside like I have for more than twenty years now." She paused as Sean went through another round of asking about our welfare. She waited until he walked away before she spoke.

"My brother and I have only started speaking again in about the last three years," she said. "He truly did believe that if I'd only kept quiet about the…uh…touching and stuff, that my father would now be the governor of the state, my mother as first lady would have been so happy she'd have quit drinking, and we'd all be having Thanksgiving dinners together." She rolled her eyes. "It's only now that he's got a teenage daughter of his own—and don't even get me started on that one," she raised a palm in a stop motion, "that he realizes what a horrible thing that was for a man to do to his daughter."

I couldn't think of anything to say to that, but she kept talking.

"Grayson—you'll meet him soon, I'm sure—is all about image. Maybe banking does that to you. Or, more likely, politics. Both of them, he and my father, want the limelight. But only in a positive way. I'm sure Gray was horrified when, his final year of college, the family made the papers so negatively." She shrugged. "I don't know how much of it got reported in Albuquerque. People here probably didn't even know about it. But Clovis—well it's such a small town. There's this certain mentality in places like that. I'm not at all surprised that Mrs. Pinkley could still remember every detail of those years. It made that big an impression."

"She told Ron that she'd seen your father just a few days ago. She must have recognized him right away."

"I wouldn't be surprised." She stopped to push her half eaten salad plate aside. "So, did she establish an alibi for him?"

"Nothing firm," I told her. "Ron's checking other sources, too. Your father may have only gone out there for a day or two. Do you know if he has a car? Does he have any resources for money, job, any of that?"

"I have no idea. He may have a few friends who stuck by him all these years. And Gray would probably help him out. Even though he's begun to believe me, he won't ever abandon Dad. He'd get him a car, maybe even try to find him a job. I don't know. I don't even know how long he's been out of prison. Could be he's already settled in."

"Why do you think he'd send you the notes now? Wouldn't time have taken away a lot of his resentment?"

"You don't know my father. Haven't you ever known anyone who just doesn't let things go? Somebody who can hold a grudge, a hateful emotion, for years?"

I had to reach for it but a name did come to mind. Brad North, who'd been my fiancé in college up to the day he eloped with my best friend. I'd ended up better off for the whole thing, but poor Stacy would never hear the end of Brad's obsessions. The man just couldn't let go. I nodded to Rachael.

"There are people like that," she said. "There's a client's son, in fact, a guy who will never get over being cut out of his mother's will. Thinks I somehow talked her into changing it against him."

This time the waiter's appearance gave me just the break I needed to put a coherent thought together.

"Is this client angry enough to threaten you? To send these notes?" I asked.

"Ryan?" She shook her head in rejection of the idea but slowly looked up at me. "Oh, no, surely not."

"But he's really angry. Really, really angry."

"Well, yes, but…"

"I just think it would be a good idea to do a little checking. We'll see what Ron finds out in Clovis, run down the leads about your father, yes. But we might also want to learn a little more about this Ryan. Is that his first name, or last?"

"First. Ryan Tamsin. I'm sure I have an address for him at home in my files."

Whether she realized it or not, Rachael was grabbing for other suspects. She truly didn't want this to be her father. And I couldn't blame her.

FOUR

RACHAEL GLANCED AT her watch. "Oh, gosh, I've got an appointment in fifteen minutes. I'm going to have to scramble."

We split the check and headed out toward our cars.

"Look, some of my crew guys are coming over this afternoon to get the balloon ready for the weekend. If you're free around five…"

"Sure." I certainly didn't have anyone to make dinner for tonight.

"Since you'll probably be spending some time around all of us these next few days, you might as well get to know everyone." She handed me a card with her address.

I watched her climb back into the Porsche and back out in a tight arc. She sent a quick manicured wave to me as I got into my vehicle. Interesting woman.

Back at the office I wished Ron were here. I'd love to have some more background on Ryan Tamsin, but I didn't have access to all his special databases. My contribution to the partnership had originally been with my accounting degree, handling financial matters for the firm. Ron was supposed to be the private investigator here, and I'd really never intended this much client contact. Somehow, over the years, things had changed. Having Drake in my life now, learning to fly and helping him run his business, had taken me even further from any actual investigations—sometimes.

I pulled in behind the downtown Victorian that houses our

offices and entered through the kitchen. Up front, I could hear
Sally's voice, speaking on the phone. Rusty greeted me as if
I'd been gone a month. He took great care to sniff every inch
of my shoes and jeans, probably knowing exactly where I'd
been and what I'd eaten for lunch.

"Enough already," I told him, pushing my way through the
swinging door and heading up the narrow hall toward the reception area.

"Ah, you're back," Sally said. She was in the process of
gathering her purse and jacket. Her desktop was clear except
for a few sheets of paper neatly stuck into her IN tray. "I was
just about to put the machine on and inform Rusty he had to
man the doors." She reached out and scratched his left ear,
which he loves.

"Yeah, I'll probably just putter around here for the next few
hours. Did Ron call?"

"Um-hmm. He's staying over in Clovis one more night.
Says it's pretty slow going, making the rounds of the motels."
Her voice rose in a question at the end.

She slipped her jacket on and handed me a stack of mail.
"Okay, I'm off to the daycare." A grimace at that. Sally and
Ross had agreed, when their daughter was born, that they'd
work their schedules so one of them could always be home
with her, no daycare. But recently Ross's work hours had increased to the point where they had to rely on outside care a
few hours each day. Sally didn't like it, but she'd stayed loyal
to us, too, and willingly put in her time here. A couple of times
I'd nearly offered to let her bring the kid with her, but when
the reality of having a three-year-old in the office hit, I knew
it was a bad plan and I'd kept my mouth shut.

She breezed out the back door while Rusty and I went upstairs where the afternoon sun cast long bars of light across
the hardwood floor in my office. By the time I'd sorted the

mail and taken care of a few calls and bills, I was startled to see that the bars of sun had turned into dim slits, obscured by the still-leafy trees in the front yard. Time to get going. I made the rounds, locking, switching on night lamps, turning off equipment.

Rush-hour traffic was in full clog as we headed west on Interstate 40, the low afternoon sun in the eyes adding an extra degree to the misery index. Rusty was thrilled to be going somewhere other than home, I could tell, even though he didn't realize he probably wouldn't be allowed to run free at someone else's house. I followed Rachael's quick directions and found her place on a quiet cul-de-sac a few blocks off Coors Road.

Although the few houses on the street revealed only small glimpses, I could tell this was one of those choice neighborhoods where the homes backed directly on the drop-off to the Rio Grande. Typically, they sat up high and offered unobstructed views of the whole city and the rugged Sandias. Late afternoons, like now, the sun turned the face of the mountains a glorious peachy mauve that could take your breath away. The distraction held my attention for a good five minutes before I realized a group of people was wondering who'd just pulled up.

"Wait here," I told Rusty, buzzing a couple of windows down for him.

I spotted Rachael just inside the garage door, talking to a tall, well-built man in a dark denim shirt. She smiled up at him in a soft way I'd not seen on her before. Her Porsche occupied one half of the double garage.

A champagne-colored crew cab pickup truck stood in the driveway, tailgate to the open door. Three husky, college-aged guys milled about, gathering ropes into coils, carrying boxes back and forth.

"Charlie!" Rachael called out. "Glad you came." She walked toward me and the other heads turned. "Come meet the crew."

She ushered me to the back of the truck and waved an arm toward the guys. "Ronnie, Justin, Danny—my oh-so-wonderful crew. This is Charlie."

They all grinned and shuffled. I registered brown hair, reddish blond hair, and black hair as my only means of keeping their identities straight at this point as I said hi to each of them in turn.

"And this is Sam Millson," Rachael said, "my crew chief and very special man in my life."

Sam seemed even taller up close. I judged him to be a few inches over six feet, with wavy blond hair that touched his denim collar. The squint wrinkles around the eyes added character and told me he was probably six or seven years older than Rachael. He shook my hand with a firm grip and had a way of slightly bowing while maintaining eye contact. "Ma'am," he said.

"Oh, please, just Charlie." I felt a slight flush work its way up my neck.

"Good enough." He did the little bow-thing again and turned his attention back to the guys, barking instructions about which order to put the boxes into the truck.

"And this," said Rachael, "is Mystic Oracle."

I followed her eyes and noticed the fluffy gray cat wrapping itself around her legs.

"Weird name, I know. Left over from my final college days. Now she's just Misty." She picked up the cat and they shared a moment of nose-rubbing. "Pets are great, aren't they? This girl's stuck with me through all kinds of stuff."

Cat person, dog person. I guess we're all suckers for those furry creatures that find their way into our lives. I glanced over at Rusty, whose panting was fogging the windows in the Jeep quite nicely.

"Let me put Misty in the house," Rachael said. "She's underfoot out here anyway. Then you can let him out if you want." She headed into the garage.

Deciding to save the distraction of the dog for a few more minutes, I walked over to the truck. To one side sat the wicker gondola for the balloon system, like a giant berry basket with handles eight feet high. Inside were two hefty fuel cylinders, which lay horizontally across each end of the rectangular space. Suede trim over generous padding rimmed the upper edges of the basket and a small panel of instruments fit neatly along one side.

"Nice system, isn't it?" Sam stood beside me, glancing around the interior of the basket, making sure everything was in order.

"Looks good to me. I've not spent much time around these things myself."

"You're not crazy enough to take off after some fool world record, are you?"

I wasn't sure whether he really wanted an answer to that question or was just letting me know his opinion of Rachael's endeavor. He turned away and rounded up the three young guys, directing them to pick up a huge canvas bag, about four feet in diameter and three feet high, obviously heavy. They each gripped a handle in the strapping that ran around its perimeter and hefted it to a spot in the garage.

Rachael came out with a six-pack in a cardboard carrier. Each of the guys took one of the cold bottles and she held the carton out to me. I'm not much of a beer drinker but I took one anyway, as did she.

"Oh, I brought you this address," she said, digging into her jeans pocket and coming up with a slip of paper. "Ryan Tamsin."

I glanced at it, thought I knew the neighborhood, and thanked her.

"I'll check him out tomorrow," I said. "Have you thought of anything else about him that might be helpful to us? Or anyone else who might have a grudge?"

"Not really." She took a long swig from her beer. "Well, the last man in my life didn't end the relationship on very good terms." She looked over toward Sam but he was engrossed in the banter of the male group.

"Name? Address? Circumstances?" I asked.

"Chuck Bukovsky. Charles, actually." She rolled the cold bottle between her palms. "I'm not sure where he lives now. When we were together we had an apartment up on Montgomery. He may have stayed there, I don't know."

"And the reason things ended badly? Sorry, maybe that's none of my business."

"No, it's fine. You're trying to protect me." Another long swallow from her beer. "Chuck got abusive, that's all. I took about three episodes of it, then I moved out."

I started to ask whether the abuse was verbal, physical, or what, but Sam walked over just then.

"Hey, babe," he said, "what time shall I tell the guys to be here Saturday morning?"

Her brain switched gears. "Better plan on four o'clock. I don't know what kind of traffic we'll run into."

He nodded agreement and turned back to the group. Rachael's eyes followed him fondly.

"He seems a little—" I searched for the right word "—negative about the whole idea of the world record."

"He's okay with it," she said. "Well, I guess you're right. Sam's a cautious guy, not a risk-taker. He gets the same way when I go climbing. Last summer, Pike's Peak, he called that a damn fool thing, too."

She shrugged and put her empty bottle back into the carrier. Noticing mine wasn't empty, she walked over to the group of men and handed off the carton to Justin. I really didn't want mine, so I strolled over and pretended to take a couple more gulps and set the half-full bottle in with the others.

"I gotta get going," I said. "I'll work on those names and see what we find."

Rachael walked partway down the drive with me, reminding me about the pilot's party tomorrow night. We decided to take our own cars and meet there. On the way home I got a sudden craving for chicken enchiladas. Exiting at Rio Grande, I pulled into the tiny parking area at Pedro's restaurant where only one other car sat in the lot. Rusty recognized the place and let out a little whimper.

"Yeah, you silly dog, you can go."

By the time I'd turned off the ignition and opened the back door, he'd worked up to full-fledged bouncing body language. He raced ahead while I grabbed my purse, waiting with one front paw slightly raised and his eyes pinned to the heavy wooden door.

"Geez," I muttered. "Little eager, are we?"

Truthfully, the ride back across the river had put me so much in the mood for Pedro's fabulous green chile chicken enchiladas that I was about ready to drool, too. This was *so* going to beat the can of tomato soup I probably would have opened at home.

Our usual table was empty and Rusty knew the drill. He could come inside as long as he went straight to that corner and didn't draw attention. Pedro met me there with one of his terrific margaritas in one hand, a basket of chips and salsa in the other.

"Your usual?" he asked, his dark eyes sparkling.

"Of course." I grinned at him and raised my glass in a one-way toast.

"You enjoy," he said. "I'll be making the enchiladas right away."

"Where's Concho tonight?"

"Her sister, she came down with some kind of flu." He raised his shoulders in a what-can-you-do gesture and headed to the kitchen at the back.

I chose the saltiest section on the rim of the glass and took a long drink of the cool green liquid. Rusty waited patiently with his ears cocked so I tossed him one of the chips and helped myself to one. Within minutes, Pedro reappeared with a plate so hot he held it with potholders. Steam rose from the pile of cheese and chile.

"Careful, very hot," he said. As if that weren't pretty obvious. "So, no Mr. Ron and no sweetheart tonight?"

"Drake's on a job in Cimarron, Ron's checking something in Clovis. So, tonight you just get Rusty and me."

He patted my shoulder and said something in Spanish along the lines of it being sad to be alone. I had to agree with that, but suddenly felt ravenous so I dug into the enchiladas instead. By the time I walked out I felt overstuffed and faintly queasy. Stupid to overdo it, I told myself. I drove home in misery and decided to take Rusty for a walk around the neighborhood, work off some of that food before I tried to settle in for the night.

The cool air definitely helped, and I arrived home just in time to hear the phone ring once and quit. The answering machine clicked on and Drake's voice came through. I dashed to pick up the receiver.

"Hey," I said.

"Hi, hon. I thought I'd missed you." His voice sounded strained.

"Long day?"

He filled me in on the job and extended hellos from the Forest Service guys I'd worked with on other occasions. I got the feeling he was making a point: I put the investigation business ahead of our own helicopter business. He cut the call shorter than usual and I went to bed uneasy.

By morning, things weren't any better. Something I'd eaten last night didn't settle well. I had this curious feeling that it still might come back up, while also feeling empty, like I wanted a big breakfast. Probably the beer followed by the margarita and the huge plate of spicy food. The tension over the helicopter job was not a good thing either.

I sat up on the edge of the bed with my head in my hands. Rusty raised his head and looked at me to see if he should bother getting up. His face was smashed on one side and I started to laugh. Suddenly, I knew what was about to happen. I dashed for the bathroom and vomited hugely.

"Oh, god," I moaned. "I do not need this, not today."

I washed my face and dragged myself back to bed. The clock told me it was nearly nine in the morning. Where had the time gone? I must have slept nearly twelve hours. I picked up the phone and Sally answered on the first ring.

"I must have picked up some flu bug," I told her. My voice came out okay, not as strong as usual but not bad. I couldn't imagine food from Pedro's spotless kitchen being tainted. "I think I better stay in bed awhile."

She agreed and assured me she could hold down the fort.

I hung up and started to lie down again, but the nausea came back. Propping myself upright on a couple of pillows seemed to work better. Within a half hour I felt better, so I grabbed some clean clothes and took a quick shower. With cleanliness came the desire for food but I thought I better take it easy. Rusty followed me to the kitchen while I toasted two slices of plain bread and brewed a cup of tea.

By ten thirty everything had settled pretty well and I felt useless just hanging around home. Maybe I'd gotten the condensed version of the twenty-four hour bug and managed to be rid of it in twelve. Fine with me; I do not make a good patient.

I pulled out the phone book and looked up both Ryan Tamsin and Chuck Bukovsky. Tamsin's address agreed with the one Rachael had given me. I knew the general area near what is nervously referred to as "the war zone." That was enough to make me think I better wait until Ron came back to town before looking for Tamsin.

Charles F. Bukovsky was listed in a middle-class neighborhood near the shopping centers. In both cases, I thought it would be a good idea to get more background before just showing up at the door. For now, I could put in some time at the office and wait for Ron to check in.

Sally looked up from her stack of paperwork, surprised to see me when I walked in.

"Better already?" she asked. She looked at me like she wanted to be sure I wasn't here to hand out germs she could take home to her kid.

"Guess so. I feel fine now. Maybe it was the food." I switched subjects. "Has Ron called in?"

"About an hour ago. He's on the road. Should get here around two." She shuffled a few pink message slips. "And Grayson Fairfield called. Set an appointment for three."

Interesting. I wondered what Rachael's brother wanted.

FIVE

I FOUND OUT SOON ENOUGH. Ron actually got in closer to two thirty, and Grayson Fairfield showed up ten minutes earlier than his appointed time. Sally buzzed Ron's office just as he was sorting through the stack of mail and messages that awaited him. He suggested that I greet Grayson and get him settled. He'd be down after he'd made one call.

If I'd thought Rachael was a take-charge person, Grayson appeared even more so. He must have come directly from his office. His thousand-dollar pinstripe suit fit his slender frame perfectly and blended with his thick, dark hair going gray. He stood in our conference room, surveying the furnishings and paintings as if he were appraising them for Sotheby's. Rachael had told me he was in banking, and I could imagine the intimidation factor as people walked into his office to ask for money. Seeing him made me wonder what his father was like.

"Mr. Fairfield?" I extended my hand. "Charlie Parker." I waved him toward the chairs at the conference table and he chose the same one Rachael had on Wednesday.

"Ron will be down in a minute. Can we get you any coffee or tea?"

He declined with a small shake of the head.

"I spoke with Rachael yesterday," I told him. "She's fairly convinced that your father is behind these threatening notes."

"She probably also told you that I'm not backing her in that assumption." His voice held a quality of patronizing gloss, despite the argumentative words. "Our father holds no animosity toward my sister, he never has."

"He's had a lot of years to stew over it."

"Ms. Parker, take my word for it. My father didn't do this." He pointed his index finger at the tabletop, punctuating the terse sentences with little jabs.

My teeth began to gnaw at a spot on the inside of my cheek and I had to force myself to quit before this pompous jerk really got to me.

"What can we do for you then? We've already explained to Rachael that we're not a large enough firm to provide adequate bodyguard services." I met his steady gaze. "And she is the one paying us."

For the first time his intent look wavered. I saw the politician in him take over, deciding to placate rather than boss me.

"I'm every bit as concerned for my sister as anyone," he said. "It just seems like we're spending resources on a dead-end trail."

"Rachael's pretty shaken by all this," I said. "Yesterday over lunch she told me that your mother killed herself after your father went to prison."

"Rachael was a child. She didn't know the half of it."

Probably true. "Still, it must have been traumatic."

Ron came into the room and I caught a flicker of anxiety on his face. He covered quickly, though, and with a quick nod toward our guest, took a seat.

"As I was telling Ms. Parker," Grayson said to Ron, "our father can't possibly be the one who sent Rachael the notes. I truly believe that we should be spending the time on developing other leads."

Ron shifted in his seat, obviously feeling the difference in authority conveyed by Fairfield's perfect business suit versus his own plaid shirt and jeans. He took a deep breath, placed both hands flat on the tabletop and considered his next words.

"Actually, we can't rule out your father as a suspect," he told Grayson, without losing eye contact. "No one's shown me yet that he really was in Clovis last week. Part of the week, yes, but not the day we're worried about."

Grayson leaned forward. "I can appreciate that, but it proves nothing. He could have been right here in Albuquerque, a block from Rachael's house. But unless he was *at* her house, he's innocent."

"Guys, look," I interrupted. "We can spar about this all day, but it isn't changing anything." They both sent irritated looks my way. "We should continue to follow leads on your father, *and* we should see if any other suspects come along. I've already come up with two alternatives."

This announcement, at least, broke the tension between them.

"Over lunch yesterday, Rachael came up with some names. I don't know how valid they'll be, but we should at least check them out." I took a deep breath. "One is Rachael's ex-boyfriend, Charles Bukovsky. She left him because he was abusive. The other is a client, Ryan Tamsin. He's gotten pretty nasty with Rachael, a dispute over his mother's will. Both have made threats against her, verbal, yes, but threats all the same."

Grayson leaned back in his chair, some of the aggressiveness receding. "I've met Bukovsky. Never liked the guy. But Rachael broke up with him more than a year ago. He must be on to other things by now."

"You would think so," I told him. "But it's amazing how some guys can hold a grudge, how often they think a woman can't make it without them. Think about the wording on the note—'You will never make it.' Chuck would think Rachael couldn't succeed without him."

"And Tamsin?" Ron asked.

"I'll admit the wording in the note doesn't seem to fit him as well, but I still think it's worth talking to him."

"Okay," said Ron, "we'll do it."

"We'll question these two and see what we find out," I said to Grayson. "But you have to know that the reason we've been looking at your father in the first place is because Rachael says the wording in the note is exactly the same thing he used to say to her as a kid. Coupled with the fact that he's recently out of prison and she sent him there…. It's pretty strong reasoning."

He looked like he wanted to launch into another argument but something held him back. "All right," he said. "Make these other inquiries. Particularly, check into this Bukovsky. I never did trust him."

He rose from his chair and shot his cuffs, heading for the door. I followed, watching his progress as he strode down the sidewalk to a dark blue Suburban parked at the curb. After he drove away I caught up with Ron on the stairs.

"You seemed pretty quiet in there," I said.

He motioned me into his office and closed the door. "Fairfield. I recognized the name, but don't know why I didn't connect it. I've gotta be careful with him."

"Huh? What did I miss here?"

"He's got the power to change my future."

"What?" This all sounded a little too dramatic, coming from my nearly-redneck brother.

"Fairfield manages the bank that's handling my new home loan. I can't afford to antagonize him."

Ah. The pieces began to fit. After Ron's divorce, over five years ago, his credit was shot. Bernadette ran up huge bills and left him stuck with them. She got the house and the kids, while he got a tacky little apartment with paper-thin walls and visitation with his three boys every other weekend.

"You know how much this means to me," he said. "I found this house and it's perfect for the boys. If I can get established, maybe the court won't see me as such a loser and I can get more time with them."

And the secret lay in finding a banker who wouldn't look too far out in his history or hold Bernadette's lavish spending against him. He'd worked hard for this chance and I now understood his nervousness.

"So, you don't think Fairfield recognized you just now?" I asked.

"I've never met him face to face before today. So far, I've only sat at the loan officer's desk and talked to her. But I've seen him walking around the bank. That perfect posture and the collection of pinstripe suits—it's him. The loan officer told me they'd review my application and the manager would have approval over it."

"So, we have to treat this guy very well." I grinned at him.

"Don't take it lightly. Please, Charlie. Don't piss the guy off. I need this."

"Okay. I'll do the best I can." I stopped with my hand on the doorknob. "What if we can't stop the threats, though? What if someone out there really wishes Rachael harm and follows through on the threats? Surely Grayson Fairfield can't hold us personally responsible, can he?"

"I've already been turned down by two other banks," he said miserably. "I'm not willing to risk it."

Oh boy, I thought as I went back to my own office.

SIX

I DUG INTO MY PURSE and found the scrap of paper on which I'd written the addresses I'd found for Tamsin and Bukovsky and carried it back across the hall. Ron sat in his chair, a faraway look on his face.

"Can you put your database magic to work on these?" I asked. "Maybe we can find something in either of their backgrounds that will help us. If nothing else, once we know whether the addresses are current we can pay each of them a visit."

He brightened at having something concrete to work on and started up his computer. I headed for the kitchen where I found Sally cutting a slice out of a cake she'd brought earlier in the week. Suddenly I felt ravenous so I helped myself to a hunk of it and made a cup of tea.

"Did you see that?" Sally asked, jutting her chin out toward a newspaper that lay on the table.

I hadn't and I spread the front page open. Nothing caught my attention.

"Go to the other sections," she said, "probably on B-1 or C-1."

A quarter page of the second section jumped out at me with a photo of a patriotically patterned red, white, and blue hot air balloon. The caption read Local woman to pilot *Lady Liberty* to world altitude record. The article went on to tell how Rachael Fairfield would be flying her balloon each day in the

Albuquerque International Balloon Fiesta and would be attempting the women's world altitude from the balloon field on the final Sunday of the event. Phrases like "with the eyes of the world watching" and "expected record attendance" sent a sinking feeling to the pit of my stomach. How were we supposed to protect someone from a stalker when she intended to make herself the center of attention in front of nearly a million people?

"Dammit, get Rachael on the phone for me," I told Sally. "No, never mind. I'll do it myself."

I stomped out of the kitchen and up the stairs, the cake and tea abandoned on the countertop.

"Rachael, what the hell is going on?" I demanded the moment she picked up the phone. "Why on *earth* would you think it was a good idea to talk about this record attempt to the newspapers?"

"Charlie? What—wait a minute. What are you talking about?"

"Have you seen this morning's *Journal?* How are we supposed to keep you safe when the entire city now knows exactly where you'll be and what you'll be doing for the next ten days?"

"No—" I heard her take a deep breath. "No, I haven't. I don't know what you're talking about."

"Did you send them a press release about your record attempt?"

"Gray probably did." Resignation lay heavy in her voice. "He wants this thing to be a big deal."

"What is the man thinking?" I ranted.

"I know, I know." She sighed. "I'm sure he sent the release out a long time ago. He wouldn't have done it once we knew about the threat."

I forced my voice down a notch, both in volume and in

tone. "I just don't get it. He was in here awhile ago, making it clear that your safety is our responsibility now, that he expects us to find this, this stalker. He informs us that it simply couldn't be your father sending the threat, he has no clue who did send it, and we're just supposed to make it all better. Meanwhile, he's doing everything he can to put you in the limelight, right out there in the public eye at the biggest event in Albuquerque. Do you see why I'm maybe just a little… peeved?"

Ron stood in my doorway, obviously having heard the commotion, looking at me with "What's up" written all over his face. I tossed him the newspaper section as I listened to Rachael. His face began to darken, as I'm sure mine had, as he read the piece. I held my hand out to prevent him from snatching away the phone and laying into Rachael as she continued with excuses for the article.

"Rachael, please." I was surprised to hear that my voice was nearly normal again. "Please just tell your brother that we can't work this way. He's more likely to listen to you, so I'm making this your assignment. You tell him that there are to be no more stories in the paper. Especially during Fiesta week. It's going to be hard enough to keep the reporters away after this one, but let's not invite them with more little tidbits."

"Okay," she finally said. I couldn't tell if it was resignation or relief in her voice. She'd already told me that she'd be perfectly happy to perform this record attempt quietly. I suspected any hesitation came more from the idea of having to confront her brother.

"Today," I said.

"Yes, right now. I'll call him at his office." She paused a second. "You're right about this whole thing. It's not about me and my record, as far as Gray's concerned. It's about his wanting to be mayor."

"Excuse me?"

"He didn't tell you? Well, no, I guess that's still a few months off. He's planning to declare his candidacy for mayor in next year's election."

"And this relates—how?"

"I think he's looking for any positive publicity with the Fairfield name attached. It's got him worried that Dad's prison time will come out. Every dirty little family secret usually does in an election, doesn't it? So, he's intent on keeping Dad's name hidden and making the most of any positive claims to the family name."

"Do you think that's the main reason he's insisting that your father isn't the threat?"

"Quite possibly so. Probably so, I'd say."

That put a slightly different light on things. I pondered this as I hung up. I quickly filled Ron in on Rachael's version of things and his jaw lost some of the tightness that had been building since he looked at the newspaper.

"Ugh," he said, "sometimes people just make me want to scream."

"Yeah, ditto to that." I reached out and automatically took the notepaper Ron held out to me. It was the scrap I'd given him earlier with addresses and phone numbers for our other suspects.

"These check out," he said. "Both current. I think we oughta pay each guy a visit."

"And you're handing them to me because…"

"Because I've received special dispensation from the queen to have the boys for an extra night. She's actually letting them spend the night in my apartment." This was rare, I knew. "I'm taking them to a movie tonight and out to the balloon field in the morning. The real reason I get them tonight is probably because she can't be awakened from her beauty sleep at five in the morning to get them dressed, but I'll take whatever I can get." He nodded toward the note in my hand. "So, I'd like for you to do the interviews. Please?"

"Can't do it tonight. Remember, Rachael gave me that ticket to the pilot's party? It starts in a little over an hour and I've gotta take Rusty home and change clothes first. Tomorrow afternoon is probably the best I can offer."

"Okay. Look, some background on Chuck Bukovsky. He's currently living with someone new, a Nora Garcia. My source at APD says she's placed at least two 911 calls from that address, domestic disturbance. The usual drill, the cops get there and things have settled down and she doesn't want to press charges. Her eye's a little puffy on one of the calls, but no one's bleeding and no one's dead so there isn't much they can do." He shuffled as if he didn't want to say the rest of it. "So, just be careful. The guy's got a rough streak."

He headed back to his own office where I heard him switching off his computer and making noises to leave. I thought about his warning and wished I didn't have to see Bukovsky tomorrow. I knew, in theory, abusers usually only acted out toward their partners but still, I'd keep my distance.

Sally had apparently left sometime during my call to Rachael, so I rechecked doors and windows and made the office ready for the night. Rusty followed my every move, his nails softly clicking on the hardwood floors, his enthusiasm picking up as he figured out that we were heading home. An hour later, I'd changed into better jeans—ones without white knees—and a western shirt and boots. The party was in the ballroom of one of the downtown hotels and I ended up parking at the Convention Center parking garage.

My ticket got me a plastic wristband and a numbered stub good for a free drink. I scanned the room, which probably already held nearly two hundred people, and spotted Rachael off to one side. She'd obviously been watching for me, too, because as soon as I caught her eye she waved.

A mariachi group in huge sombreros and black blousy shirts strummed away enthusiastically in one corner, and a table with an enormous spread of Mexican food bordered one entire end of the room. A good part of the crowd had begun to gravitate that direction.

"You made it!" Rachael greeted me with a warm smile. She wore jeans, as did nearly everyone in the room, but while many of them leaned toward T-shirts or jumpsuits covered with gaudy ballooning patterns and scads of brightly enameled lapel pins, Rachael presented her usual understated elegance in a turquoise sweater and fitted black leather jacket. A simple gold chain with a balloon-shaped pendant hung around her neck.

"Want to get in the food line?" she asked.

"Not just yet." Mexican food didn't seem quite the thing right now.

"Well, the line's shorter at the bar anyway," she said, indicating portable bars set up in each corner of the large room. We moved slowly toward the nearest one and I opted for a Coke when we got there.

"Did you get a chance to talk to your brother this afternoon?" I asked.

"Yeah." She sipped at her glass of merlot.

"And?"

"No more press releases." She shuffled slightly and looked hesitant. "See, the thing is, he's already got some reporters lined up to fly with me several days during the Fiesta."

I pondered this. Doubtful that any reporter would be the one threatening Rachael, but what would they talk about once they knew she had this cloud over her.

"Ron wants me to go along with you each morning, keep

an eye on you," I told her. "How are we going to keep this situation quiet if there are reporters hanging around all over the place?"

Her mouth did a thoughtful little pucker. "Okay, I think Sam and I are the only two on the crew who know about it. I certainly haven't told the younger guys and I'm pretty sure he wouldn't either. But I better make sure. Sam's not exactly all for this whole altitude record idea anyway."

"I picked up on that at your house yesterday. Why?"

She struggled not to say anything disloyal. "Sam's just a traditional man. He has his little farm and he'd be very happy to end up with a little farm wife."

"So, how on earth did he end up with you?" I said. "Sorry, that didn't come out right. But, really, you're hardly the checkered-apron type, canning her own tomatoes."

"True, true, I'm not." She took a longer swig of the wine this time. "I really don't know how things will end up with Sam and me. We have this very powerful attraction, probably because he is protective and such a far cry from most of my experiences with men. But our lifestyles are so different. He's up there in the mountains with his dairy goats and I'm trying to run my little law practice in town. I don't know."

"Hey, girl, how ya doing?" A woman glided up to Rachael and pulled her into a fierce hug, which Rachael sort of stumbled into.

"Liz, good to see you. Let me introduce you to Charlie Parker. Liz Pierce."

Liz turned to me and extended her hand. She was model-pretty, with long blond hair and a body that *Playboy* could have commandeered for the centerfold. Large brown eyes and pouty lips made her look about twenty.

"Kevin's here somewhere," she said to Rachael. "Did Sam come?"

"No, he had work to do at his place. Considering that we'll all be up before dawn for several days now."

"Oh, Charlie, you should see Sam's place," Liz said. "We all went up there for a barbeque this summer. Gorgeous, just gorgeous mountain property. And the goats. He took us to that lower pasture where they stay. They're just so *cute!*"

I supposed that, with some imagination, goats might be called cute but I didn't voice this.

"Oh, here's Kevin now. Kevin! Kevin, over here, honey."

I caught Rachael's eye and she sent me a tiny wink. Clearly, Liz was a little on the gushy side for her, too.

Kevin Pierce didn't look like the kind of guy who could score once with a gorgeous girl like Liz, let alone marry one. He was four inches shorter than his wife and slightly on the chunky side, a result no doubt of many libations like the beer he held in one hand. His receding blond hair was pulled back into a scrawny ponytail and he had one of those strips of facial hair that looks like a fuzzy caterpillar crawling toward his lower lip. I resisted reaching out to pluck it off and stomp on it.

"Hi, babe," he said to Liz, handing her a glass of wine. Rachael introduced him and I noticed that his T-shirt already had a dribble of salsa down the screen-printed, hot pink balloon on the front. The name *Beauty's Beast* was written below it in scrolling script.

He took a long gulp from the beer can, clearly not his first for the evening. "I'm the luckiest guy in this room," he said, barely suppressing a belch. "Who else is married to a beauty queen?"

"Oh, Kev, those pageants were years ago." Liz snuggled into the arm he draped around her and dabbed at the salsa spot with a cocktail napkin. She turned back toward Rachael and me. "Really, it was only Miss Dallas. I didn't get all the way to Miss America."

"Yeah, but honey you could still do it some day," he said, looking into her eyes.

She giggled and actually blushed. I stretched a smile over my lips and wondered how many times they'd performed this little routine.

"And that beauty ain't just skin deep," he said. "She's a great mom to Kevie Jr. and a brave lady, too." Liz shot him a look and elbowed him into silence. This time he didn't manage to suppress the belch.

She's probably loyal, trustworthy and can light a campfire without matches, too, I thought.

"Well," said Rachael with a slight clearing of the throat. "That buffet line is looking a little more reasonable now. Charlie?"

"Yeah, I think I will."

We scooted across the room as quickly as we could.

"Liz really isn't quite that vacant," she murmured to me as we took our places at the end of the line. "I've known her for a couple of years and, yes, she comes across pretty forcefully at times. But she really only goes into that dumb blond beauty queen routine when Kevin's around. Usually when he's had a few."

"Yeah, I got that impression."

Her eyes skipped beyond me and she perked up with a look of familiarity. "Butch, how are you?" The dark-haired man came up behind us in line, along with a woman wearing a denim jacket that held a glitter of enameled balloon pins all over the front. Rachael introduced them as Butch and Sara Haines.

"Are you a pilot, too, Charlie? Which balloon is yours?" Sara asked. Her blue eyes sparkled with fun.

"Oh, just helicopters, actually. I've never piloted a balloon. I'm going to be on Rachael's crew this week."

By the time I'd passed through the buffet line, taking nothing stronger than salad and a flour tortilla, I'd learned that Butch and Sara flew *Early Morning Delight,* a multi-colored spiral patterned Aerostar AX-8, and that they were from Kansas. As they chatted on with Rachael about gores and single turbos and upright tanks, I realized this sport had a language all its own.

We found a table for four among those scattered around the big ballroom. While the others continued to talk flight strategies for the next morning, I munched my salad and realized it was the first thing I'd eaten since having toast this morning.

"How are your record attempt plans coming along?" Sara asked Rachael. "I heard that someone—" A brunette with spiky hair and a jacket full of pins bounded up to Sara and interrupted. Hugs and greetings went around the table and it became obvious that the Haines's were certainly popular among this crowd. Rachael maintained a reserve that seemed typical, and nothing more was said about her upcoming altitude attempt. Most of these pilots from all over the world obviously hadn't seen the Albuquerque papers, yet. Maybe she'd done a better job of keeping it quiet than I'd realized.

By eight the crowd began to thin and it struck me that we would all be up by four in the morning. A wave of fatigue rushed over me at the idea.

I said a quick goodbye to Rachael, and she confirmed our plan to meet at the field in the morning. I located my car again, headed home, and was in bed by eight thirty. As I closed my eyes it dawned on me that I hadn't heard from Drake all day.

SEVEN

WHAT GOES UP MUST come down. It just doesn't necessarily come down anywhere near its takeoff point. In the world of hot air ballooning, this is especially true, I'm discovering. This partially explains why I found myself hunched in the bed of Rachael's champagne colored pickup truck, frozen hands jammed under armpits, waiting for the sun to warm up enough to have an effect on my poor body that had been functioning, if not awake, since an ungodly hour of the morning. When that first digit on the alarm clock is a 3, well, we won't go there.

No sensible person subjects herself to this pre-dawn, frosty adventure when the sun had barely cleared the top of Sandia Peak just minutes ago. I guess the bigger question is why nearly fifty thousand people from more than a dozen countries would do the same. Why would national TV, local radio, and nearly every travel magazine in the world send its glamour people out to an open field before dawn, in a place that half of them don't yet recognize as part of the United States? I took a deep breath, leaned my head back against the cab of the truck, and really opened my eyes at last.

Against the backdrop of New Mexico's incredible blue firmament, somewhere around six hundred multicolored globes hung like bobbing Christmas ornaments, decorating the city sky so beautifully that it made my throat tighten. Around the perimeter of the launch field, heavenly smells of coffee, frying bacon, and freshly roasted green chile wafted through the air as vendors began tantalizing the crowd with breakfast.

Rachael's important passengers showed up promptly and presented satisfactory ID. I would ride along with the chase crew. The reporters from *Aviation World* and *People,* were Grayson's idea of those who garnered premium seats on this, the opening Saturday of the ten-day Fiesta. The story of the first high altitude record to be attempted from Balloon Fiesta Park, during the world's largest gathering of balloons, pulled media worldwide. I just wished we'd known about the threats in time to chill the publicity machine a bit.

Back in the late 70s and early 80s other New Mexico women had set world ballooning records for altitude, distance, and duration. But these were relatively low-key events, known only within the aviation community until after the fact, and then receiving little more than local news coverage. Rachael's high-power brother had seen to it that her aviation record attempt made the headlines well before it actually happened. With connections in politics, media, and Hollywood, Grayson Fairfield arranged it so the world would be watching Rachael's record attempt. Whether she wanted it that way was another story. The fact that her life was on the line didn't affect Gray's obsession with the limelight.

I'd spoken to her briefly before the flight this morning and sensed that she simply wanted to concentrate on the task before her. The hovering media people seemed an irritation. She wouldn't even address the death threat. I shifted my position in the back of the truck, keeping her balloon—the red, white, and blue *Lady Liberty*—in sight. If someone decided to take a shot at her, there wasn't a lot I could do about it from here.

Contrary to what most people might think, a bullet hole through the fabric envelope won't bring down a balloon. The shooter would have to be pretty damned accurate to hit the pilot from close to a mile away. Rachael had instructions to fly high and land quickly. Sketchy as it might be, that was our plan for now.

The truck hit a bump, as we shifted from dirt road to paved street. The jouncing ride smoothed considerably, and Justin and I adjusted our collars to keep the chill wind off our ears and necks. Four more crew members rode inside the plushy Chevy extended cab pickup, but I'd opted for the outside slot with its better visibility.

Lady Liberty was well ahead of us now, altitude about three thousand feet above the ground, floating somewhere over the North Valley. Sam drove like a bat, sailing through cordoned off intersections, making his way toward *Lady*. Although the crowds attending the Fiesta might be stuck in traffic for hours, it was crucial that the crews be out of the melee and near their balloons when they landed. Radio contact and the foresight of the Fiesta planners in routing crew traffic in and out by restricted exits accomplished this with amazing smoothness. I shifted position, leaning against the cage of the inflator fan, making sure I kept Rachael in sight. So far, so good.

"You ever crewed before?" Justin shouted over the roar of the wind as we picked up speed on Paseo del Norte.

"Yeah, once. But it was a long time ago," I told him. "A friend took me on a flight. It sure wasn't anything like this." I nodded upward, indicating the masses of color overhead.

"Fiesta's special, huh?" he said. "You can't describe it to anybody. Gotta be here."

"That's for sure." I'd been stupid not to bring my camera. Being disgruntled at playing ineffective bodyguard was no excuse to miss out on the fun part of this adventure. I hoped Ron's kids were maxing out on funnel cake and breakfast burritos.

A horn that played *La Cucaracha* blared behind us. Justin grinned at the other crew and flipped them the bird. "Crew from *Scarlett's Dream*," he explained. "Their chief's my roommate at UNM." In the other truck a passenger raised a beer can. Ballooning is one of the few activities in the world where they break out the booze before eight in the morning. When you've been up since three thirty, eight feels almost like lunchtime. The red truck blazed past us.

Lady Liberty seemed suspended over the Rio Grande. Sam pulled to the side of the busy six-lane and waited. Rachael's plan was to catch an upper wind out of the south-southeast and ride it to the west side of the city, with a landing near the town of Rio Rancho where there was more open space and plenty of roads for the crew. Unfortunately, her mandate to stay high put her into the prevailing westerly and it was holding her pretty much stationary. She'd have to descend a bit to get back on track. I duck-walked toward the cab of the truck and tapped on the back window. Four heads turned. Sam stepped out and walked back to me.

"Sam, does Rachael know to keep the radio chatter to a minimum?" I asked.

"Yeah, we talked about that before." He kept his voice low. "So far, we've kept it pretty quiet. And she knows to use only general information."

"Good. I think she's safe for now. The worst time will be when she starts to land."

"Yeah, a seventy-foot-tall ball of red, white, and blue isn't exactly easy to hide." His eyes sparkled when he smiled. Although he remained wary, gone was the gruff demeanor from a couple of days ago.

I followed his steady gaze over the river. Rachael had maneuvered into a wind that carried her to its western banks. Sam slipped a tiny digital camera from his jacket pocket and zoomed in on the view of *Lady Liberty* poised over the vivid green cottonwood trees at the river's edge. After clicking off three shots, he chuckled. "Sorry, I guess that toy is like Rachael's kid. Her walls are covered with photos already."

"Is Rachael using *Lady Liberty* for the altitude record or does she have some other...something custom made for that?" I asked.

"Yep. *Lady*'s doing it with her. Course, she'll have extra fuel tanks, oxygen equipment, parachute, bunch of other stuff you don't normally take on a flight like this." He nodded upward, indicating the sky full of balloons, each at a different altitude. "Looks like next Sunday's the day. Unless the weather patterns change."

I tried to think ahead to what I'd heard for the prediction. Since weather played such a big part in our own helicopter business, Drake and I watched it constantly. As I recalled, there was a front coming through mid-week, clearing after that. Next weekend should be ideal.

From the cab, radio static crackled. Sam leaped forward with a giant step and reached in through the open window. I heard voices blended with static but couldn't make out the words.

"Shit!" Sam yelled, flinging his door open. "Sit down, everyone!"

I'd barely planted my butt when he yanked the gearshift. The truck zipped into traffic with a screech of rubber. I stared down the expanse of the Rio Grande. In the distance, *Lady Liberty* appeared to be falling from the sky.

EIGHT

FOUR SETS OF EYES stayed glued to the balloon, which had lost more than twenty-five hundred feet in altitude by now. Sam divided his attention between the radio and the road, while I watched all of them.

"Why's she coming down so fast?" asked Justin, hunched beside me in the bed of the racing pickup. "That doesn't look normal. She usually waits till we get right below her."

It didn't look normal to me either, the balloon's shape was now elongated into a long, inverted teardrop. It still held air, but there was something decidedly strange about Rachael's maneuver.

Sam took the exit at Coors Road too fast and we veered toward the embankment. Luckily, it held and he whipped into the traffic lane between two startled motorists. The car behind us slowed to accommodate the move and the one ahead of us slipped to the right, giving us a clear path. One thing about Albuquerque drivers—they may drive with their heads in dark places 90 percent of the time, but during Balloon Fiesta they become extremely polite. Realizing the critical relationship between chase crew and balloon, our drivers extend every courtesy to those trucks flying the distinctive Chase Vehicle flags. Sam made the best of it and raced north on Coors, barely making the light at Rio Rancho Boulevard. Fortunately, the police are also somewhat forgiving at this time of year.

Justin and I held on for dear life, unable to keep the balloon in sight because of the wind in our faces. I caught one glimpse of her just above the treetops, still at least a mile away. What the hell was going on?

At Southern Boulevard we were forced to stop for a red light, the police not being quite *that* accommodating. Through the back window I could see that Sam had a cell phone to one ear and the radio microphone near his mouth. He clicked something on the cell and dropped it into his lap. I chafed at the fact that I was stuck here in the back, not knowing what was happening. Had the killer managed to get to Rachael after all? Had he engineered some malfunction in her fuel system or burners? Where was she now? The balloon had completely disappeared behind the trees and buildings.

"The park," Justin said, as the truck roared to life again. "Ronnie just shouted back that we're heading for the park."

I couldn't think of any park out here but trusted that they knew what they were doing. Two minutes later Sam turned beside a small industrial warehouse complex, pulled alongside the building, and—amazingly—there was a small park hidden back there. Completely out of sight from the road and most of the neighboring buildings, the balloon lay, sadly flat now, on the grass. The wicker gondola was on its side, nothing abnormal there, but what caught my eye was a body lying on the ground. I leaped over the side of the pickup the second we stopped and raced toward the prone figure.

It wasn't Rachael. I nearly crashed into her, kneeling beside the reporter from *Aviation Week,* who was lying on the grass clutching at his left arm. His face looked gray and his mouth clenched in a grimace of pain. Someone was holding a wide sheet of paper above him to keep the sun out of his eyes. The reporter from *People* stood off to one side, scribbling notes furiously.

"Are you okay?" I panted in Rachael's ear. She nodded. "What happened?"

She stood up and backed away from the little crowd that had gathered.

"Passenger started having chest pains. They came on so suddenly, I couldn't think what else to do but land. Sam called an ambulance."

Sam walked over and put his arms around her. Sirens blared, nearby.

"I think I should ride to the hospital with him," Rachael said. "I don't think he knows anyone else in town. I should try to call his office."

"You go," Sam said. "We'll get everything handled here."

An ambulance pulled into the park, its sirens winding down with a slow moan. Two EMTs jumped out and hauled an equipment kit over to the victim. As they worked over him, Sam rounded up the chase crew and issued quiet orders.

Like a well-oiled machine, they went to work bundling the voluminous nylon fabric into a neat column. Within minutes, they'd unhooked the connection cables, stood the gondola upright, and backed the truck up to it. By the time four of the crew had stuffed the hundreds of yards of fabric back into its storage bag, the basket was in the truck, inflator fan restowed, and everything neatly secured with tie-down straps.

Sam kissed Rachael at the ambulance door and she stepped in. The vehicle was rolling before she sat down. I scanned the area. The few curious bystanders dispersed as soon as the ambulance left, and our crew were standing around waiting for instructions.

"Okay, everyone," Sam announced. "Everything's going to be fine. Let's get back to the field."

The *People* reporter took the front seat, so Justin's buddy Ronnie joined us in the back. They chatted while I allowed myself to wind down. Relief flooded me. Thank goodness Rachael hadn't been hurt. I felt an increased respect for this determined lady who took the time to see to her passenger's comfort and safety, while under threat herself and while planning her own world-record flight, barely a week away. As our truck wound its way back to Rio Rancho, I spotted a news truck from Channel 7.

Back at Balloon Fiesta Park, life went on in happy pandemonium. Once the six hundred-plus hot air balloons left the area, other activities took over. A parachute team from one of the military forces had just spot-landed, one after another, in a center bullseye.

I managed to find the obscure spot where I'd parked my car, retrieved it, and headed toward Presbyterian Hospital. Just inside the ER entrance I ran into Rachael.

"Thought you might need a ride home," I told her.

She fumbled a minute for an answer. The early morning and disorienting trip to the hospital was beginning to show. "I think Sam was planning to come," she said. "But I'm not really sure at this point."

"Give him a call and save him the trip. Getting out of the balloon field right now is not fun."

Once she'd settled the arrangements with Sam I suggested that we find some coffee.

"Sounds good," she said, "but not here."

"How's the passenger doing, by the way?"

"As we suspected, heart. He'll be okay and his wife is on the way. Nothing more I can do here."

We decided to grab coffee at the Pancake House and headed that direction. Traffic on the streets wasn't bad at all; half the city was probably still at the Fiesta activities. At a corner table, with a carafe of steaming brew between us, I decided to put forth the idea that nagged at me since Rachael's sudden landing.

"You know Ron and I are concerned about all this publicity. We can't seem to get your brother to realize that the exposure is probably not a good thing."

She toyed with a paper napkin, alternately twisting and smoothing it. "I know. I can't get that through to him either."

"What if one of these journalists is doing this to create a story?"

"Trying to kill me? Isn't that taking it a bit far?"

"Only if they actually do kill you. But the threats, the escalating danger. Makes for great press coverage."

"So far they haven't covered that part of it."

True. "I don't know, maybe it's a dumb theory."

Our waitress came back to see if we wanted to add actual food to our breakfast. "Hey, you're the lady from the paper," she said, giving Rachael a good look for the first time.

I groaned inwardly. But the article last evening only showed the balloon. There was no photo of Rachael. "What paper?" I asked.

She held up one finger and hustled away to the cashier's station, came back a few seconds later with a newspaper in hand.

"See? Front page." She thrust the paper toward Rachael.

Yep, front page. A nice publicity photo of Rachael and a headline. LOCAL BALLOONIST OBJECT OF DEATH THREAT.

Rachael dismissed the waitress and we both stared at the story.

"How did they know about this?" I growled through clenched teeth. My mind raced. "Only a few people know about that note. You, me, Ron, Sam, the police, and your brother. Any guesses who leaked this?"

Her face had gone white. "But, why?"

"Publicity. Isn't that what he's all about right now?" I

fished for answers. "Either that or some unscrupulous journalist has taken it upon himself to create the biggest story of the year. They've been caught trying to throw presidential elections, why not create a fake death threat for a local celebrity?"

I caught sight of our waitress standing to one side, whispering behind her hand to two others.

"We need to get out of here," I told Rachael. She stared at the center of the table, uncomprehending.

I tossed some money on the table and took her elbow, reaching for the newspaper at the same time. Outside, I buckled her into the passenger seat of my Jeep and headed to my own side. By the time we'd come to the freeway entrance, she'd turned from a zombie into a livid mass of anger.

"I can't believe Gray would do this to me!" she shouted. "Why? Because of my dad, because Gray never did believe my story and now it's payback time?" She twisted in the seat to face me. "Could Dad have…" She slumped back, obviously awhirl with myriad thoughts.

I negotiated traffic on Interstate 25 while my mind did the same thing. It seemed unlikely to think that her father, just out of prison, could have managed to plant a news story—that was much more likely to have been Grayson. But the notes themselves, where had they come from?

No clear answers came to me. I once again squeezed through the traffic at Balloon Fiesta Park and found a parking spot. We made our way through the masses at the concessions, where the smells of bacon and chile made my knees weak. I'd had nothing but coffee and one donut since sometime last night.

We found Sam and the crew at Rachael's launch spot and I took Sam aside. "We need to get her away from the crowd," I told him with a quick explanation about the newspaper headline. "Take her home as quickly as you can reasonably get away. I'll make contact with Ron and we'll come up with a plan." I left her in his capable hands.

Announcements blared from speakers, letting us know about the amazing array of fabulously tasty junk food available and the rest of the day's entertainment, including an after-dark balloon inflation. I pulled a crumpled twenty from my jeans pocket and headed for the breakfast burrito booth.

Three bites into the best burrito on earth, Ron and his kids found me.

"How'd it go?" he asked. "Everything okay?"

"You mean the part about Rachael leaving in an ambulance?" I bit into the burrito again. I turned sideways to avoid being bowled over by two kids who thought they needed to race at top speed through the thick crowd. "Or the part about her picture being on the front page of this morning's newspaper?"

His face went white. "What!" he sputtered.

"Chill, Ron, she's fine." I swallowed and gestured toward the middle of the grassy field. "Let's move out of the line of traffic," I suggested. I quickly recapped the morning's events and explained why Rachael had gone to the hospital. He visibly relaxed.

"The newspaper thing bothers me more," I said. I posited some of my rambling thoughts on it. He looked concerned at the development but didn't have any other ideas to offer at the moment.

"Look, I gotta get these kids home. Joey's got a tummy ache," he said.

No surprise there.

"How many cinnamon rolls, caramel apples, funnel cakes, and cotton candies did he eat?" I couldn't resist the dig. Ron's a great dad, but getting the kids only a couple of weekends a month tends to make him guide with a light hand. Face it, he just can't say no.

"I know, I know," he said. "I just gotta get him well before Bernadette gets them back at six tonight or I'll never hear the end of it."

"Good luck. Look, I'll see you in the office tomorrow. Maybe we can get some of our suspects interviewed."

"I think it would be a good idea for you to spend the night at Rachael's tonight," he said.

I opened my mouth to protest but he cut me off.

"She's got her mind on a hundred other things right now. I just don't like her being all alone."

I grumbled but agreed to do it.

He looked down, where Joey stood with a chubby arm wrapped around his dad's leg. His face was pretty green. Ron patted my shoulder and gathered his little brood. I watched them head for the parking lot, making a silent bet as to whether Joey would throw up before or after they reached the car. If it happened after, Ron would not be a happy man.

I strolled the field for another hour, polishing off my burrito and adding a chunk of funnel cake, as much as I could handle of it, on top. Vendor booths rimmed the edges of the large field and the crowd was loading up on T-shirts, pins, funny looking hats, and tons of junk food. An announcer with a sense of humor kept them entertained as they waited for the next airshow entry to arrive. I pulled my phone from my jacket pocket and tried Drake. No answer and I left a message to let him know that I'd be at Rachael's tonight and that I hoped we would have a chance to talk before then.

Feeling somewhat at loose ends, I decided I might catch a decent nap at home so I'd be somewhat awake for my evening duties. I headed for the parking lot.

The morning paper on the backseat caught my eye and I

remembered that the *Journal* offices were just a few blocks from the balloon field. Reaching for the paper, I noted the by-line. Tom Smithson. It was worth a shot.

I wound my way through the quiet streets of Journal Center Business Park. Most of the parking lots were empty, the buildings looking quiet and echoing emptiness on this Saturday morning. The Journal itself seemed nearly the only exception. I pulled into a visitor space, entered the reception area and asked about Smithson. Yes, he was in, could she say what this was about? I mentioned the Rachael Fairfield story and she asked would I please wait?

Like I had much choice.

I took a chair at one side of the lobby and waited fifteen minutes. Tom Smithson seemed the antithesis of my idea of a hard-driving newsman. At five-five, with thinning sandy hair and thick glasses in invisible wire frames, he didn't come across as the investigative reporter who put fear into the hearts of gigantic corporations. But that's how the town saw him.

"Can we talk privately?" I asked, handing him my business card.

He ushered me into a small room that contained a bank of enclosed cabinets and a copy machine. A small table in the center of the space provided a spot for collating copies and dumping miscellaneous forgotten projects.

"Sorry," Smithson said, shoving a stack of papers aside. "The main conference room is outside security limits on weekends."

I started to ask what he meant by that but he'd already pulled a chair out for me and offered coffee, which I declined.

He sat opposite me, forearms resting on the table, a notepad and pen at hand. "I understand this is something about the Rachael Fairfield story this morning?"

"Our firm has been retained to investigate the threats against Ms. Fairfield," I told him. "We've been trying to keep the whole thing quiet while we try to find out who's behind them."

"And who is?" he asked. His right hand twitched toward the pen and pad at his side.

I ignored the question. "Where'd you get that story, Mr. Smithson?" I leaned forward in my chair, taking a more aggressive posture. "Doesn't the paper have some responsibility about putting something like this in print?"

I shoved the headline page toward him. "Bringing this out seems extremely irresponsible to me."

The otherwise timid-looking face didn't budge. He shrugged. "You know how we newspaper people are about our sources."

I chewed at the inner corner of my lip and remembered the old bit about flies and honey. "Okay, fair enough," I said, expelling a breath of resignation. "Rachael thinks her brother probably sent out a news release to gain publicity for her upcoming record attempt."

His head tilted in a tiny gesture of acquiescence.

I nodded an I-thought-so and a responding flicker from him let me know that we were on the same page with this.

"But to treat it as a front-page headline?" I asked. "If you believed it was a publicity stunt, why would you do that?"

He picked up the pen and began doodling a series of squiggles in the upper corner of the notepad. "Let's just say that other sources confirmed the existence of the notes."

Other sources? Had Sam or one of the crew talked to him? Or maybe the sender had anonymously contacted Smithson himself?

He saw the conflicting theories play across my face.

"Not what you're thinking, Ms. Parker," he said. "And, no, I have no idea who sent them."

The police. It had to be.

"Let's just say I know someone who was working another case, we got into a little conversation, this person confirmed the first note."

"And said they couldn't do anything about it because no one had actually approached Rachael yet."

A tiny shrug.

"My guess is that Grayson Fairfield sent a press kit with the announcement of the record attempt, complete with glossy photos, maybe a couple of weeks ago. Then, sometime in recent days, a second contact—something more subtle this time—with the juicy tidbit about the threats. You make a call to a buddy in the police department and the existence of the threat is confirmed. So, you're free to go with the story. Hit the streets first day of Fiesta with this...this..."

"Headline. It's a lead story, that's all."

"It brings out the very thing we're trying to keep quiet." I fought to keep my voice level and didn't succeed very well.

"C'mon, Ms. Parker. Be real. My editor loves a weekend headline with the word death in it. I'm just doing my job." He leaned toward his notepad again. "So, let me in on who your suspects are?"

I stood abruptly, tipping the chair, which refused to slide on the carpeted floor. "Forget it." I stomped out of the room and past the receptionist.

In the parking lot I fumbled through my purse for my keys.

"Look." Tom Smithson had followed me out. "I don't wish Rachael Fairfield any harm," he said. "Maybe I could help uncover more information if you'd tell me who you're looking at."

Standing, I had nearly two inches height advantage over him. I gave him a long, hard stare and he actually had the grace to look uncomfortable. Without a word I climbed into the Jeep and started it. He stood there among the fallen syca-more leaves until I'd driven out of the lot.

I joined the traffic flow on Paseo del Norte and found my-self on I-25 southbound within minutes. Now what? Clearly, Smithson hadn't instigated the threats. That had been a dumb idea from the beginning. Grayson Fairfield, for a man of sup-posed high position and discretion, had certainly pulled a stupid move. Or had he? Bringing the situation to light could either cause the stalker to make a bad move and reveal him-self, or to retreat and leave Rachael alone. Or it could simply escalate the whole thing.

NINE

THE FAMOUS WORLD WAR II generals got street names in Albuquerque, in what was probably the newest part of town around that era. I merged into the eastbound lanes of I-40 at the last possible second, remembering that Ryan Tamsin's address was somewhere on one of these general streets—Bradley, Arnold, Marshall—I couldn't remember which.

Traffic was heavy but moving and I stayed with it for another fifteen minutes or so until I was able to exit at Wyoming Boulevard. East on Copper and I found a spot where I could pull over and rummage for my notebook. Deep in the recesses of my shoulder bag I came up with my notes and the address. I wound my way through a neighborhood of small houses, some well kept and others obviously given over to rentals, mixed with boxy low-income apartment buildings and the occasional trailer park.

Drug transactions took place in more than one parking lot here. The area of town known as the War Zone, where graffiti held more square footage than business signs did, was just the other side of Central Avenue, less than four blocks away. I found the right general and located Tamsin's address, a 1950s-era bungalow with chipped tan stucco and a dirt front yard. Clearly a rental. Next door to it stood a pale gray version of the same floor plan, this one surrounded by a short picket fence enclosing a neat patch of lawn and pots of vivid purple chrysanthemums beside the front door. I felt sorry for the owner, probably some little old lady who was struggling to hold the trashy neighborhood at bay.

Tamsin's place looked closed up tight. Mismatched curtains covered the windows and the door to the single car garage had a large padlock through the crude hasp that held it down. No vehicle seemed to be associated with the place.

I pressed a doorbell but heard no corresponding sound on the inside, so I pulled open the rickety screen and knocked firmly on the front door. Twice. Nothing. A side yard cluttered with dried tumbleweeds from previous seasons led to a high wooden gate and presumably a walled backyard. I picked my way through the weeds and fiddled with the gate latch, only to be greeted with ferocious barking from something that sounded huge and mean.

Tamsin clearly wasn't home but probably would be later, at least to tend to the dog. Any animal with that much energy was being fed regularly. I walked back to the front sidewalk and took a moment to give the house a puzzled stare. As I'd hoped, the woman next door had, by this time, become curious and stood in her doorway.

"Is at work, that guy," she said.

I took this scrap of conversation as an invitation to approach her gate. She took my approach as her one chance this week to have some company. She walked down the porch steps, drying her hands on a flowered apron. Tiny, Hispanic, probably old enough to be my great-grandmother, she smiled at me from a face creased with years of outdoor work.

"Do you know what time he comes home?" I asked.

Her eyes crinkled in concentration. "He is not a friend of yours, no?"

"Well, no. I'm supposed to ask him some questions. For my job."

"You a bill collector?" Again, that sharp scrutiny.

"Can you keep a secret?"

She grinned, showing perfectly even, white dentures. "I keep many secrets," she said, pointing to her head. "I know many things."

"I don't doubt that for a minute." I chuckled and she did the same. I pulled out a business card and handed it to her. "I really don't want Mr. Tamsin knowing that an investigator is looking for him. Not just yet."

She nodded solemnly.

"I need to ask him some questions but I'd rather he didn't know ahead of time."

"Catch him off guard, you mean. Like those guys on *Law and Order.*"

"Uh, something like that, I guess. So, do you know what time he usually gets home?"

"Usually...today is Saturday. Usually a little after six."

My guess was that she could tell me it was exactly 6:14 every night.

"Tonight, I don't know." She leaned closer to me and lowered her voice. "Last night, Friday, he come back from work 6:15, 6:30. Come out a half-hour later, all dressed and cleaned up. Going out with that girl. Rode away on that motorbike."

"Bike?"

"One those loud things. What do they call it? Rumble, they rumble through the neighborhood."

"Like a Harley?"

She shrugged. "I guess so. He works at that place they sell them."

"Thanks," I said. "Maybe I can catch him there."

"Would you like some lunch? I made beans." The look on her face was so hopeful, I almost said yes. Little old ladies, grasping for company. But I already had one of those next to my own house.

"I really can't," I said. "I have to be out on the west side pretty soon."

She glanced again at the card I'd given her. Why did I have the feeling she'd put it away with the stack of old birthday cards she undoubtedly kept in a shoebox somewhere.

"Remember not to say anything to him?" I tilted my head toward the house on the north.

"Oh, no, nothing." She reached out to shake my hand and seal the bargain. "Maybe when you come again, after you talk with him…"

"I'll stop in and say hello."

She seemed happy enough with that as she stood watching me get into my car. I pulled away from the curb feeling guilty somehow. My notebook on the passenger seat caught my eye and reminded me that the other person I wanted to interview, Chuck Bukovsky, lived only about fifteen minutes away. But somehow I just didn't want to do it right now. My early morning was catching up with me and suddenly I desperately wanted a nap.

There were a couple of stops I had to make—a short grocery list including dog food was a must. I headed toward my own neighborhood. My cell phone rang just as I pulled into the parking lot of my local market.

"Hey, where are you?" Ron asked. I told him my plan to stop at home first then head out to Rachael's.

"Good. I'm there now. Decided to turn the kids in early so we wouldn't have to leave her unguarded. That newspaper headline this morning left her kind of shaky."

"Where're Sam and the other guys?"

"Sam's taken Rachael's truck and the balloon over to Justin's house. Didn't want it parked out front here overnight. In case someone tried to vandalize it."

"Good idea."

"I've got a bit more information on some of our suspects and we can go over that when you get here. Soon, I hope?" So much for that nap.

I assured him I'd be there before dark, but felt myself bristling at what felt like having to account for my every move.

An hour later I was pulling into my driveway at home. Rusty bounded out from the yard next door, which told me that my neighbor Elsa had been watching. Sure enough, she stood on her back porch when I walked around to that side of the yard. I roughed up Rusty's ears and he bounced and twirled with joy.

"How's everything going?" I called out to Elsa. My neighbor, now in her late eighties, still keeps her own house, plants a garden every year, and generally treats me like the grandchild she never had.

"Fine, Charlie, just fine. Rusty's been a good boy. Good company for me." She pulled a tissue from her apron pocket and dabbed at her nose. "Can you stay for dinner?"

I worked up a smile. "I wish I could. But Ron ordered me to get out to the west side for the night. And you know how the traffic is this time of day."

Actually, I felt a hankering for a Big Mac and would willingly pick up fast food on the way to Rachael's, but Ron had assured me that Rachael had made a big pot of green chile stew that had been simmering all afternoon. Dinner would be ready when I got there.

Turning to Elsa, I said, "Walk over to the house with me. I need to look through my mail and check messages. We can visit for a minute."

She gave a quick backward glance toward her kitchen before coming down the porch steps. Rusty tagged at my heels as we cut through the break in the hedge. I unlocked my back door to be greeted by that silent, slightly dusty feeling of an empty house.

"Drake hasn't been home for a few days, I noticed. Out on a job?" Elsa said. "You sure got yourself a good man there, Charlie."

Again, a quick flash of impatience that everyone else seemed to have an opinion about our lives. I buried it before she could see my face.

"I know," I sighed. Thinking about the way this week had turned out, I wished again that I'd been free to go with him. Neither of us liked being apart.

I flipped through the pile of mail I'd brought in. A quick sort into his and hers piles, left me with just a few bills that could wait until next weekend and a newsletter from a tax consultant. Heady stuff.

Elsa followed me through the house as I double checked windows and doors, retrieved my Beretta nine millimeter pistol from the wall safe in our office. I gave her a quick recap of the reason I wouldn't be home tonight. "Is it okay if Rusty stays with you?"

"You know it is," she said. She gave me a pensive look. "People always come to you with their problems, don't they?"

I pondered that as I locked up the house and said goodbye to her and Rusty. A powerful urge hit me, an urge to take them both back inside, lock the doors, and not answer the phone. Being home for awhile would feel really good right now.

But I didn't do it. I climbed back into the car and pulled out of my quiet neighborhood and into the crush of traffic on I-40 west across the river. I remembered the way without notes this time, and spotted Ron's Mustang in her driveway.

Her front walkway led to an ancient looking gate, the portal to a Spanish-style courtyard surrounded by a six-foot wall. The gate, more of a door really, stood open a couple of inches so I walked in without ringing the buzzer mounted in the adobe wall. Inside the courtyard, a small fountain poured a stream of crystal water through a series of hammered copper bowls into a tiny pond surrounded by desert plants. A grouping of four chairs stood to one side. When she saw me, Misty the cat jumped down from one of them and came to rub against my ankles. I bent to scratch her ears and she sniffed suspiciously at the dog smells on my fingers.

I headed for the ornately carved double front door but stopped short. A rectangle of white lay on the flagstone patio five feet away.

TEN

My PULSE DID A LITTLE skip as I approached it. With the very tips of my nails, I picked it up by one corner. No doubt what this was. Same m. o.

The green chile stew smelled wonderful the minute Ron opened the front door. He took one look at the envelope, which I held dangling as if it were a dead rat, and steered me into a formal dining room. I could hear Rachael clattering pans in an adjacent kitchen.

"What does he say this time?" Ron muttered, grabbing the envelope.

"Shouldn't we—"

"Worry about fingerprints? Like the police are worrying about them?" He dug in his jeans pocket for the little penknife he always carries and slit the envelope in one quick move.

He had a point about that. Spreading the tri-folded page on the dining table he let me see it. BITCH, GIVE UP NOW said the magazine letters.

I almost wanted to. The authoritative tone, the note of inevitability.

"How's Rachael coping with this?" I was surprised to hear a catch in my voice.

He shot a hard stare toward me. "How are you coping with it?"

Instant tears stabbed at my eyelids and I shook them

back. This was getting ridiculous. I swallowed hard and met Ron's gaze.

"I'm doing fine." My voice came out steady.

"Good. Don't show Rachael any of that other...whatever it was that nearly came out just now," he said. "She's got a lot on her mind and we're here to protect her."

I sighed and kept my voice low. "I thought we were here to get evidence against her father, track him down, and turn him over to the police?"

"I'm still working on the possibility that William Fairfield is behind these notes, but I'm not completely convinced," he said. "I'm pretty sure he's back in Albuquerque now, but haven't actually set eyes on him. I'll be watching his place tonight. Once I find him, I'll be on him like white on rice. He's not getting close to Rachael or her house again."

"And what if it's not him?" I pointed out, quite logically, I thought. "We'll be after Fairfield and somebody else gets right in."

He shuffled a little uncomfortably. "We're not the FBI, Charlie. I've been over this with Rachael but I'm not sure she gets it. All we can do is what we were hired to do. She thinks it's her dad, we're hired to keep him away from her."

"But we have other—"

"Suspects. Aside from Bukovsky or Tamsin, not many."

I told him about my unproductive trip to Tamsin's house.

"And I tried to catch Bukovsky this afternoon but didn't find him home either. Here's a photo."

He handed me a vacation snapshot of Chuck and Rachael, smiling, somewhere in a bar or restaurant. Chuck had thinning dark hair, brushed straight back from a glowing forehead. It bushed out in thick waves from behind his ears. Within his self-important smile, his teeth appeared to be capped, too thick and even to be natural.

"Any more?" I asked.

"There've been a few other clients over the years, but none that I really like for it. Rachael can tell you more over dinner."

"You said you'd also asked her brother."

"Yeah. Grayson volunteered the information that he'd recently had a bank client threaten him. Wilbur Johnson, a guy they'd foreclosed. Gotta understand he'd be upset over losing his home, but would he go this far over it? I don't know. Grayson took the threat seriously though. Stayed home two days after the guy called, and he's been really watching his back ever since."

"Is the guy unstable enough to stalk his banker's sister, though? That's a stretch."

"I thought so too, but it doesn't hurt to know about it." He gave me a written description of Wilbur Johnson, too—an older man, farmer, who seemed best identified by his battered Stetson and the gun rack in the back of his Ford pickup.

I took the small stack of papers and photos and followed him as he gave me a tour of the house. The front wouldn't be difficult to defend. It was a traditional adobe with high walls around the entry courtyard, a deadbolt lock on the gate at the entrance. Since the house was on a cul de sac, any cars on the street would be easily recognized if they weren't neighbors. Past the cool, dim entryway, the space opened dramatically with two steps down into a sunken living room. To the right of the living room was a large, open kitchen with Spanish tiled backsplashes and countertops. The dining room we'd first stepped into adjoined the kitchen. Three bedrooms and a home office branched off a hallway to the left of the front entry.

The biggest security problem was the wall of windows the entire length of the living room, dining room, and kitchen.

The view showed a small backyard with covered patio of pine *vigas,* large pots of bright flowers, and a raised fire pit. Beyond the retainer wall, the earth dropped away to the Rio Grande River. What remained was an unobstructed view of the Sandia Mountains, in full lavender and coral glory now as the final minutes of sun shone on them, playing up their vast ruggedness.

"Charlie?" Ron snagged my attention away from the view that ranked among the best I've seen from anywhere in the city. "Earth to Charlie."

I shook my head and turned my attention back to him.

"We need to talk about these windows," he said. "Notice, no drapes."

"Yeah I'd picked up on that."

"As soon as it gets dark those will have to be covered. Have Rachael get some sheets, blankets, anything. It's not safe for her to be walking around in here, backlit, with a stalker out there."

"I agree. We'll figure out something."

"Hi, Charlie. Thanks for waiting," Rachael said, joining us in front of the glorious view outside. She looked remarkably fresh for someone who'd been up since before dawn several days in a row. The highlights in her blond page framed her face perfectly. "I put cornbread in the oven, so we'll be eating in fifteen minutes or so. How about out on the patio?"

I glanced at Ron.

"Should be okay," he said. "It's still light out. Table's up close to the house and we've got a good view of the property."

"I just can't get used to this," Rachael said. Her voice shook. "I *hate* having to be careful all the time."

"Soon," Ron said. "He's gotta show his hand sometime."

Ron stayed for dinner, three bowls of the fragrant stew for him, before leaving me alone with Rachael for the night. We came up with enough spare sheets to cover the wall of windows and, while it severely cut back on the ambiance of the home, the makeshift curtain made me immediately feel more secure.

"Charlie, thanks," Rachael said, almost shyly. "I know this really interrupted your life."

I didn't want to get into it so I made a half-gesture of it's-okay.

"No, really. You had plans and this...this..." Her voice cracked as she picked up the newest note. She breathed deeply and waved a hand in front of her welling eyes. "Just tired, don't mind me."

"How about if I make us some coffee?" I headed toward the kitchen.

She gave a wan smile. "That would be great. Second canister there on the counter. And the filters are in the drawer right below the coffeemaker."

I found everything and even managed to push the correct button without incident.

She sank into one of the lush leather couches in the living room. "God, that feels good," she sighed. She shimmied deep into the cushion. "I haven't done this in about a month."

Taking the other large couch, I did the same.

A few minutes later, over coffee, I decided it was about time to get more information out of Rachael.

"The other day at lunch you were going to tell me about Chuck," I said. "Sorry, but Ron and I are looking at any and all suspects at this point."

She raked her hair with one hand, streaming the strands through her fingers.

"Chuck." She set her coffee down and pulled an angora afghan over her legs. "The more I think about it, I suppose it could be him. Calling me 'bitch' in this note. That was very Chuck. Telling me I'd never accomplish anything."

The rest of the note, "Give Up Now," nagged at me, too. Give up what? The record attempt? One of her legal cases?

Rachael continued, "Well, I don't know if you've ever gotten involved with a man like that, but it ain't pleasant. Chuck can be a charmer. He started our relationship on a very romantic note. Flowers after the first date, mushy little notes, *extravagant* gifts. Kind of bowls a woman over, if you know what I mean. The euphoric period lasted about six months. By then we'd moved in together and once he felt I belonged to him, things changed. It started gradually, with a temper fit directed at someone else. I was absolutely stunned the first time I saw it, but I convinced myself this wasn't the real Chuck. When I didn't walk out, the rages escalated.

"We'd been together over two years before he actually directed one of them at me. I don't know why I believed he'd change, but I did. I stayed with it another year before I realized how much he'd chipped away at my self esteem. He'd tell me I was stupid, didn't dress well enough, couldn't remember basic things like unplugging the toaster. Basically, if his hundreds of petty rules weren't followed to the letter, I paid.

"He'd usually start the rampages late at night, often waking me up to start in on me. Screaming, berating, breaking things—the only place he drew the line was that he didn't hit me. I don't know why. The anger was certainly there."

"He's graduated to that now," I said. I told her about the background check Ron had run.

She blanched. "Then he might really—" She ran both hands down the sides of her face. "The only reason I didn't suspect him was the fact that he never actually acted out his violence. It was all words."

"Not any more. The woman he lives with now has called the police twice. Who knows how many times she didn't call them."

"Oh, god," she whispered.

She flung the afghan aside and stood up. "I need more coffee. You?" Without waiting for an answer, she picked up my mug and strode to the kitchen. "Now I don't know what to think," she said. "I'd always banked on the idea that he wouldn't really do anything. I thought once I moved out of his house and bought my own, he'd finally be out of my life. Since I've been dating Sam, everything's been so wonderful for me."

"Have you ever seen Chuck hanging around? Has he called or approached you?" I stood up to take my newly filled mug from her.

"No, nothing recent. He called for weeks after I first moved out. But then he met someone else and the calls ended. I guess that's why I felt safe." She clasped her mug with both hands, warming them.

I yawned largely. "Sorry, I really don't mean to..."

She waved off the apology. "No need. It's getting late and tomorrow's another early morning, I'm afraid. We ought to get to bed. I guess I puttered around in the kitchen longer than I realized."

I chose the guest room that faced the street and deposited my duffle there. In the adjoining bathroom, I managed to brush my teeth and wash my face before another giant yawn took over. I made myself perform one last check of all the doors and windows before returning to peel off my clothes and fall onto the soft bed. I was conscious of nothing else until the alarm clock rang in the dark.

I wanted to reach out and hit the snooze button but I heard Rachael moving about in her bathroom and knew the day was going to start, whether I wanted it to or not. I sat up slowly and rubbed at my eyes. Our plan was that Ron and I would trade off today. I'd stayed with Rachael for the night, he'd take over this morning. I just had to get her over to Justin's, where she would join the crew for the trip to the balloon field. Ron would meet up with them there. The plan was for him to ride along on her flight. I could go home if I wanted, but knew that once my brain kicked into gear and I got a cup or two of coffee into me, I'd not go back to sleep. Given that, there wasn't much point in going home to sit around and look at the walls, so I decided I'd tag along with the crew again.

At the thought of coffee, I caught a whiff from the kitchen. Rachael, bless her heart, had set up the machine's timer to produce the magic brew at three thirty, and it seemed to be right on time. I slipped into my jeans, a T-shirt, and a sweat-shirt over that, and padded barefoot to the kitchen.

My hostess had beaten me to the punch and stood at the counter, pouring coffee into two travel mugs. She lifted one to me, which I accepted gratefully. The liquid was still too hot to sip, so I carried the mug back to my room as I fumbled with shoes and socks and brushed the morning taste out of my mouth.

"Ready?" Rachael asked from the doorway.

"As much as I'll ever be," I said. "Do you ever get used to this?"

"Uh, somewhat, I guess…well, not really." She laughed. "The average weekend isn't so bad, but the nine straight days of Fiesta week get to be a bit much."

I rummaged through my bag for car keys and we set out into the frosty darkness. At Justin's house, things were begin-ning to swing into motion. The guys had pumped up with cans of caffeinated sodas. They piled into Rachael's pickup truck and I followed them to the field.

By the time the pilot briefing was over, the sky had light-ened sufficiently for the first wave of balloons to begin inflat-ing. We would be in the second wave, so we stood around and Ron joined us at Rachael's launch space, T-12.

"This is one of our vulnerable times," he said, nudging my side and eyeing my coffee. "Keep your eyes open."

That's asking a lot at five in the morning, but I did it. We'd decided that Rachael should stay in the truck or be surrounded by several crew members until the moment she absolutely had to take over her duties as pilot. Ron and I scanned the crowd, watching for the faces we'd memorized, fearful that the real danger would come from one we hadn't considered.

An hour later, I finally relaxed. *Lady Liberty*'s inflation had gone perfectly, the balloon becoming airborne with Rachael, Ron, and one of Grayson's reporter buddies aboard. I'd settled into my familiar position in the back of the chase truck, with Sam at the wheel again. The flight plan was similar to yesterday's, and we managed it without any health incidents this time. I met up with Ron afterward.

"Plan?" I asked.

"I'm going to keep an eye on Bill Fairfield the rest of the day. Rachael's going to hang close to her crew and Sam promises to keep her away from the crowds. Grab a nap if you need to, and plan to spend the night at her house again." His orders might have rankled, but the promise of nap time sounded so good that I didn't say anything.

By five thirty that evening, I was back at Rachael's, making myself at home with a clean set of clothes in her guestroom. She'd ordered Chinese to be delivered, and I eagerly sprang for the front door when the bell rang.

Over Kung Pao chicken and egg rolls, our conversation drifted back to the place we'd left off last night, Chuck Bukovsky. I was pleased to see that Rachael was loosening up with me each day, trusting me with more confidences.

"Chuck's abuse must have been pretty hard to take," I said. I had brewed a pot of green tea and we'd settled once again on the comfy sofas in the living room. "Especially after what had happened with your father. You were pretty young, then."

She withdrew into her cushions. "Twelve. The first time was kind of an otherworldly experience. I remember coming out of a deep sleep, being really fuzzy. I smelled my dad's cologne and felt really happy that he'd come home from his business trip. He snuggled up to me in my bed and I fell back to sleep with his arms wrapped around me. The next morning he wasn't there and I asked my mom about it. She said he wasn't back from his trip yet and I must have dreamed him being there."

I reached for my mug but it was already empty.

"The next time the experience was similar but this time he rubbed his hands over my breasts and I was wide awake. I didn't know what to do. I just kind of froze. He kept whispering endearments and telling me this was our special secret." Her face had become soft and childlike as she spoke. "Months went by and I began to think I'd imagined it all. Then he came back. Always in the dark, always touching and whispering. I felt repulsed and stimulated at the same time. It was just..." Her voice cracked.

My skin crawled in horror. I couldn't imagine how awful it must have been for her.

She took a deep breath. "I don't know how long it went on before he began to ask me to touch him. He guided my hand. I—I couldn't do it. I rolled out of bed and ran for the bathroom. The next day I told my counselor at school."

"How absolutely horrible," I said.

"When my mother found out she insisted that I tell the story to the police and testify in court. Without her support I probably would have been too scared to say anything. On the other hand, as an adult now I can see that she wasn't happy in the marriage anyway and was probably looking for an excuse to leave him. It would have worked out well for her if she hadn't died so soon afterward."

"And your father's attitude?"

"Oh, he pleaded his innocence all along. Never did even admit to coming into my room." The afghan fell aside as she waved off the statement. "As much as anything, his lying destroyed all credibility with me. I mean, it's bad enough that he did what he did but not to face up to it, not to even apologize." Her words trailed off.

Something about the whole situation nagged at me. Unanswered questions from twenty years ago… I couldn't pin it down. But I still wasn't convinced that Bill Fairfield would take this threatening tactic now, this many years later.

I walked over to the kitchen counter where I'd left the pictures and descriptions Ron had left with me. Rachael had gone to the bathroom and came back looking steadier, back once again in the present day. She saw me shuffling through the pictures.

"Back to our other suspects," I said. "I'm not discounting your father or Chuck, but let's keep them on the back burner for a minute. Assuming that as long as Chuck's got someone else to batter, he'll leave you alone. He may still be a threat, but there could also be others." I spread out the papers. "Let's talk about them for a minute."

Picking up one of the descriptive sheets, I said, "Wilbur Johnson, your brother's disgruntled customer."

"I doubt it," she said. "I've never even met the man. If he was this angry at Grayson, why wouldn't he be threatening him? For that matter, why wouldn't he be down at the bank, shooting at everyone?"

Good point.

"Our list is getting short here. How about Ryan Tamsin?"

"Well, he stood to inherit quite a lot of money, and I'm

sure he thought he would. But his mother made her wishes—"

The phone interrupted her and she reached for it absently.

With a sharp intake of breath she dropped the receiver on the couch. I leaned over the huge coffee table that separated us and grabbed the fallen instrument, jamming it to my ear. Nothing but a dial tone.

ELEVEN

"RACHAEL, WRITE THIS DOWN!" I ordered, punching *69. I repeated the number given to me by the mechanical voice. Immediately, I dialed it, hoping the person would be dumb enough to pick it up. It rang fourteen times.

"One more try," I said. I dialed Ron's home number and was about to give up when he answered. "Can you get your buddy inside the phone company to trace a number?" I asked before he had a chance to take a breath. I read it off to him.

"With any luck, we'll have an answer sometime tomorrow," I told Rachael. "Now, while it's fresh, what did the voice sound like? Male, female, what did they say?"

"Nothing," she said. "There was someone on the line, but all they did was breathe. Strong, heavy breathing. It was so creepy, Charlie. Just like the other times."

"Other times? Ron didn't mention others."

"Yeah, there've been a few. Once there was a whispery voice that I thought was male, but couldn't be sure. I yelled at him that time, thinking it was Chuck. All the other times, though, it's just this breathing."

"Have you ever tried to have the calls traced?" I asked.

"No, didn't think of it. I'm sorry I freaked tonight. I guess with the lack of sleep and all this talk about the suspects, I'm just extra jumpy."

"Hey, perfectly understandable. Speaking of lack of sleep…"

"There's no way at this point. My mind won't settle down for another couple hours. Maybe if we changed subjects. I have a Scrabble board," she suggested.

By the time we finally went to bed around eleven, I knew that four thirty would come way too early. I took one of the bedrooms that faced the street, hoping I'd hear anything out of the ordinary. It felt like mere minutes after pulling the luxurious puffy comforter over me that the bedside alarm went off.

I wanted so badly to roll over for another two or three hours, but that wasn't my job. I sat up groggily and rubbed at my eyes, forcing them open. Rachael had told me that she planned to leave the house by five, and since her truck was at Justin's house it would be my duty to get her out to the field to meet up with her crew this morning.

We found them huddled on launch space T-12, Thermoses of coffee being passed around, and anxious eyes focused on the sky. In my early awakening haze I hadn't noticed that a breeze quickened from the east. Now that the sky had begun to lighten over the Sandias, thick gray clouds became more apparent with each passing minute.

"Looks like we may get weathered out," Sam said, sliding an arm around Rachael's shoulders.

She stared at the sky and flinched as a raindrop hit her eye. "I'll go see what they're saying up front."

I followed her to the large tent where the pilot briefing was just getting underway. We caught the last few numbers on the winds-aloft report. A few pilots bothered to jot them down but most just stood around with hands in pockets, scuffing their boots against the fine, powdery dirt floor. I glanced at Rachael.

"The rain wouldn't be that big a deal," she whispered, "if it were just a few sprinkles. It's the wind. I think they're going to call it."

Sure enough, after a show of discussion among the officials and a halfhearted vote among the pilots, the decision came down to put the day's flying on hold. "Hold" was a fancy way of saying that if by some miracle the weather improved in the next hour, people could fly if they wanted to. The forecast didn't indicate much chance of this, but only those in the tent knew that. No such announcement would be made to the crowds, who by this time were queued up by the thousands at the vendor booths to fortify themselves with burritos, cinnamon rolls, and coffee.

"What're you going to do?" Liz Pierce had edged closer to Rachael and showed her a scrap of paper with the winds-aloft written on it.

"Guess I'll see what Sam and the guys think. They might appreciate getting home early and sleeping a little longer."

"Us too." Liz's eyes scanned the crowd until she spotted Kevin. She headed his direction.

"So, do you think you'll actually fly today?" I asked Rachael as we walked backed to the truck.

"In this?" The wind had picked up to a steady ten knots by now, with spatters of rain sending occasional drops our way. It wasn't the kind of weather that would keep you off the streets or even off the beach if it had been warmer, but balloons are sensitive craft and any wind over five knots, especially in a crowd this size, would be too dangerous.

"So, will everyone pack up and go home?" I think a touch of wistfulness crept into my voice.

"The official line will be that we're holding until the weather improves. That will keep the crowds here because they've paid their money and are hoping to see a show. It also gives the vendors a chance to recoup a little something for the day. They lay out big bucks for booths out here, not to mention thousands of dollars in product, and they bitch like crazy when the crowd goes home early. Took a few years, but the Fiesta officials finally figured out they'd make everyone happier if they stalled and kept the people around. It works. Look at 'em."

True, few of the spectators were wandering around the middle of the field full of parked pickup trucks. They were all milling around the edges where the vendor booths were happy to snap up their money. It wouldn't net them a full day's income, but they might salvage an hour or two worth of sales. If some of the stunt planes flew, it would help keep everyone happy.

We trudged back to T-12 and found several of the guys huddled inside the cab of the truck. Justin and Danny were slipping a rainproof cover over the wicker gondola, cinching it in place as we walked up.

Sam slid the window of the driver's seat down and stuck his head out. Rachael filled him in on the verdict while I stepped back to see what the guys were doing. They'd covered the inflator fan with a small plastic tarp and secured the other equipment.

"I had a feeling about this," Justin said. "Forecast was right on."

A meteorology major in school, Justin would have been the logical one to ask. Silly me, I hadn't even thought to check it last night.

Rachael had climbed into the cab of the truck beside Sam and I felt somewhat at loose ends.

"Think you guys can watch each other for the day?" I asked through Sam's open window, even though I was pretty sure I knew the answer to that one.

With their assent and after some cautionary words about her safety, I gratefully extracted myself from the Balloon Fiesta scene and found my Jeep. A few other people, obviously having figured out the weather, were also leaving but most would stay until the official announcement came in a couple of hours. My first thought was how nice it would be to go home, retrieve my dog, and snuggle in for a rainy day of reading and catching up on little chores. But the more I considered it, the logical choice seemed to be following up with a couple of our suspects.

Six o'clock on a Monday morning turns out to be an excellent time to catch a person off guard. I retrieved Chuck Bukovsky's address from my purse stuffed under the back seat of the Jeep and headed his direction. Traffic on the freeways was picking up but hadn't yet reached the full-on mess it would be in another hour. I found the house on Valencia Drive and parked across the street.

Drapes across a large front window, probably the living room, were closed tight, as were the mini-blinds on a smaller one that I guessed might be the kitchen. A newspaper in a plastic sleeve lay in the driveway. Even the paperboy had noticed the forecast. A red Lexus and a silver Toyota sat in the driveway. I backed up, positioning myself so I could see their property clearly but wouldn't be the first thing they spotted when they looked out. I didn't have long to wait.

The mini-blinds cranked open—the first sign of life—and about a minute later the front door opened and out stepped Chuck. He wore some kind of sweatpant-type pajama bottoms, in a plaid fabric with a cord at the waist. His black T-shirt was either several years and many washings old, or he actually thought the skin-tight look enhanced his muscles. He bent to pick up the newspaper and the plaid slid dangerously low. He hiked it back up, scratched at his crack, and walked back toward the front door.

My goal was to find out whether he was current on Rachael's whereabouts, but this didn't seem like the best time to approach someone from whom I wanted information. I waited in the car another hour until the transformed Chuck appeared—showered, shaved, and wearing a business suit. He climbed into the red Lexus in the driveway. I knew he worked for one of the smaller brokerage houses with offices in the Uptown business park, only about ten minutes away. I followed discreetly and saw my chance when he whipped into a Starbucks along the way. He angled the Lexus across two parking spaces and walked toward the coffee place, his step jaunty, his metro-business persona in full evidence. I followed him to the door, managing to get there in time for him to hold the door for me.

"Hey, Chuck. Wow, it's been awhile."

He struggled to figure out how I knew him, working to balance confusion with his natural inclination to flirt.

"How's Rachael?" I asked. "Haven't seen you guys in ages."

He fumbled for an answer and I kept up the chatter.

"Did she end up taking that position with...what was the name of that firm?"

We approached the end of the line of five people standing at the counter. He clearly didn't have a clue who I was. But he wanted to keep the conversation going.

"Uh, well, Rachael and I split. Awhile back," he said.

He grinned stupidly and got ready to make a move.

Uh-uh, I thought. I know too much about you, buddy. "So, what's she up to these days? Have you seen her recently?"

"No, uh, I've been pretty busy," he said.

Yeah, busy beating up on someone else. "I've been wanting to call Rachael for ages," I said. "I really need to do that. Wonder where she's living now."

"Can't help you there," he said.

I studied his face while he studied my sweater. My turn at the counter came up and I ordered a double latte. He cleared his throat, like he was about to say something but I handed some money across the counter and brushed past him.

"Well, it's great to see you again," I said casually. "I really will call Rachael one of these days."

"Uh, maybe I can give her a mess—" The rest of it was cut off by the closing door.

I got to my Jeep and ducked low until he came out. He scanned the parking lot but didn't see me. I followed the red Lexus to the Morgan Stanley building and watched him carry his Starbucks cup and a briefcase inside. I sipped at my latte and fought back the urge to settle deep into my seat and nap. I tended to believe that Chuck didn't know where Rachael lived now. The spontaneous meeting, catching him completely off guard just now—I thought I'd actually caught him in a moment of honesty. Plus, the man was a flirt. If he could have kept me in conversation longer he would have. But, he was also a charmer, and they'll say anything, truth be damned. I might do a little follow up.

The silver Toyota in their driveway hadn't moved. My dashboard clock indicated that it wasn't yet eight o'clock. I rummaged through some papers I'd left on the back seat and came up with a lined pad and a manila folder. I padded the folder with a sheaf of random papers, mostly financial reports from Drake's business, added four or five blank pages ripped from the lined pad to the top of the stack and wrote Garcia, Nora, on the folder's tab section. I actually didn't hold much hope that this hokey ruse would work but I'd give it a shot.

She came to the door only after my second press at the doorbell. The door opened a few inches, revealing half of a tan-complected, dark haired woman in a pale blue fuzzy bathrobe. The scent of herbal soap drifted toward me.

"Yes?" Her tone clearly conveyed that she had no intention of opening the door farther.

"Nora Garcia?" She nodded. "I'm with the Department of Family Services. We have a report that you called the police a couple of weeks ago about a, a situation, here. Our department does a follow up call to see if there is…" I glanced up and down the street. "Could I come inside? It won't take five minutes."

Across the street a neighbor walked out to her car, openly staring toward us.

Nora glanced over my head at her, then pushed the screen door open, and stepped back. The living room drapes were still closed and she left them that way. Light from an overhead fixture in the kitchen cast a beam into the dim room and a glow from a hallway to my left probably came from the bedroom beyond. Even in the dim light I could tell she had a puffy, blackened eye.

My semi-plan of asking her to verify Chuck's whereabouts when the notes had showed up at Rachael's went out the window. So did the cool, professional manner of the government social worker. I took her hand and pulled her into the kitchen where I could get a better look at her face.

"I have to get ready for work," she said, staring at the floor in that if-I-can't-see-you-you-can't-see-me attitude.

"Nora, how long are you going to let him keep doing this?"

She pulled away from me and picked up a mug of coffee from the counter. It shook so badly that she set it down again.

"It's up to you," I said gently. "You call the police but you won't let them do anything. You put makeup over the bruises and a smile on your face and act like it's going to be okay?"

"He says he's sorry and he won't do it again," she pleaded.

I let a full minute go by. "They all say that, Nora. They all promise to change and they rarely do. I'll bet he's made that same promise more than once, hasn't he?"

She stared at the floor again.

"You have to get out. Put your things in the car and drive away."

"It's my house. He moved in and I can't make him move out. I've told him to, he just laughs at me."

"The law can help you there. Cooperate with them and they can make him move."

"I can't make it without him. He tells me that. I'll never make enough money to—" She stopped abruptly, her eyes darting to the doorway behind me. I spun, half expecting to see that Chuck had returned.

A little girl stood in the beam of light in the living room, her jeans and sneakers neat, her pink jacket unzipped, her school pack squarely on her back. Eyes like liquid chocolate stared at me from an unsmiling face.

TWELVE

NORA BUSTLED FORWARD and zipped the child's jacket. "Got your lunch money?" she asked.

The girl nodded silently, not taking her eyes off me.

"Okay, the bus is coming in just a minute," she said. The doorbell chimed twice, quickly. "There's Megan now." She kissed her daughter and attempted a hug around the bulky pack, then opened the door and guided her daughter out to join another pink-jacketed girl on the porch. "You girls have a good day."

She stood there watching until they'd covered the length of the sidewalk and turned toward the corner. Closing the door with a firm click, she turned toward me.

"I have to support her," she said. "You see why I can't leave Chuck."

"No, Nora. I see exactly why you do have to leave him. How can you let your daughter grow up watching this? You think she doesn't hear the fights? You think she doesn't see your face in the morning? How long have you been with him? He's not her father, is he?" I hammered her with questions.

"Her father died last year. A car accident. He was a kind man, a good father. He…" She walked back into the kitchen and made another attempt with the coffee cup.

"Sit down. Take a deep breath," I said. I set her mug on the table and guided her to a chair. Pulling another mug from a rack on the wall, I filled it and topped hers from the carafe on the counter.

"Steven was a good man. A hard worker. We were married ten years and we barely came up with enough to buy this house. I cleaned houses and took Christy with me until she was old enough for school. When Steven died there was no insurance…the mortgage company was calling…" She raised the cup and took a small sip.

"And Chuck came along and helped out financially," I prompted.

"He's so generous. We have everything now. I don't have to scrub other people's toilets anymore. I work in an office and they let me leave at three so I can be here when Christy gets out of school." She glanced up at a clock on the wall above the stove, stood up, and took her mug to the sink. "I have to get ready."

"Another minute, Nora. You really have to seriously think about your situation here. It isn't healthy now and it's going to get worse."

She stared out at her front yard, spine stiff.

"Do you have relatives? Or a friend Chuck doesn't know about? Someplace, anyplace you can go until the police can get him out of here. Your life and your daughter's probably depend on it, you know."

She nodded silently. I picked up my folder that I'd laid down near the coffeemaker and headed for the door. I wanted to dash down the hall, pack a bag for her, and shove her into her car. I wanted to take her to her mother, to a battered women's shelter, anyplace. I wanted to magically heal her bruised eye and her bruised ego so her daughter would never have to look at them again. But all that was up to her. First, she had to want those things or she'd simply come right back.

I reached out and rubbed her shoulder. "I don't want to read about your untimely death in the newspaper one of these days. Where will Christy be then?"

Her shoulder shook and a tear dripped from her chin, only one of thousands she'd already shed, I felt sure. I quietly walked out the front door and got in my car. When I looked back at her kitchen window she was gone.

I started the car and drove a block before I realized my hands were shaking. I pulled to the curb on this quiet residential street and shoved the gearshift in Park as my vision blurred. My emotions had been way too near the surface in recent days. There were women like Nora Garcia all over this city, this country, and the world. I couldn't save them all, and I doubted I could even save this one. I swallowed hard and took a sip of the latte that sat in the cup holder. Stone cold.

Get with it, Charlie. You did what you could back there.

I got out of the car and walked around it twice, shaking out my limbs and breathing deeply of the chilly fall air. Damp brown leaves lay in the gutter and I kicked a bunch of them. They settled into soggy clumps on the pavement.

Back in the car I reviewed my plan. This might be a good time to try Ryan Tamsin again. Most retail stores opened around ten, so he'd probably still be at home. I blended into a crush of traffic on Wyoming and headed south. The semi-crumbling house looked exactly the same as before. Closed up tight. Next door, drapes stood open and a lamp glowed softly in the living room window.

This time when I knocked at the door I heard vague sounds inside, a creaking floor, a radio somewhere in the background with a thrumming beat. About the time I'd raised my hand to knock again, a creak sounded much nearer and the doorknob wiggled loosely. The man who opened the door was probably approaching fifty. His dark hair was pulled straight back and bound in a ponytail at the neck. Parts of his face hadn't been shaved this morning, other parts probably never. A stylized Fu Manchu dripped from the corners of his mouth, showing strands of gray that matched his fluffy sideburns.

"Yeah?" he growled.

"Ryan Tamsin?"

"Who wantsta know?"

Suddenly I wished Ron had taken this interview. Like the dog out back, Tamsin exuded the attitude that he would snap your head off the second you showed any weakness. I took a second to pull a card from my bag and to arrange a hardened look on my face. Tamsin glanced at the card but didn't take it. His sullen stare challenged me.

"Rachael Fairfield," I said. "Had any contact with her lately?"

"The little lawyer bitch? Why would I?"

"You had some business dealings with her a few weeks ago, didn't you? Something about your mother's will."

"You already know the story, why come here? Her with her blond hair and high heels. That snotty attitude. She sure don't give a shit about me."

"She handled the will and you disagreed with what it said, I hear."

"Well, wouldn't you? My own mother cuts me off and I'm just supposed to let this prissy little thing tell me that's how it is. No choice, just take it." His voice rose a couple of steps. "What a laugh, that uppity attitude of hers. What a big fucking laugh. All this 'I'm so pure and honest' shit. And her old man's in prison all this time she's playing all highbrow with everybody else. I know what that little blondie's about, heard the whole story."

"What whole story? How?" A chill crept up my spine.

"From the old man's cellmate at Santa Fe." He noticed the surprise I couldn't conceal. "Oh, yeah. Buddy of mine, knows old Fairfield *real* well. Knows the little bitch was puttin out for him when she was twelve. Suddenly she gets religion or whatever and nails him in a different way. You think *I* hate the bitch. Talk to her old man." He shot me a smug grin and slammed the door. I jumped at the sharp sound and I'm sure my tough-girl expression flipped right off my face.

Through the door I could hear Tamsin's chuckle. A minute later the huge-sounding dog bounded against the side gate barking like crazy and sounding like he could rip the gate right off its hinges. I made a prudent retreat to my vehicle and reached for my cell phone as I turned the key in the ignition.

Ron's voice reassured me with its normalcy. "Find out who was William's cellmate in prison," I said.

"What's the matter? You sound kind of shaky."

"I just met a friend of this cellmate. Not a pleasant guy."

"I'll get on it," he said. "By the way, I got an address and place of work from Fairfield's parole officer. He's a stock clerk at the Wal-Mart on Carlisle, on the night shift. I'm sitting outside his apartment building now. I'll follow him to work tonight."

I let out a pent-up breath as I ended the call. Nine in the morning and I felt like I'd already put in a full day. I pulled into a McDonald's and treated myself to two Egg McMuffins, a very large orange juice, and big coffee. I consumed all this in my vehicle while listening to a newscast on the radio to put my mind on other people's problems for a change. About the time I was wadding up my used wrappers, I saw Ryan Tamsin roar by on his black Harley. He'd strapped a Nazi-style helmet, complete with pointed top-spike, over his dark hair and added leather jacket and chaps for a complete black-all-over ensemble. He rumbled by, shaking the entire neighborhood, on his way to work.

The pre-dawn low clouds continued to thicken and I liked

the idea of having part of a day to myself. I headed back toward I-40, wanting to get to my own part of town as quickly as possible. Before I'd made it halfway, the sky opened and my wipers barely kept up with it, even on fast speed. I pictured Tamsin on his bike and suppressed a tiny smile. Traffic began doing weird things and I slowed, holding back to let the weavers and lane switchers have their way. By the time I got to my own driveway it had slowed to a steady drizzle.

Rusty recognized my Jeep by sound and bounded out of Elsa's back door to meet me in the driveway. I let his enthusiastic greeting make up for my recent encounters with humans. It's wonderful how a dog brightens your day.

I waved to Elsa in her doorway and headed for shelter as I unlocked my front door. My clothes felt damp and wrinkled, like I'd been wearing them for two days straight, which I nearly had. I felt ready to shed them and head for the shower but decided to check the answering machine first.

Two messages: One from Ron (call me) and one from Drake (Hi, hon, we're in a lull this morning and I just wanted to hear your voice). Our last conversation had been a little tense and I dialed his number with a little flutter of trepidation. "Hey, is this a good time?" I asked when his soothing voice greeted me.

"Perfect." He sounded ready to chat, buddy to buddy, like we usually do. I let him go on about how the helicopter crew was having to wait around until a government guy from Fish and Game arrived to give them the go-ahead to take off. "Like I don't know what direction the wind is coming from and can't pull pitch on this thing without some bureaucrat with his two-week's training here to tell me it's safe," he complained.

I knew the story—make-work jobs within the bureaucracy so someone's untrained nephew could wave a signal flag and command a million-dollar piece of equipment, flown by a pilot with over twenty years experience. And the uncle who'd gotten him the job no doubt kept his own by sitting around in the off seasons dreaming up more rules to give jobs to more untrained nephews. I half listened while I rolled my head from side to side working cricks out of my neck.

"So, how's your day going so far?" he asked.

I jumped back to reality. I didn't think he really wanted to hear the whole raft of details about people he didn't even know, much less the fact that I'd had encounters with a couple of pretty nasty ones already this morning. "Fine," I said. "Just wishing we were both back home again."

"Me too. How about us taking a vacation during the winter lull this year, a real trip somewhere that has no helicopters and where no one can possibly ask you to investigate something." His voice sounded so wistful, I knew he was serious about it.

"Sounds great to me. Think about where you'd like to go."

"You too. Miss you."

For a fleeting moment I wanted to walk right out to my car, drive north, and go to his job site. Pick him up and just hit the road. I wondered what it would be like to just quit life for awhile and become anonymous in some little ski resort for the next six months. We exchanged some more mushy stuff and ended the call by making suggestive promises about what our reunion evening would consist of when he got home. I'd peeled off my damp clothes as we talked and the shower was running, hot and steamy, by the time we hung up. Lather and shampoo and thoughts of Drake filled the next ten minutes but work loomed ahead. I toweled off and bundled into my thick terry robe.

Shaking off the warm, glowy feeling, I dialed Ron's number.

"Got your message. What's up?" I asked.

"Not much," he said. I sensed weariness in his voice. "Finally got the chance to speak to Bill Fairfield."

"How'd that go?"

"About like I expected. He denied knowing anything about any notes to Rachael. Said he hasn't seen her since he got out of Santa Fe."

"What's his attitude like?"

"Wary. The guy isn't about to open up to me. He's got that defensive attitude that prison usually gives them. Comes through like, 'You're not the law and you're not my parole officer and I don't have to talk to you.'" He sighed deeply, like he was wondering exactly what we were doing with this case. "I don't know. Maybe Fairfield would open up more to you. Confide something."

"Like what? I'd just use my feminine wiles on him and he'd completely spill the beans?" What beans? I wondered as I formulated the question. We knew what he'd done. Did I honestly think he'd just blurt out a confession about the threats?

"There's more to this story than we're seeing," Ron said. "I don't know what it is, but this isn't just about Bill's doing time and Rachael's receiving a bunch of notes. I can't exactly put my finger on it."

"Clovis." I said. "Something back there, something from years ago." I told him how my alarm bells had gone off when it seemed that Mrs. Pinkley, the neighbor, didn't know anything about Linda Fairfield's death. "Come on, Ron, we find a woman who's got her nose in everything but she doesn't know how her neighbor died? I think there's more to that whole story."

I heard the crackle of some kind of food wrapper being wadded. "So, you think I ought to go back there and do a little more checking?" he said without enthusiasm.

"I could." Even as I said it, I wondered what I was thinking. But the idea began to grow. Ron could certainly keep an eye on Bill Fairfield without my help, and Rachael had decided to stay at Sam's today and skip flying tomorrow. It would be the perfect time to go.

I glanced out the window as I clicked off the call. The rain had stopped but clouds still blanketed the sky. Although I'd left Ron with the impression that I might just jump in the car this minute, it seemed a little late in the day to drive halfway across the state, not to mention that the early mornings were taking their toll. My body felt ready for a good, long sleep.

I opened a can of soup and managed half of a crime scene show on TV before my eyelids began drooping. Bed felt great and I dropped out of consciousness until full daylight streamed through my windows. I allowed myself the luxury of a leisurely cup of coffee and long shower.

I slipped into jeans and a sweater and pulled a duffle bag from the top closet shelf. A change of clothes and minimal overnight toiletries didn't half fill it. By the time I'd added a jacket and gloves, a couple of scoops of dog food in a baggie and Rusty's bowls, we were ready. My canine partner danced with joy when he saw these last items and he even picked up his leash and waited near the front door.

It was barely noon when I reached the eastern outskirts of town and I cruised into a fast-food drive-through where we grabbed burgers and fries for two and a Coke for one. Rusty finished his in roughly four seconds, then stared at me as I took my time. By the time we'd passed through Tijeras all edibles were gone and he settled into the back seat for the three-hour ride.

Ron had given me the Fairfield's old address but otherwise I hadn't much idea where I'd go. Turns out three hours on relatively straight highways is a pretty good time to plan strategy. Unfortunately, the only new idea I came up with was to visit the local newspaper and see what kind of news the Fairfield family was making back in the 1980s. I pulled into the parking lot of said newspaper office after a quick stop at the edge of town for directions.

"The offices close at five," the receptionist told me as she escorted me to a room that looked like it served as a conference room in addition to holding reels of microfiche and two readers. "But this is Tuesday. Somebody'll be around until at least eight."

I shot her a puzzled glance.

"Paste-up day," she said, like that explained everything. "We scramble all day to get the final layout done on Tuesday. It gets transmitted to the printer tonight by nine, papers come back tomorrow and hit the streets by three. We're a weekly. That's how it's done."

"Ah." I slipped out of my jacket and got a quick rundown from her on the filing system for the fiche.

"I'd offer you some coffee," she said, "but it disappeared hours ago and no one's had time to make more. There's a Coke machine down the hall, girl's room right through there." She pointed. "If you need help you'll have to trip somebody as they dash by."

"No problem," I assured her. She'd offered me exactly what I wanted, hours of uninterrupted time without anyone staring over my shoulder.

I located an index file that let me look up subjects alphabetically and it was a matter of minutes before I'd determined the dates of Bill's trial and sentencing. His arrest had happened three months before that. Small town justice seemed pretty swift.

With the reels at hand I sat at one of the machines and played with the controls until I could scroll through the pages without feeling like I would throw up. There's a technique whereby you close your eyes in coordination with your finger hitting the buttons that send the film flashing forward and backward.

Rachael had mentioned that their father was running for mayor so it should have come as no surprise to me that the year of the big scandal was also the election year, but it did. I scrolled through headlines until I came to campaign photos—the smiling Fairfield family on a dais somewhere, all caught in mid-wave to the crowd.

Bill Fairfield looked almost exactly like his son does now—tall, slender, salt-and-pepper hair. Linda was a pretty blonde, her hair styled fashionably large, her smile looking only slightly forced. Grayson must have been about twenty, a dark haired, young-faced version of himself today. Rachael looked at the camera from beneath lowered eyebrows, shyly, a smile that refused to show her teeth because they obviously were encased in braces. Hard to believe the polished present-day version had sprung from this gawky, colt-like beginning.

The accompanying article spouted the usual political stuff that all campaigns are made of, conservative version, with loads of patriotic feel-good-ism and promises that one guy couldn't hope to actually keep. The bottom half of the front page sported much of the same (even more conservative) from the opponent, Dean Patterson.

Patterson's family looked equally good in their photo, obviously taken from the same dais on the same day. The candidate was also tall, also good-looking, and also accompanied by a wife and son. No daughter for this one. The son was probably about Rachael's age because of the obvious acne and brace-smile.

I scrolled through the weeks as the election began to draw near. The smiles became more tight and the promises began to be ignored in favor of jabs and smears at each other. One photo of a political forum caught Linda Fairfield with a wine glass not quite concealed in her hand as she posed with her husband. I wondered where the paper kept its outtakes, or whatever they called them, the photos their photographers snapped but which never made it to print. Undoubtedly, there would be some good stuff there.

"Ma'am?" The voice startled me and I nearly fell out of my chair. "I'm sorry. I just wanted to tell you that it's five o'clock and I'm closing up."

My face must have registered disappointment. I'd not gotten through a fraction of the issues I wanted to.

"You said someone would be here late?" I asked.

"Well, Sarah's in her office and a couple of the reporters still have to e-mail their stories. But—"

"I really just have a few more places to check," I said. "And I drove all this way…"

"You can always come back tomorrow."

"But that's just the thing. I have to be back in Albuquerque tomorrow." I tried to make my eyebrows do that pleading thing. "Please? Just a little while longer?"

She fell for it. "Okay, but stay in here and if anyone asks what you're doing just say that Gerald said it was all right."

"Gerald."

"The office manager. He's gone already but nobody will question it."

"Right."

She closed the door behind her, exposing a file cabinet that I hadn't seen before. File cabinets are kind of my specialty and it didn't take me more than two minutes to figure out where the photo archives were. This was way better than the public stuff any day. I silently pressed the thumb button on the door, locking myself in, and took the first folder labeled "1984 Election" to my work table.

The pictures covered the same events I'd found on the front pages but these revealed a lot more about the players. Linda Fairfield seemed to frequently get caught with drinks in her hand. Dottie Patterson, Dean's wife, must have stubbed out dozens of cigarettes for those staged photos but the evidence right here showed the truth. Since her husband had apparently campaigned hard on the issue of making all city restaurants non-smoking, it didn't take a rocket scientist to figure out the many shots of the two of them looking apathetically at each other. This was not an ideally matched couple.

By the time I'd flipped all the way through the folder, I'd put together a picture of the Pattersons: he being preachy, polished, and very conscious of his image (evidenced by some blurred shots where he'd obviously reached up to smooth his perfect hair); she being a secret smoker, also conscious of her image (as evidenced by the shots where she didn't know the camera was on her and she'd not sucked in her tummy bulge), and not a very happy woman. Here she was, on the verge of becoming the first lady of the whole town and her candid shots revealed sad eyes and forced smiles.

The Fairfields also presented a different picture: Bill's political zeal showed through, with a hard edge to his mouth and a fearsome stare in his eyes. Grayson showed up again as his father's little clone, eyes watching his dad's moves, emulating his postures. Rachael looked bored in every shot where she wasn't required to smile. Linda looked…well, in several of the shots she looked more interested in Dean Patterson than in her own husband.

THIRTEEN

WELL, WELL. A little something going on between Linda Fairfield and her husband's number one rival? That certainly could prove to be interesting, after all. I wondered if the feelings were mutual.

I pulled out the few photos in which the two families mingled. Nothing overt, just hints, body language. Maybe I was imagining it. As I got to the back of the folder I realized it had a built-in pocket, the kind of file folder where you could separate the contents and put special items in the little pocket. Someone certainly had. Jammed down out of sight in the pocket was a single photo. It was a group scene in which people mingled with drinks in hand. Linda certainly had hers, obviously not her first of the evening, judging by the giddy look on her face. Dean Patterson stood at the left side of the picture, talking to a short man in a tux. More accurately, the short man was talking to Dean. Dean and Linda were exchanging a look that spoke volumes. If a picture is worth a thousand words, that steamy look was worth one: blackmail.

My mind whirled through possibilities and couldn't settle on anything. Voices in the hall interrupted my reverie and, without thinking, I jammed the photo into my bag along with the four or five others I'd separated out. In one swift move I closed the folder, three-stepped across the room, and jammed it back into its space in the drawer, closing the drawer as quietly as I could.

I held my breath as the voices went on by and I returned to my chair. Could we be looking at another motive for someone to want Bill Fairfield out of the way? Maybe Linda didn't really want to be the town's first lady and she'd sabotaged his chances. Maybe she'd had a thing going with Dean Patterson for a long time. So many things didn't make sense.

A glance at my watch told me that I better hustle as I returned to the microfiche. Now the election itself took on new importance, as I wondered whether the dirty little secrets of the two families ever became public and how Bill's arrest figured into it. I scrolled quickly to the weeks nearer to the election. The campaign continued to heat up, the issues of the day being hotly debated. Then came the day of Bill's arrest—three weeks before the election.

MAYORAL CANDIDATE WITHDRAWS UNDER CLOUD read the first headline. The article, obviously written minutes before press time, gave no details and promised more later. By the following week, the story made the lower half of the front page, with a notice that William Fairfield, former candidate for mayor, had been arrested on suspicion of child molestation. The headline that week was about the newcomer who'd shown up to run in Bill's spot on the ballot. The next week carried the news that Patterson had won in a landslide. Nothing about Fairfield.

I pondered that. Was it simply a matter of the small town grapevine being quicker than the newspaper? Everyone already knew the skinny on the whole thing so why take up space? Or was it a case of the paper shoving the real dirt under the carpet, protecting one of its prominent families? Small towns were funny that way. I'd probably never know the answers.

A tap came at the door and I opened it.

"I saw the light on in here," the young guy said. He sent me a puzzled look.

"I guess I better get going," I offered.

"Unless you want to spend the night. We're all heading out."

"One second." I put away the reels of film and gathered my jacket and purse, with the evidence of my thievery inside. I hoped nothing showed on my face but he didn't question me.

Outside, it was getting quite dark. Gray clouds formed a low ceiling over the flat terrain and the smell of ozone told me to expect rain shortly. Streetlights had already come on. Rusty greeted me happily, sticking his head out the window I'd left open for him, smearing the glass with lovely doggy slobber. No such thing as a clean car for a dog owner, I guess. I shoved him out of the way so I could climb inside. Two blocks over I located a motel that looked big and clean and would allow dogs with a twenty-five dollar deposit.

We settled into our room, which was the standard version of such rooms all over the country, this one including a hair dryer and a teenie coffee maker. I dumped some nuggets into Rusty's bowl and pondered my next move while he wolfed them down. Ron had given me the name of the older bank teller, the one he'd been unable to reach on his visit. Since it was now well after banking hours, I took the chance and looked up her name in the phone book.

The beauty of small towns is that the phone directories are also small and people don't seem to have that big-city paranoia about having unlisted numbers. Debbie Fuller didn't even bother to disguise the fact that she was a lone female. And she answered on the first ring. I introduced myself and gave my prepared story about how I needed to get in touch with Bill Fairfield and understood that he used to work at the bank.

"Yes, ma'am," Debbie said. Her eastern New Mexico accent was just one tiny y'all away from its West Texas neighbors. "Mr. Fairfield worked at the bank years ago, but, heavens, I haven't kept up with him. After the, uh, unpleasantness of that election he left town."

"Did Mrs. Fairfield and the children leave at the same time?"

The line went so quiet that I thought she'd hung up.

"Debbie?"

"Who did you say you were again?"

"I'm with RJP Investigations in Albuquerque. We're working on a case involving the daughter."

"Well, I didn't know the family all that well. You could check with Miranda Clement. She retired from the bank a few years ago but she was Mr. Fairfield's secretary."

"Is she still here in Clovis?"

"Yes, ma'am." She closed down with this note of formality and I knew I wasn't getting anything more from her. I thanked her and hung up.

Back to the little phone directory, where a listing for Riley Clement gave me an address. I consulted the sketchy street map in the front of the directory and thought I could find the place. Fifteen minutes later I pulled up in front of a modest ranch style home with a wide lawn and neat borders of brick-edged flower beds. The storm that had dumped rain on Albuquerque yesterday had now reached the eastern edge of the state. Gusts of damp breeze rolled through the treetops, sprinkling my windshield with droplets. I left two windows cracked a couple of inches for Rusty before getting out and facing the chill.

A stocky woman in her late sixties opened the door. She had probably been to the beauty parlor that day. Her blond hair held the just-sprayed tightness of a new set meant to last for a week. I revised my story, leaving out the part about our investigation, pretending instead to be an old school friend of Rachael's who hadn't seen her since fifth grade.

"Oh, my goodness," Miranda said, ushering me into an early American living room. She insisted on bringing iced tea and saw to it that I was comfortably settled into a cushy flowered chair. "I've so often wondered about Rachael myself."

"I heard there was a terrible scandal and her father went to jail," I said, edging a conspiratorial whisper into my voice. "Did Rachael and her mom stay in town after that?"

"Not for long, I'm afraid. Her mother died just a few weeks later, you know."

"A few weeks?" Odd. I hadn't at all gotten that impression from Rachael herself. She'd led me to believe her mother went into rehab and there was a steady decline over a period of years.

"…suicide, but a lot of us never believed that."

"Excuse me? I… I didn't catch that."

"I just said that a lot of people around here never really believed that Linda Fairfield killed herself."

"She drank a lot, didn't she? We kids never really talked about it, but you kind of knew."

"Yes. Poor Mr. Fairfield. He'd come into the bank some mornings, distracted. You knew he had problems at home but he never talked about them."

"And I guess his election campaign must have been rough. We heard a little about it on the news in Albuquerque. My parents loved to catch any little news item about people they knew from back home." Careful, Charlie, you'll start believing your own fiction.

Miranda remained perched at the edge of the plaid sofa. She reached for her tea glass before addressing my question.

"The election was a terrible time for all of us. I often wondered whether it was smart for Bill to get involved at that time, his wife being so fragile and all. The pace of it, the cameras, and reporters all the time. They had some social function nearly every night of the week and it wasn't doing her any good."

"The drinking picked up, I guess."

"Well, yes. And then Bill's arrest. You heard about that, I imagine."

I nodded.

"That just about split the whole town. He dropped out of the mayoral race immediately, of course, even though he didn't do the horrible things she accused him of. I never did understand that. Never will. Bill Fairfield might not have been a saint, heaven knows. He ran a pretty tight ship at the bank and he probably angered some people along the way. And he'd do just about anything to get ahead politically. Wanted to be governor someday, you know. But to touch his little girl like that? No, not Bill. I just never will believe that."

"And Mrs. Fairfield died very soon afterward?"

"That's the other thing I started to say. I'll never believe she killed herself. Maybe it was the drink. That's the devil's work, you know, that liquor. But I could almost understand in her case. She was unhappy in the political life."

"Maybe she really was unhappy enough to kill herself," I said.

"But it doesn't make sense, does it? Bill was, truthfully, the cause of her unhappiness. He'd been arrested, her time in the political spotlight was over. I always thought she'd finally be able to take her daughter and pick up her own life, do whatever she wanted."

So, why would she kill herself when she was on the verge of being free of the life she didn't want? The woman had a point.

"Well, you came here for information about Rachael, didn't you?" she said, popping up from her seat. "I'm pretty sure she ended up in Albuquerque. Never hear from her myself, but I do get a Christmas card every year from her brother. Let me get you his address." She bustled out of the room.

I let out a pent-up breath. Why, indeed, would Linda Fairfield have killed herself? She'd been in love with Dean Patterson and suddenly, with her husband out of the way, she could have had her dream. Except that Dean had a wife. And Dean was clearly going to become mayor, with dear Dottie at his side. Dottie, not Linda.

Miranda reappeared, a sheet of small notepaper in her hand. "Here you go. This is Grayson's address. I'm sure he'll know where Rachael is nowadays."

"Thanks." I stuck the note in my purse without really looking at it. Miranda didn't sit again and I took this as a hint. "Whatever happened to the man who ran against Bill in the election. He won, I guess."

"Dean Patterson. Oh yes, he won easily. Let's see…" she glanced upward. "He served just one term as mayor. I'll never forget his wife. She was another who never wanted to be in politics. They'd send her out to give a speech somewhere and she'd manage to offend someone every time. They divorced shortly after he left office. Still lives in town, I think. We don't exactly move in the same circles."

"And Dean? Is he still in town?" Who knew, I might get something useful from one of them.

"No…gosh, I have no idea. I'm sure he's not still in Clovis. I'd know for sure if he was. But I have no idea where he went. Isn't that strange?"

She stood in her doorway as I stepped out onto the wet sidewalk. The downpour would be only moments away, and I scurried to my Jeep. As I left the quiet residential neighborhood it hit me that I hadn't eaten in over seven hours so I made my way back to the commercial district where I found a drive-in burger place, one of those old fashioned ones where you park your car under an awning and talk to a little speaker. While I waited for my double deluxe cheeseburger, tater tots, and Coke to arrive, I pulled out the phone directory that I'd brought from my room and looked up Dottie. There was a D. J. Patterson listed, and the address looked to me like it would only be a couple of blocks from the Fairfield's old place. It seemed like a reasonable assumption that she'd be the one.

Thirty minutes later, sufficiently full and having waited out the initial downpour of rain, I headed toward the once-posh country club section of town. I cruised past the Fairfield's former home and agreed with Ron's assessment—upscale, as seventies-style homes in small towns went. The block of split-level and two-story homes remained very well maintained, with wide lawns and subtle landscape lighting. Three blocks down and two over I found the Patterson's place, a two-story house with dramatic arches across the front and a pitched roof done in wood shake shingles. Lights glowed at several windows, upstairs and down, and a ten-year-old Cadillac sedan sat in the driveway. I parked at the curb and wondered briefly if Dottie would even open the door to me after dark.

As it turned out, she didn't have much choice. I'd reached for the bell when the door opened and the quiet night air erupted with hen chatter from a set of women who were clearly on their way out. I stepped aside as three women in pastel pantsuits with darling little embroidered embellishments, purses hooked over their arms, and plastic bonnets over their bouffant hair, stepped out. Pointed stares reminded me that my normally straight hair had probably kinked in the humidity and that I could probably be taken for anything from a salesperson to a wayward hippie at this point. I sent a cryptic smile at each of them and maintained my position within arm's length of the door.

By the time they reached the edge of the covered porch they realized it was still sprinkling rain, so this prompted a quick dash to the Cadillac.

"Dottie?" I asked, stepping into her line of sight while her attention was still on her retreating guests.

"Do I know you?" She firmly gripped the edge of the door with her right hand. Her once fiery red hair was now a pale apricot, styled in a neat cap of feathers, and her fair complexion still contained a few freckles. The wide-smiling mouth that had just bade her friends goodbye now turned into a straight line framed by deeply etched verticals leading toward her chin. I guessed her to be somewhere in her seventies.

"I'm Charlie Parker. A friend of Rachael and Grayson Fairfield."

Her ginger-brown brows crinkled, bringing back the names from the past, clearly wondering where this was going.

"My company is investigating some threats Rachael recently received." I shifted from one foot to the other, not really wanting to go into the whole thing out here on the porch. "Bill Fairfield recently got out of prison. You may have heard about it. Could I come in for a minute?"

The news about Bill's release seemed to surprise her, and with her guard down she stepped aside to admit me.

We stepped into a foyer with baby-blue walls and blue floor tile. Directly in front of me a staircase led to the second floor. The focal point of the entryway was an oval rock garden tucked beneath the stairs, bordered by a tiled edge and accented by a mirrored wall behind it. Nestled among the white rocks sat a couple of garden gnomes and a stone bunny. I worked to suppress a smile but she'd already turned toward the living room.

Through a wide archway, a sea of baby-blue carpet stretched across a living room of blue and cream furniture that looked as if it had never seen the weight of a human butt. The one sign of life in the room was a card table surrounded by four chairs, a deck of neatly stacked cards in the center. This was clearly the hub of the evening's activity.

"If you don't mind, I need to get this cleared away," Dottie said as she bustled ahead of me.

"No problem. I just have a couple of questions." I dropped my purse on a stiff Queen Anne chair and trailed her into a dining room—also done in baby-blue and ivory—where she began to gather the remains of a spread. Silver bowls of pastel mints and mixed nuts, a platter of decimated tea sandwiches, a silver coffee service. She began picking things up and carrying them through another doorway to the kitchen.

"You seemed surprised that Bill Fairfield is out of prison," I said, raising my voice as she went into the kitchen. "I guess you didn't see him when he was in town last week?"

A rattle sounded, dishes being set into the sink, then she returned. "No, I haven't seen Bill Fairfield in twenty years."

"But you knew them well at one time. Bill and your husband were political rivals. Your husband won the election and was mayor of Clovis for awhile."

She picked up the sandwich platter and a handful of linen napkins. "That was a very long time ago. I can't see what it would have to do with anything that's going on in Rachael Fairfield's life today."

She zipped back to the kitchen and made some more noise. I wished she'd just settle down for a minute.

"Look, this gets kind of touchy," I said when she came back. I reached out and touched her forearm, stopping her in mid track. "Rachael thinks Bill is threatening her now because she testified at his trial."

She made a humph sound and turned toward the table again. "Not Bill. I can't see him thinking that would change anything now."

I stepped into her path. "Neither can I. So I'm wondering what's really going on. And the more I learn about that family, the less I think I know."

Her lips tightened and she itched to be moving again.

"How did Linda Fairfield die?" I asked.

Her eyes darted toward her china cabinet, then at the table. Finally her gaze settled on the floor.

"Dottie? How did she die?"

Her fingers twitched and settled on her upper arms as she folded her arms and closed me out.

"Officially, it was suicide. Now I think you'd better go."

"Who determined that? Was there a coroner or medical examiner who made that assessment?"

I waited out a long beat of silence.

"Old Doc Hardin was the medical examiner and mortician back then." Her lips nearly disappeared into the tight line of her mouth.

"Where can I find him now?"

"The cemetery over at Bovina. He died ten years ago." The tight line became a smirk.

She sidestepped me and went back to clearing the table. I mumbled a thanks, retrieved my purse, and left. Outside, the rain had become a mere sprinkle, whipped now by winds at the back edge of the storm front. I flopped into my car seat wondering what to do next. Rusty licked at my ear and I roughed up his fur. Enough for tonight. We headed back to the motel.

I switched on the room's TV set for company and took a hot shower, slipping into comfy sweats afterward. I pulled the photos from my purse and laid them out on the bed, shuffling them into different order from time to time but not coming to any new conclusions. I still had a strong hunch about there being something between Linda and Dean Patterson but had nothing else to go on. I'd hoped to learn more about that situation from Dottie, but she clearly didn't care to open up to me. My mind jumped around for answers, for ideas on what to do next, but I didn't come up with anything firm, and by ten my eyelids were drooping. I pointed Rusty to his usual mat on the floor and switched off the TV.

I stayed unconscious until the phone jarred me awake. The bedside clock told me it was 5:43. I fumbled for it and uttered a groggy hello. A perky voice asked for Tiffany and I slammed the receiver back in place and let go with a few sailor words. Rusty padded over to my side and laid his chin on the edge of the bed, his deep brown eyes questioning me. I rubbed his ears and the brown eyes closed in contentment. Mine would have, too, but my stomach began talking urgently about breakfast. I forced myself to roll over and plant my feet on the floor. A sudden wave of nausea hit and I dashed for the bathroom. Nothing much happened but I hovered over the bowl with weak knees, wondering what the hell this was about.

I studied myself in the mirror and decided I'd had too many combinations of strange food recently. Dark circles under my eyes also attested to the fact that all the early mornings were catching up with me. My damp hair had dried in bizarre kinks and bunches while I slept. I ran a brush through it, which blended the bunches and did nothing for the kinks. Forget it.

I put my sweats back on and clipped a leash on Rusty's collar. We headed for the rear edge of the parking lot. I saw that the sky had nearly cleared and the rain, which last night puddled everywhere, had rapidly soaked into the ground completely. The air felt crisp and clean. I let the dog make his rounds and realized that my stomach's shakiness seemed completely gone and I felt ravenous.

Back in the room I gathered our few possessions and put them in the car, checked out of the motel and headed for the Denny's next door for breakfast. I lingered over my omelet and toast, saving a few crusts in a napkin for Rusty, who was fogging my car windows quite nicely by now. The phone book had given me an address for the Hardin Mortuary, and that was going to be my main stop this morning once they opened.

Since that wouldn't be for another hour—according to their yellow pages ad—I busied myself by taking Rusty for another short walk and calling Drake to touch base. As expected, I got his voice mail. He'd undoubtedly gotten up in the pre-dawn and was now somewhere over the treetops, flying over the most gorgeous country in the state. I felt a pang of…something. Something like being left out, like the kid who's afraid to go on the giant roller coaster but then feels jealous watching all the other kids have a great time at it. I really needed to get back into the pilot's seat. Drake was right about that.

For now, back to the current case. I pulled into the mortuary's parking lot, surprised to find it full. The stream of dark-clad people told me which way the funeral chapel lay, and I headed the opposite way. Surely someone must man the offices during services. I hoped it would be Riley Hardin, son of the late Doc, whose thoughtful face adorned the company's phone directory ad. And I hoped he'd remember something of the Fairfield death so many years ago.

I located the office and was told by a woman in a navy suit that Mr. Hardin was presently tied up. After I presented my business card she punched a couple of digits into the intercom on her phone and asked someone named Sean to come up. Sean turned out to be another Hardin, a guy barely out of his teens, whom I assumed to be Riley's son or maybe a nephew. He had the clean-cut look of a kid raised in a fairly strict conservative family—dark hair that was short but not radically so, navy twill pants and navy polo shirt with the Hardin logo embroidered on the chest. He gave me a tentative smile showing perfectly orthodontured teeth and his gaze slid shyly off to the side.

"Ms. Parker will need to see the M. E. records from…what year did you say it was?"

"Eighty-four, I think," I told them.

"Records that old will be in the second basement," she said, probably for both Sean's and my benefit.

"Right," he said. "Come with me."

I trailed him through a series of back hallways and down some stairs. Closed doors along the way probably hid all manner of activities that I didn't even want to know about. At the bottom of the stairs we entered a large room, which contained rows of storage shelves, mostly flower vases, folded cloths in a variety of colors, and assorted office supplies.

Sean headed down one of the aisles and came to a door against the far wall of the room. It opened to reveal shelves of file boxes, all neatly labeled by year and letters of the alphabet.

"There's space in the front offices for about three years worth," he said. "After that, nobody hardly ever wants to see them again so they come down here."

We passed boxes from the new millennium years, then headed back through the nineties.

"Here we go," he mumbled. "1984." He pulled the box from the shelf and carried it to a table across the room. With a flop and a small cloud of dust, he set it down and raised the cardboard lid. Over his shoulder I could see tabs on neatly labeled manila folders. "What was the name you needed?" he asked.

"Fairfield, Linda Fairfield."

His fingers had just reached the folder I wanted when a voice echoed from the storage room, calling him.

"Here you go," he said. "That's Uncle Riley. I'll be right back."

A man in a perfectly tailored charcoal suit stood in the doorway. He sent one quick glance in my direction then beckoned Sean toward him and began to issue instructions in a practiced, low tone that kept the words strictly private. I turned my attention to the folder Sean had given me.

Linda Fairfield. A copy of the death certificate was the uppermost document. Cause of death: overdose of barbiturates. I flipped past it, came upon a photo of the body which I quickly went past, and found a page of handwritten notes. I caught the words again: overdose of barbiturates. This time they were followed by a dash and the note—self inflicted? Apparently old Doc had questions about it. But he'd put his verdict firmly, without question, on the death certificate.

I glanced up. Sean had left, apparently sent on some errand but Riley Hardin was puttering with something on one of the shelves, discreetly keeping an eye on me.

"Mr. Hardin? Are you familiar with this case?" I asked.

He stepped forward and took the folder from me. "Fairfield. I vaguely remember it, but it was a long time ago."

I pointed to the handwritten page. "I found this note. It looks like Doc had some question about the suicide. See how he put a question mark here? Wouldn't that indicate that he wasn't sure whether she took the drug herself or if someone else might have somehow given it to her?"

He set the folder on the table and began to ruffle through the pages. "Here are the autopsy findings," he said. "Everything seems consistent with barbiturate poisoning. Doc microscopically examined the liver. Also requested tox tests from the state lab. Fatal overdose. Conclusive. The method the drug was administered seems to be the question."

He gazed across the room and tapped his fingers restlessly. "I vaguely remember this case now. Dad—Doc, everyone called him—said there was something Marilyn Monroe-like about it. No pills remaining in the stomach, a very large amount of the drug in the bloodstream, but no sign of her having taken it herself. He speculated as to whether someone else could have given it, injected it maybe."

"But no mention of a needle mark?"

"They're not always easy to find."

"So, ultimately, he just listed the death as an overdose, with no opinion about the method."

"Right. As I recall, the Fairfield family was in turmoil. Something had happened to the father and the children were dealing with it. The son was of legal age but young and inexperienced with this kind of thing. Family friends came along and helped out, I think. The Pattersons." He gave a little shake of his head. "Wow, where did that come from? Amazing how old stuff can just pop into your head, isn't it?"

"Uncle Riley? Brenda says they're ready upstairs." Sean's voice interrupted my roiling thoughts.

"That's it, then?" Riley said. He put the folder back into the box and slid the box into its slot on the shelving. I noticed that he switched off lights and closed doors along the way as they escorted me out.

Back in the car I sat for a few minutes pondering everything I'd learned. For the life of me I couldn't see what any of this had to do with Rachael's current problem and the threatening notes. Bill Fairfield was still the big unknown and I began to think it was about time I had a conversation with the man.

Before heading back to Albuquerque, I decided to call Ron.

"Got the name of Bill Fairfield's cellmate for you," he

said. "The most recent one anyway. Seems he had several over the years."

"Anyone who'd likely be a buddy of a Harley-riding biker?"

"Buddy, hardly. He's Tamsin's brother."

FOURTEEN

"HENRY TAMSIN. Affectionately known on the inside as Hank the Tank."

"Hank the Tank?" I had a hard time picturing a tank as the confidant of William Fairfield, banker, politician, and Clovis's man of the year.

"Doing time on aggravated battery and attempted murder," Ron said. "I went back into the newspaper archives and found that he put two guys in the hospital, one of them in critical condition, in a bar fight. Get this—the fight started when Hank busted up the place, raging drunk, on the night of his mother's funeral. After the reading of her will."

"The same will that cut Ryan out without a cent did the same to his brother?"

"Exactly. Dear old mom saw through both her sweet boys and didn't approve of their lifestyles. Left her entire estate to her favorite charity. Score: battered women's shelter, a million, Tamsin boys, zero."

"Oh boy. So Hank the Tank finds out he's paired with Rachael's father and learns all he needs to know to go after her."

"And Hank got out two months ago, get this, on good behavior. Just lucky for him that neither of his victims died," he said.

"And little brother Ryan is still running wild and free. Obviously, they talk."

"May have even paired up. We don't know, although

Hank's records show that he's living in Santa Fe. We should probably check that out. Can you make a run up to Santa Fe tomorrow?"

And face The Tank alone? I told him there were probably a hundred good reasons why I shouldn't do that.

"I wasn't suggesting you confront him yourself," he said. "Just check out where he's living, is he really there, is he holding a job. You know, check with the neighbors, stuff like that." I grudgingly agreed and brought up another thought.

Ryan obviously hadn't cooled a bit in his attitude toward Rachael. I'd seen that first-hand. But I couldn't see a series of threatening letters fitting his style. Wouldn't he be more likely to just track her down and drag her into a dark alley somewhere? Taking the time to cut words from magazines and deliver notes to her house didn't seem like the Ryan Tamsin I'd met and I told Ron so.

"So, maybe it is her father after all," he said. "Maybe Bill got the story about the will from Hank and added it to his own list of grievances."

"We better keep tracking him then," I said.

"I've been on him pretty constantly." He didn't sound exactly thrilled. "He comes and goes from work, keeps a regular schedule, hasn't done anything suspicious yet. At least Rachael's safe for now. I just talked to her a couple hours ago. She's gone with Sam out to his place in the mountains. Plans to skip tomorrow's flying. I guess a lot of the crews do that, pick a day in the middle of the week and get some rest. She'll stay at Sam's until sometime tomorrow."

"I'm heading back to Albuquerque now. I can watch Bill for part of the time."

"Yeah, good idea." He sounded relieved.

"How about if I take over for the afternoon and evening?"

We agreed that it didn't seem necessary to sit outside Wal-

Mart all night while Fairfield did his job. Ron had worked out a deal with the supervisor to call him if Bill left anytime during his shift, and this hadn't happened all week. I'd stake out his apartment and see that he reported for work at eleven that night. We could each get a good night's sleep and Ron could take over again in the morning.

The drive back to Albuquerque passed uneventfully. The previous day's showers were nowhere in evidence, I had the sun at my back, and traffic was light. What more could I want? Figuring that Rusty had endured about all he wanted of life in the car for awhile, I stopped at home to give him free rein of his own territory, to drop off my small duffle, and to gather a small cooler full of drinks and snacks to get me through the next eight hours or so.

It was a little after three when I pulled up to the very average looking stucco apartment building that Bill Fairfield now called home. I couldn't help but make the comparison to the two-story brick with white colonnades where he used to live in Clovis. A place he might still be living had events turned out differently. I gave another glance at the tan building with its three floors of all-alike windows and boxy construction that offered nothing architecturally interesting, then scanned the parking lot. I spotted Ron's car near the street, beside a second driveway that I'd not noticed when I pulled in.

"I am *really* ready to go home and stretch out in front of the TV," he said with a yawn.

I pushed aside at least six fast food bags and took his passenger seat. "You ought to be ready to spend an hour at the gym." I stared pointedly at his stomach. "Getting a little gut on you there, buddy."

"I've always had a gut on me and an hour at the gym isn't going to change that."

He had a point there. He quickly filled me in on Fairfield's activities for the day (no sign of him since he'd come home from work at eight o'clock this morning), the location of his apartment (third window from the left, second floor), and his vehicle (a white Nissan that was easily ten years old) parked directly under his apartment window. I shifted back into my own vehicle and watched Ron drive away after I promised that I'd see Fairfield safely off to work at eleven tonight.

I diligently watched the building and parking lot for a good, solid fifteen minutes to get the feel for the pace of life here, the comings and goings of the people. There wasn't a lot going on in the middle of the afternoon and face it, I got bored pretty fast. I opened one of my bottles of spring water and pulled an apple from my stash of goodies. I'd brought the morning paper from my front porch so I decided to give the headlines a quick glance. Nothing about Rachael or her record attempt, thank goodness. Maybe Grayson had taken us seriously after all.

A full-page ad about a huge shoe sale at Mervyns had pretty well grabbed my attention when I realized that Bill Fairfield's car was on the move. Yikes! I jammed the newspaper aside and wedged the water bottle between my thighs as I reached for the key and started the Jeep. He'd turned left out of the driveway by the time I'd managed to start rolling and was nearly a block away before I reached the street. That was fine. With little traffic at this time of day, I could easily keep an eye on him. I let two cars pass me before I entered the street and I stayed a block or so back as I watched his moves. He signaled a left onto Candelaria and a few blocks later, another left on Carlisle. When he made another left on Montgomery, I realized he was probably heading for the freeway and I closed the gap slightly. He surprised me by pulling into a gas station instead. I hung back, not wanting to be the only other person standing at the pumps while he fueled his car. A parking spot opened up beside the convenience store portion of the building and I took it.

Fairfield got out of the Nissan and went into the store, presumably to prepay for his gas. Through the windows I saw him hand over some kind of bill and come back out. The pictures I'd seen of him didn't really convey the essence of him at all. I knew he'd be tall, slender, with hair that was mostly gray. His face was thinner than before and there was a sadness around the eyes now. He moved with graceful smoothness. Even pumping gas, there was a fluidity of motion, a certain style. If I'd ever imagined Fred Astaire pumping his own gasoline, he might have done it like this. I could easily see how the man might have become a huge political success. The charisma was still there, despite all he'd been through.

Careful, Charlie. The guy molested his own daughter and may have had a hand in his wife's death. He's spent twenty years in prison and surely is no Fred Astaire.

He'd finished pumping his gas now and was in the process of replacing the nozzle onto its slot on the pump. I cranked my ignition and got ready to move. But when I glanced up he was walking straight toward me. His eyes met mine and he signaled for me to roll down my window. My foot hit the brake and the Jeep rocked. I slid the window down two inches.

He ambled up casually and stopped a polite distance away.

"I thought, since you've been following me, that I should introduce myself. Bill Fairfield." His voice came out smooth as honey and the smile that followed could make female hearts feel like warm butter.

I felt totally flummoxed. My mouth flapped a couple of times but no sound came out.

"I figured you'd show up sometime. The chubby guy had to get tired at some point. You must be Charlie." Again, that smile.

"Uh, yes." Witty, I know, but it was all that came out.

"I know you're private investigators and I know you're following me because there've been threats against my daughter." He reached out and rested a hand on the top of my car, but his body language was casual and not at all threatening.

Thanks a hell of a lot, Grayson. For a banker, his sense of discretion was completely lacking.

"Look, I understand why you're doing this," Fairfield continued. "I can tell you all day that I haven't sent any threats. I didn't do the original crime, either, but that didn't stop the system. I paid the price. I have no reason to want to get into trouble again."

"I—"

"You've got a job to do. I know that. Just wanted to get acquainted."

With that, he flashed the smile again and turned. He went into the convenience store and came out five minutes later with a jug of milk and a sack. He raised his chin toward me as he climbed back into his car. I let out a huge breath. This was definitely the weirdest surveillance I'd ever done.

I followed him back to his apartment where I watched him get out of the car and climb the stairs to the second floor. At dusk, a light came on in his window. From five until around eight, cars came and went, but nothing more happened with Bill Fairfield until ten thirty when he came out, lunch sack in hand, and I followed him to Wal-Mart. He gave me a little wave as he walked into his workplace.

Once Bill had been safely in place for thirty minutes, I phoned Ron and he released me to go home. I told him how Fairfield had approached me at the gas station but didn't mention the effect his smile had on me. No one would ever know that.

FIFTEEN

I GOT HOME FEELING RESTLESS and agitated. Too many encounters with strangers and too much time in the car left me
wanting to run, to exercise, to punch something. I wanted to
talk to Drake, to let his strength and even disposition make
me feel centered again. But it was way too late to disturb him.
On these jobs he was always up well before daylight and bedtime came correspondingly early. I settled for exercising to a
thirty-minute video of aerobics followed by thirty more minutes of Tai Chi.

By this time it was so far past my usual bedtime I knew
my internal clock would be screwed up for days. I showered
and fell into bed.

When the alarm sounded at six, I slapped the button and
went right back into a deep sleep. Insistent prods from a dog
nose finally got my attention around nine and I groaned and
rolled off the edge of the bed. I'd probably missed my window
of opportunity to talk to Drake but I dialed his cell anyway.
Sure enough, the voice mail came on and I left him a message.

Next, Ron. I knew he'd spent the early morning hours
staking out William Fairfield's apartment and I really didn't
want to end up having to take over that duty, although it
would have been the right thing to at least offer. I'd try the
office first, then his cell phone, but only if necessary. With
any luck I could stall him by letting him know that I'd be at
Rachael's tonight as we'd discussed.

"Charlie, where are you?" he demanded. Sally'd said he was on the other line, but he'd obviously put that call on hold long enough to share some stress with me.

"I'm home now, Ron, you know that," I said in my calmest, sweetest voice.

"Yeah, well. I need you to get to Rachael's."

"What's going on that can't wait until this evening?"

"There's been a new threat on Rachael and she's pretty shaken up."

"What happened?" I visualized sabotage to her balloon or a near-miss in traffic.

"Another letter like the last one." He paused for effect. "But this time they left it on her doorstep, along with the body of her dead cat."

I felt my stomach do a high flip. "Oh, geez." Poor little Misty.

"She found it when she returned from Sam's this morning. I can't tell if she's more shaken by the note or the cat. She needs company right now and I've got a deposition at two that I can't miss."

"Do you think it was her father?" Could he have left his job after I'd watched him check in?

"When I got there at six this morning he was still on the job and I followed him home."

"Could he have left during his dinner break?"

"Supervisor says he didn't and his time card wasn't punched out."

I tried to come up with other possibilities and the only thing that came to mind was Ryan Tamsin.

"Plus," he continued, "we don't know when the, uh, message was left. Rachael hadn't been home in about twenty-four hours."

"So, basically, anyone could have come and gone."

"Guess so. I'd like to canvass the neighbors on the cul-de-sac to see if anyone saw anything."

"I can do that," I said. "I'll go to her place, see how she's doing."

I hung up and decided to call Rachael before driving out there. I had a hard time picturing her hysterical. Anyone who was willing to pilot a big piece of fabric more than thirty thousand feet in the air was no wimp. Rachael's voice got a little shaky when she answered but she sounded in control.

"I'll be there in a couple of hours," I assured her. "Lock everything and stay back from the windows." She assured me she would.

Meanwhile, I needed to check a few things here and secure the place for another overnight away. I heard the mailman's truck and stepped out the front door to meet it. I remembered that I hadn't checked the mail the previous day either. Somehow time kept managing to sneak away from me.

The neighborhood, with its streets lined with tall, old trees, conveyed peace and serenity. The cottonwoods and sycamores were beginning to turn, fall shades of yellow and orange against the vivid October sky. Cicadas thrummed in the distance and a late robin darted over the lawn, poking around for stray bugs. I exchanged hellos with the mailman and took the little stack he handed me, went back inside, and found Rusty nosing toward the kitchen trash. He jerked back guiltily when he saw me.

I'd just begun fingering through the mail when a tentative tap sounded at the back door. I jumped, even though it could only be Elsa.

Her small face and puff of white hair showed at the glass panes. She smiled broadly when she saw me turn toward the door.

"Hi," she greeted. "I didn't know if you were still home."

"Just for a minute, I'm afraid. I have to get out to Rachael's again and stay with her tonight."

Her smile faltered just a fraction but she didn't let the disappointment make it as far as her voice. "I was hoping you could come over for dinner."

I made a disappointed sound. "Balloon Fiesta is done on Sunday and Rachael's record attempt will be in the history books by then. How about dinner over here Monday night? If Drake's home by then it'll be something really good. If not, it'll be something quick and easy."

Her wide grin said all. Despite my lively neighbor's many interests and friends, I knew she got lonely at times. She considered me her granddaughter and loved time we spent together. Now that she was well into her eighties I couldn't afford to wait for "someday" to include her in our activities.

"What's going on with this lady balloon pilot?" she asked. "Charlie, is this going to be dangerous?"

"Um, I don't think so. I really don't know." I laid the mail on the table and opened the door for the dog, who'd begun his subtle way of whining. He dashed out and ran to the woodpile. "Someone has threatened her and Ron wants me to spend the night at her house, just to scare off any potential intruders, I guess. That's why I thought it would be a good idea to take Rusty. Maybe I'll actually get some sleep if he's there to alert me to anything serious."

"Take care of yourself?" She said it tentatively. Even though she's spent a good portion of her life worrying about me, I guess it never gets any easier for her. I crossed the room and hugged her. She rubbed my back, making circles with both hands, and I wanted to stay there for the next week instead of leaving again right away. With a tight feeling in my throat, I finally pulled back.

"I will," I said.

We each made some it'll-be-all-right noises and she headed back through the hedge to her kitchen door. I gathered food and water bowls for Rusty and locked up. He was thrilled to hop into the back seat of my Jeep.

By the time we were on the road again, heading across the river, the rush-hour traffic was already beginning. An accident on the bridge brought two lanes to a complete stop and the others to a crawl. As I inched along, I pulled out my phone and called Drake again. His voice mail came on; he must have been out on a flight. I left a message that I'd be at Rachael's tonight and gave her number. Then I dialed Rachael and suggested that I could pick up a pizza on the way. I envisioned something with thick crust and every topping known to man. She agreed and gave directions to the place nearest her house. She said she'd call in the order now. Finally, the traffic began to move. It took me twenty minutes to negotiate the drive to the pizza place, but having the fabulous scent as company for the final six minutes of the drive made it all worth it. Rusty was drooling heavily by the time we arrived and parked in Rachael's driveway.

Rachael's appearance, when she opened the door, clearly showed that the week was taking its toll. Her complexion had faded; her hair lay limp. Her eyes were puffy from lack of sleep and grief at the loss of her pet. Although it seemed an effort, a smile worked its way to her mouth as she greeted us at the door.

"I'm so glad you had the idea to bring your dog," she said, reaching out to pet Rusty, whose complete attention rested on the pizza box I held shoulder high.

I carried our dinner to the kitchen counter, while Rachael pulled plates from a cabinet.

"He's a great alarm system," I told her. "Once he settles in and isn't completely focused on ways in which to lay claim to spare pizza crusts, he'll alert us to any noises from the outside. I'm sure you can use some sleep by now."

"I know, I look awful today." She touched at her hair. "Give me a second." She scurried off to her bedroom before I could assure her that I didn't really care whether she combed her hair or wore makeup at dinner. Heaven knows, I certainly didn't.

She came back in under three minutes. A fresh dash of lipstick added color to her face and she'd pulled her hair up into a clip. The transformation had actually made her smile, too.

"Okay, dinner," she announced. First things first, which was good with me. I'd poured wine from an open bottle into the two glasses she'd obviously set out for the purpose.

We sat on stools at the kitchen counter bar and each polished off two slices before another word passed between us. Rusty perched strategically between us, mouth at the ready to catch anything that might accidentally drop. I aimed a small segment of my crust toward him and he made a neat mid-air catch. By the time I'd picked up my third slice, I was able to pace myself and speak too.

We made idle chit-chat about the weather and the forecast for the rest of Fiesta week while we finished eating. Once the prospects of more people-food had ended, Rusty became interested in his surroundings and began to explore the house. He picked up my scent in the bedroom I'd used a few nights ago and seemed content with that. I took him briefly out to the backyard and we walked the perimeter of the house. He initiated a few bushes and sniffed closely at the places jackrabbits like to hide, thick shrubs and a pile of firewood. He paid special attention to the front doorstep, where Rachael had made her grisly discovery this morning. I noticed a fresh mound of earth with a single chrysanthemum lying on it in a corner of the backyard. This wasn't going to be easy.

I left Rusty closed inside the courtyard as I heard a car pull slowly into the driveway next door. This would be my chance to follow up on my promise to Ron. I walked over to the house across the cul de sac to the south of Rachael's. A woman had pulled her white Subaru into the garage and was just stepping out of it.

"Excuse me," I called out.

She jumped as if I'd shouted the words right in her ear. Her eyes went wide and she tugged her short jacket down over generous hips.

"It's okay." I stayed at the end of her drive, as non-threateningly as I could, but had to raise my voice. "I'm staying at Rachael's. Across the street?"

Her eyes flicked toward the other house and back at me.

"I'd just like to ask you a couple of questions, if I could."

A look of impatience, one of those not-another-survey attitudes flashed across her face but she didn't bolt. Yet. I approached carefully.

"Rachael Fairfield, your neighbor over there, had some strange notes slipped under her gate during the past few days," I said. "We're just wondering if you might have seen anyone over there, any strange vehicles on the street?"

A look of irritation creased her brow. "There are strange vehicles over there all the time," she said. Her voice hinted at Midwestern, conservative middle class. "Trucks, young kids, that whole balloon contraption."

"Rachael's crew. Those are normal. Have you ever noticed a black motorcycle there, one of those noisy Harleys?"

"No, nothing like that." She closed her car door and started toward the connecting door to the house. "But then, I'm not always here. Can't say who comes and goes when I'm at work."

I started to ask whether anyone else was home, a husband or kids who might've noticed something, but she'd made it to the safe haven of her door and pressed the button for the garage closer. I hopped back to avoid being closed in.

No help there. I looked at the other two houses on the street. One had a For Sale sign in the yard and appeared to be uninhabited. At the other place no one answered my rings or knocks so I gave up and headed back to Rachael's.

By the time Rusty and I got back inside, Rachael had stored the leftover pizza, rinsed the dishes, and made coffee. She offered a plate of bakery cookies to go with it and we sat in the living room facing the wall of windows with that fabulous view of the Sandias. Rusty surprised me by visiting his own bowls, which I'd set up in a corner of the kitchen, rather than pestering us about the cookies.

"I guess we'll have to get into this soon," I said. "Ron said there was another threat this morning."

Her eyes reddened but she covered by clearing her throat and getting up. "I'll show you the note." She went to her office and brought back a flat nine-by-twelve envelope, which she handed me without a word.

I brushed grit from the back of it, opened the flap, and pulled out a single sheet of paper. As before, it consisted of plain white paper with cut-out magazine words and letters.

IT WON'T BE THAT HARD TO GET YOU.

The eight words stood out starkly.

"You found this by the front door?" I asked.

"Yes. Right by M…by Misty." She swallowed hard. "It was about noon. I'd just gotten back from Sam's place."

"It was inside the courtyard, right?"

"Yes, and the gate was still locked." She paced to the kitchen and back. Rusty raised his head, sensing her agitation. "Charlie, I can't tell you how vulnerable I felt right then. Someone had done this horrible…horrible thing. And they'd gotten right to my front door. I always felt so safe here. I—"

I slipped the note back into the envelope, giving her time to compose herself.

"We'll figure this out," I said with more assurance than I actually felt. "Meanwhile, I'd suggest that you skip the rest of the Fiesta. It's, what, three more days? I don't like all the publicity surrounding the Balloon Fiesta and the record attempt. You can do the record attempt next week, after all the hoopla is over, do it quietly somewhere away from the crazy atmosphere of the big event. If someone wants to take away your moment in the spotlight, we can simply disarm them."

"This is all crazy. If they kill me that will keep my name out of the papers? I hardly think so. If anything, wouldn't that turn me into some kind of heroic figure, cut down in the prime of life, so much to achieve if not for these tragic events, blah, blah."

She had a point.

"So if it's not just about preventing you from setting the record, it's personal. Someone who wants to see you hurt."

"Dead, Charlie. You can say it—he wants me dead. My own father wants me dead."

"We don't know that for sure." I told her about Ron's surveillance of her father and the fact that he seemed to be accounted for all night. I also did a quick recap of my visits to Chuck Bukovsky's place and the connection with Ryan Tamsin and his brother.

"But why now?" I mused. "Chuck or Ryan could have killed you any time. Why during Balloon Fiesta, why with all this publicity? Unless it's not one of them. It could be someone who's looking for notoriety himself."

"So any garden variety nut case, then."

"Could be. Rachael, why aren't we calling the police? There are stalker laws, they could be doing something about this."

She picked at a cuticle. "Gray won't let me."

"Won't *let* you?" My voice rose and I fought to keep it

calm. "Rachael, it's your life, not his. He isn't getting these notes." His pets aren't being murdered.

"I—I don't…" The doorbell interrupted her. Rusty leaped to his feet and raced to the door, barking madly.

"Go in the back bedroom," I whispered. "Lock yourself in. I'll handle the door."

Retrieving the Beretta from my duffle near the kitchen counter, I stuffed it into my waistband and pulled my sweater over it. I glanced out the peephole and remembered that visitors rang from the courtyard gate. Had I relocked it after taking Rusty for his inspection tour?

The bell rang again.

I opened the door and let Rusty race to the gate, his frantic barking filling the quiet evening. I grabbed his collar and he quieted, although he pulled relentlessly toward the closed wooden gate.

"Who is it?" I shouted.

A man's voice said something too muffled for me to catch. I opened the little peep window in the gate and scanned the sidewalk. He was alone.

It was Grayson Fairfield.

SIXTEEN

I OPENED THE GATE, keeping a grip on Rusty's collar. The harder I tugged at him, the more he lunged, a maneuver simply designed to get out of my restraint. He's never actually attacked anyone. But they don't know that.

"Where's my sister?" Fairfield demanded, edging away from the dog. Considering I'd only met the man once, I thought it would at least be polite to say hello first.

"Inside," I told him.

He threw a disdainful look at Rusty, then marched past us.

I quieted the dog with some overly perky words and he settled down. I relocked the gate and the front door. Grayson and Rachael stood in the living room, already in the midst of a conversation that looked intense.

"...would be smart," Rachael was saying.

"Nielson is an important client." His voice was firm.

"Charlie, you remember my brother." Rachael, at least, managed some of the pleasantries.

I nodded. I definitely remembered that he'd done nearly everything he could to sabotage our efforts to keep Rachael's whereabouts quiet and to watch their father.

"Gray thinks I need to be flying tomorrow, and I was just trying to tell him that we'd been discussing that."

I turned on him. "How can you ask your sister to put herself at risk, all for publicity?"

"Ms. Parker, this world record is a once-in-a-lifetime

event. We've worked for months getting it set up, getting the media to pay attention, making sure she's got coverage from top publications. We cannot afford the huge letdown, which will undoubtedly make it into the news, if she simply quits now."

I couldn't believe I heard him correctly. I glanced at Rachael. She'd backed up to the kitchen counter and stood nervously twisting her rings on her fingers. I turned back to Grayson but he was already on his way to the door.

"Tomorrow morning," he said to Rachael, dismissing me as if I were just a pesky insect. "Nielson will be there and so will you."

He turned on his heel and walked out.

"Rachael?"

She busied herself at the kitchen sink, rinsing our coffee mugs and wiping a spotlessly clean counter.

"I'll just say one thing, then it's your decision." I took a firm stance in the living room, not taking my eyes from her. "You're a successful woman in her thirties, ambitious, smart, and pretty. I don't know why you're still taking orders from your older brother, but your life is on the line here. Not his. Yours. Make your own choices."

I walked out the front door. Rusty trailed along, probably hoping we were leaving now. Fairfield's car was gone and the street looked quiet. I relocked the front gate, then the front door, then stomped through the house and went room to room checking windows and doors. Rachael had returned to the living room and staked out one of the leather sofas, her gaze blank and focused somewhere in the empty space in the middle of the room. It was fully dark now and I tacked up our curtain of sheets across the back wall of windows. When I'd finished that, I pulled my pistol from the waistband of my jeans and pointedly set it on the coffee table between us.

Rachael's face seemed more drawn than before. Tears dampened her cheeks and one round droplet threatened to plop from her chin at any moment.

"Charlie, you're—"

From deep inside my purse, my cell phone rang. I held up an index finger indicating for her to hold that thought while I turned to locate my bag.

Ron started right in. "I just had an irate phone call from Grayson Fairfield," he said. From his tone of voice I knew this wouldn't be pleasant. "Our client didn't like your attitude. He says you mouthed off to him."

I glanced at Rachael and decided this wasn't the place. I walked down the hall and closed myself into the guestroom. "I thought Rachael was our client. And I didn't like his attitude either, Ron." I recapped my side of it, hating the defensive tone in my voice.

"Just remember that the financing for my new house depends on him. I'm not going to live in this crappy apartment forever, and if my house deal falls through it's on your head."

He hung up and I childishly dialed him right back, launching on him before he'd said a word.

"Just tell me, Ron, what's our job here? Are we trying to keep Rachael safe? Or are we merely here to suck up to Grayson Fairfield? I just need to know what I'm *really* here for. Think it over and let me know in the morning because I'm completely tired of this bullshit tonight." I clicked off and tossed the phone on the nightstand.

My neck twinged with pain and I sat heavily on the edge of the bed, holding my head with both hands. Great job, Charlie. Now who's the one taking orders from her older brother? Now the client's mad at me, the client's brother is mad at me, Ron's mad at me, and my husband hasn't been any too happy recently, either. To emphasize the point, Rusty whined out in the hall, unhappy that he'd been shut out. Great, even my dog's mad at me.

I opened the door and he greeted me with his special I-love-you-no-matter-what doggie kisses. My heart softened and hot tears prickled at my eyes. I blinked them back and strode out into the hall.

My duffle and purse lay on the floor near the kitchen counter. I gathered them up. "Everything is secure," I said to Rachael. "Sleep well."

"Charlie, wait." She stood up and took my arm.

I spun around.

"You were right," she said quietly. "I have to make my own decisions. I can't let Grayson keep pushing me around."

"We all make our choices," I said.

"Yes, and I've been dumb about mine, that's for sure." She indicated the two leather sofas and we each took one, facing each other. "I want this world record. I want it a lot. But I've let myself get caught up in Gray's whole publicity machine and the idea of making it a big event. The idea that it should take place at Fiesta, with national media and a hundred thousand people watching…that's all dressing. The record will be official as long as the FAA observer records it on that little instrument of theirs. Really, other than my crew, I don't need anyone else to be there." She dabbed at the corner of her eye with the cuff of her sweater.

"But, it's been a big rush, hasn't it? Admit it, the reporters and the well-wishers, it's all been pretty heady."

"Yeah. It has." She sniffed loudly and walked to the kitchen counter for a tissue. After a discreet little nose-blow she returned to her seat. "So, what now?"

Fatigue had begun to drape over me like a shawl. My brain felt like mush.

"Let's sleep on it," I said. "I don't think you should fly tomorrow, not after the message you got today. Let's sleep as late as we can in the morning and wake up with a fresh perspective. I'll come up with something."

A wave of gratitude flushed over her face, relaxing the ridge between her brows. She was merely substituting my orders for Grayson's, I realized, and we'd have to have a talk about that. Later.

"Unplug your phones unless you want them all to be ringing before dawn," I said.

"Good idea. He'll be mad as a hornet, won't he?"

"Yeah, but he'll survive it."

With a plan finally established, she gathered her mushy Kleenexes and took them to the kitchen trash. "I'll call Sam and tell him to get the word out to the crew that they have another day off."

I picked up my bags once more and headed toward my room. Rusty would sleep near my bed as usual, but by leaving the door open I hoped he'd prowl around the house if he heard any noises. For myself, I didn't plan to hear a thing until at least eight. Beyond that, I'd have to come up with something—I just didn't know what.

SEVENTEEN

My CELL PHONE VIBRATED gently on the nightstand at some point while it was still dark in the room. A one-eyed peek at the clock told me it was five in the morning. Hunh-uh. Not yet. I let it go. At eight thirty, I yawned and stretched and checked the messages. Two, both from Ron. I'd slept through the second one. I dialed his apartment.

"Gonna bite my head off again?" he said cautiously. "Geez, Charlie, you've been a guy's nightmare lately. All these moods. Up, down, bitching one minute, crying the next. You pregnant or something?"

"No!" The denial popped out automatically but my mind went into some kind of white zone. No, couldn't be. Ron was still talking and I forced myself to catch up.

"...you and Rachael didn't go out to the field this morning," he said.

"Uh, yeah." I fumbled to bring myself back to the conversation. "That's right. It was an executive decision on my part, but her safety was worth more than her brother's publicity plan. Plus, the lady is frazzled. It's been a hard week for her."

"I agree. When Fairfield woke me up, at *4:51* this morning, I told him to give you ladies a break and to chill. He wasn't happy but I had to stand firm and agree with you."

Well, well. Chalk up another name to the list of Those Who Are No Longer Mad At Me.

"Thanks, Ron. I appreciate the support." Finally. "So, what

now? Should Rachael pull entirely out of the Fiesta? Is there anything we can do to catch this guy by the weekend?"

"Working on it." I heard papers rustling. "I got back the trace on that phone number you gave me. It was a phone booth near Winrock."

I visualized the massive shopping mall. There were apartments and residential neighborhoods all around it, plus hundreds of offices and shops, and freeway exits feeding right into it. The trace didn't help us a bit.

We talked a little about the notes with their cutout magazine lettering, but decided without police involvement and the ability to check fingerprints, those wouldn't provide any help either.

"So, what's our next step?" I asked. There were still so many unanswered questions.

"The balloonists will be finished flying in another hour or so, then there are airshow events, and I'm not sure what else. This evening there's a barbeque for the pilots and crews. I think we may learn something if Rachael goes. But we need to be there with her. It'll be a big crowd and it's going to take some manpower to spot any danger."

"Can we get into the party?"

"Talk to Rachael about it. Every pilot got a packet of crew tickets. If she hasn't already handed them out, get a couple for us."

"And if they're already gone?"

"Tell her it's urgent. Get her to figure out a way."

"I heard water running in her bathroom a minute ago, so she's up. I'll find out about the tickets soon." I closed my bedroom door and lowered my voice. "Ron, there's something else I need to ask you."

"Uh huh."

"Grayson Fairfield. He was really, really upset last night when I suggested that Rachael back out of the Fiesta."

"And?"

"Why? Why is he so set on this world record being done so publicly? As Rachael pointed out to me last night, the record is real whether it happens in a public place or not. With Grayson it seems like this whole thing is about the publicity. He's completely adamant that she becomes a celebrity over this. Why? What's he got to gain? Can we trust him?"

"Trust him? God, Charlie, he's trying to save his sister's life!"

"Are we sure about that?"

He spluttered then got quiet.

"Something to think about. That's all I'm saying." I could almost hear the cogs turning in his head. "Look, we always watch for motive, means, and opportunity, don't we? Well, who else has better opportunity, who else has the means whenever he wants. All we need to know is the motive. We know he took his father's side against Rachael in the past."

"I think this is going a bit far, Charlie." The protest in his voice wasn't quite as strong as before.

"Okay, just keep it in mind. I know you don't want to piss him off because of your loan application, Ron, but let's be realistic. You can find a mortgage somewhere else. I'll help you if you want. But right now let's not rule out any possible suspect. Anyone."

He agreed, albeit grudgingly. "I'll keep you posted," he finally said.

I looked at my stomach as I slipped into jeans and a sweater. Nah. I put Ron's stupid suggestion out of my mind and padded barefoot through the quiet house. Rachael's shower was still running so she hadn't overheard any of my conversation with Ron. Better to keep my suspicions to myself for now. I took down the makeshift sheet curtain and let Rusty out through the French doors to the backyard. While he made the rounds of the walled yard, I stepped out the front door and examined the front of the property. No new messages and nothing seemed disturbed.

Back in the kitchen I started some coffee and found a package of poppyseed muffins in the breadbox. From Rachael's end of the hall came the blare of a hair dryer.

I tidied my room, brushed my teeth, and swiped on a smear of lipstick. By the time the coffee was ready, I'd repacked my duffle and filled Rusty's bowl with doggie nuggets.

Sun filled the big living room and kitchen, warming the tile floor and brightening the potted flowers in the patio area. I filled a mug with coffee and took it out to one of the comfortable padded chairs. The sun over the Sandias accented the city's whitish morning haze, and a few balloons in the air showed as dark dots over the north end of town. I sipped at my caffeine and wanted to savor a peaceful moment but Ron's offhand comment kept nagging at me. I struggled to remember my cycle but couldn't come up with a date. Surely I wasn't really late yet. Surely, if I was, it was only because of the crazy schedule I'd been keeping and everything would straighten out next week. It would. Drake and I had talked about the possibility of having children and pretty well decided we liked our lives without them. But neither of us had taken steps to make that decision permanent. I closed my eyes and refused to think about it.

While the past twenty-four hours had been busy, the next twenty-four could potentially bring much more. I thought about driving to Santa Fe and fought against it. It would be so much more pleasant to sit here in the sun for about six hours, ignoring everyone else's problems. Rusty came over and laid his big reddish head on my lap.

"Huh, you agree, don't you, kid?"

He rolled his eyes then sat back with ears perked in that I-want-a-treat mode.

"Later."

Rachael walked out with a steaming mug in hand. "Wow, I hadn't realized how completely fatigued I'd become over the past couple of weeks," she said, setting the package of muffins on the table between us and lowering herself into a chair.

"I'll bet." I briefly filled her in on my conversation with Ron this morning, including the plan about attending the barbeque this evening but leaving out the parts about her brother.

"If I can just stay home all morning, catch up on a few bills and a bit of paperwork this afternoon, and relax, I'll be ready to socialize again this evening," she said. "You and Ron will both be there?"

"If you have two extra tickets." I took one of the muffins and bit into it.

"I put them on the dining table," she said.

I excused myself to take a potty break and to put the tickets in my purse.

Ron had told me he had a few more things to finish up at the office then he'd come spend the rest of the day at Rachael's so I could get to Santa Fe. I returned to the patio to find Rachael nursing another cup of coffee and soaking up the morning rays. Rusty sat at her side, eyes on the horizon, head positioned in alignment with the hand that dangled over the arm of her chair as she massaged his ears.

"Well, you two look comfy," I said.

Rusty craned his neck to look back at me but didn't give up the special treatment.

Rachael smiled lazily. "Everything okay at the office?"

"Fine. Ron's doing some more computer checks and keeping an eye on your father. He's assigned me to a task in Santa Fe." I didn't elaborate. "I'll leave Rusty here with you. Unless your brother spread the word, most anyone would assume that you were out at the balloon field, somewhere in that crowd. You should be safe enough at home, but I'd like you to be inside with everything locked up tight. Take the dog in with you and don't answer the door. He'll alert you to any odd noises."

"We'll be fine," she said. "Much as I'm enjoying this sun, I've probably had enough for the day anyhow."

Thus assured, I tossed my duffle into the car once again. The way things were going, I had no idea where I'd be sleeping tonight. I ruffled Rusty's fur and assured him I'd be back for him later. I had this brief fantasy that we would somehow find Rachael's stalker, get the police to pay attention, and lock him up, and I'd have my own life back pretty soon. But I didn't see that happening.

Aside from a snarl of traffic around the exit for Balloon Fiesta Park at the northern edge of Albuquerque, the drive to Santa Fe went smoothly. It was after eleven when I arrived, so the first thing I did was to satisfy my fast-food craving with a Big Mac and Coke. Back in the car I found my note with Hank's address on it and studied my map of Santa Fe to figure it out. No wonder they called this place "The City Different." Whoever laid out these streets had to have been under the influence of something pretty strong. I'd been here hundreds of times and never managed to master more than the basic main roads.

Ron's groundwork had netted Hank's parole officer's phone number, the address of an apartment building, and place of employment with a landscaping contractor. I pulled out my phone and called them first. A perky sounding receptionist answered.

Yes, Henry Tamsin was employed there. He was out on a job right now, could she take a message? I faked my way through the call by saying I was an assistant to his parole officer and it was my job to find out about his attendance record. Had he missed any days of work? No. Had there been any problems with coworkers? Not that she knew of. Did Mr. Tamsin have his own car or use of a company vehicle? She hesitated at that one, finally letting me know that he came to work on a motorcycle. If he drove the company trucks it was only during work hours. He certainly wasn't allowed to take one overnight. I thanked her and quickly disconnected before she put together that these weren't exactly normal parole officer questions.

The apartment complex wasn't difficult to locate. It was one of those cinderblock structures that dated back to the sixties and rented cubicle-sized apartments by the week or the month, the kind that avoids the tag "slum" only because it's not located among hundreds of other such buildings in a mass of dark, inner city alleyways. This one sat on a decent-sized piece of real estate with a parking lot that only held a couple dozen cars this time of day. The complex consisted of four buildings, set at ninety-degree angles to each other so they formed a square. A huge letter on the side of each labeled them, appropriately, A, B, C, and D. I parked outside B and followed the scent of frying onions to a narrow walkway that gained me access to the inner courtyard.

An empty swimming pool surrounded by a metal fence with a padlocked gate filled most of the open space. Apartment doors on three stories faced it. No doubt the developers in the early days had used this feature to sell the tiny abodes as "poolside" or "garden view" or some other such hype. I climbed a clanking set of stairs to the second floor and found B-210 without too much trouble.

Knowing that Hank was on the job made me bolder than usual. After a quick tap on his door, I slipped it open with a thin strip of plastic I just happen to carry in my purse. I won't admit to owning it specifically for this purpose, but let's just say it's come in handy more than once.

I stepped into an all-purpose living-bedroom about the size of a decent walk-in closet. A daybed stood against one wall, a metal chair with a fourteen-inch TV opposite. Biker magazines littered the floor near one end of the bed, with a scummy mug of cold coffee stuck to the top one. Yes, I did pick up the magazines and flip through them looking for missing words and letters. No, I didn't find any. I gingerly placed the cold mug back where I'd found it.

Beyond the main room a narrow doorway led to a kitchen with half-sized appliances and four more mugs in the sink. Mold had begun to grow in a couple of them. A large plastic trash bag on the floor overflowed with fast food wrappers. The fridge contained three beers of an open six-pack and a hunk of cheddar cheese. The freezer compartment above it held a partial bag of store-bought ice and a mysterious foil-wrapped package. It held five hundred dollars in twenties, a small plastic bag of white powder, and a wrapped condom. I didn't *even* want to think what that was about. I gently folded the foil again and put the whole packet back. Surely this guy had learned some more original methods in the slammer. I'd have to give him a failing grade on home security if even I could find his money and stash this quickly.

I stepped out of the kitchen and discovered that the rest of the apartment consisted of a tiny bathroom, which I couldn't bring myself to walk into, and a five-foot stretch of closet rod. Two pair of jeans and two shirts with the landscaper's logo embroidered on the chest hung there. On the shelf above, a black Harley-logo T-shirt, neatly folded, sat all alone.

No generic white paper or envelopes, no traces of dead cat

hair, no picture of Rachael tacked to a dartboard. I wasn't sure what I'd expected to find, but it wasn't here.

The rumble of a Harley grabbed my attention. The kitchen window faced out to the parking lot and I caught a glimpse of a larger version of Ryan Tamsin. He swung his leg over the bike and hitched up his jeans, pulling a bag from Taco Bell out of his jacket. Shit! Why had I assumed that all landscapers ate sack lunches from home while sitting in the shade of a tree on the job?

I dashed to the door and popped through it, pulling it shut behind me just micro-seconds before Hank rounded the corner. I did a quick side-step, hoping it would appear that I'd just walked out of the apartment next door. Luckily, his attention had focused on a man coming out of the laundry room on his right. I made myself stroll leisurely away from him and prayed that I blended in.

I made it to the corner of the building, where another flight of stairs led to another narrow corridor going to another section of the parking lot. I risked a peek and saw Hank apply his key to his lock. I ducked around the corner until I heard his door close firmly.

"You hidin' from that guy?" A kid of about six stood in the first doorway of the row of apartments that were ninety degrees from Hank's. His high-pitched kid-voice echoed along the cement pathways.

"Shh," I cautioned.

"Is it a secret?" he whispered.

"Yeah, something like that. You won't tell, will you?"

"I'm home cause I got the chicken pox," he bragged. He wore pajamas with Spiderman on them and his bare feet danced on the concrete sidewalk.

"Does your mom know you're outside?"

"Nah, she's at work. She calls me when I'm home, but she

can't miss work, else we'll run out of money and we'll lose this apartment. That's what she says. I'm not supposed to open the door to strangers."

"How do you know I'm not a stranger?"

"Cause you're a girl. And I saw you go in that guy's place."

"Well, I won't tell your secret if you don't tell mine. Okay?"

He shrugged. "Sure, I guess." He scratched at a red bump on his arm.

"Want to tell me another secret?" I asked. His eyes sparkled. "That guy, he rides a big motorcycle."

"A Harley, the Wide Glide."

"Wow, you're pretty smart."

"My daddy has one. I've seen pictures of it and my mom says that's what my daddy rides. I kind of remember it. My daddy doesn't live here though."

"Ah. But this guy," I tilted my head toward Hank's place. "Do you know if he went someplace yesterday or the night before that, someplace after work, I mean?"

He scratched again and stared skyward. "I watched SpongeBob last night. But I got sleepy. I heard the Harley right before I went to sleep."

"Was he coming in or going out? I bet you can tell the difference."

"Sure, I can. He went out."

"Did you hear him come back?"

The blond head shook ruefully. When kids sleep, it's true and deep. My dad used to say a bomb could go off in the room with me. I began to worry that Hank would wolf his food and come right back out, and I didn't want him to see me quizzing his neighbor. I thanked the kid—he said his name was Adam—and reminded him about keeping secrets.

Once he was safely inside I trekked down the stairs and took up a vigil in my Jeep. Within minutes Hank strolled out and climbed aboard the Harley again. I followed his slow rumble through town and watched him glide into the parking lot of his employer. From another parking lot across the road I saw him get off the bike and climb into the passenger seat of a company pickup truck. The driver acted impatient as he wheeled the vehicle toward the street and made a left turn. Hmm.

On a whim, more than anything else, I drove back to Hank's building and once again used my key. The Taco Bell wrappers lay in a wad on the daybed and the top of the TV set felt faintly warm, but I didn't think Hank had come home for lunch merely to catch his favorite soaps. A glance into the freezer told me I was right. The foil packet was gone.

EIGHTEEN

SO, A FEW WEEKS out of prison and Hank was clearly in violation of his parole. I made a note to have Ron check his past again and find out if drugs were part of it, but I'd bet money they were. I sat in my Jeep for awhile, wondering if it would be worth my time to stick around and see what he did after work. My phone rang before I'd come to any definite conclusions.

"Where are you?" Ron asked.

"Santa Fe, just like you ordered." It came out sounding snottier than I'd intended.

"Anything happening there?"

I filled him in on the little I'd learned so far and he confirmed that Hank's long rap sheet had included drug charges—coke and pills mostly. He didn't seem surprised when I told him Hank was back at it.

"We might get him off the streets again with a discreet call to his parole officer," he said. "I'll take care of it."

"Other than the five hundred dollars in cash, I didn't find anything that could remotely tie him to Bill Fairfield or Rachael. I'd kind of pictured him as the muscle behind Bill's revenge plot, but there's no evidence."

"Yeah, I know. I'm sitting out in front of Bill's apartment right now and there hasn't been a peep out of him all day." He crunched on something and I envisioned his usual surveillance companion, a bag of Oreos, at his side.

"Well, he works nights. Probably sleeps all day."

He muttered something about what a waste it was to watch a guy sleep, with which I privately agreed. "Why can't you leave until this evening, right before he goes to work?" I suggested.

"I'm just wondering whether this whole line is off track," he said. "I've been watching the guy for days now and haven't seen him make a wrong move yet. He just looks like your average clean-cut guy who goes to work and comes home. Put a suit on him and stick him in a fancier house and he could still be a banker."

I agreed with him but was careful not to let my personal reaction to Fairfield play a part in my opinion.

"Have we actually matched up anybody's movements with the times when the threats came?" I asked.

"Not really."

"None of these leads seem to be panning out. Can I make a suggestion?" I didn't wait for permission. "Why don't we switch tactics and watch Rachael. My guess is that whoever is threatening her is also watching her. They know when she's home and when she's not. They can leave all the notes they want but if they don't get close to her they can't actually do anything."

He didn't say anything for a minute. "Then we're back to the problem of not having the manpower to really guard her. She's out there in big crowds. A well-placed bullet, a bump from someone with a knife, it wouldn't take much to get her."

"Then she needs to hire bodyguards, not private investigators," I said.

"Yeah, well, we already had that conversation, too."

"So, am I sticking by Hank the Tank in Santa Fe, or can I come home? I really need to get Sally's paycheck done."

He muttered again. "Yeah, come on back," he said. "You

can relieve me here at Fairfield's place for a couple hours. I've got paperwork to catch up on at the office and we both need to be at that barbeque tonight. Starts at six."

I didn't want to be sitting in a warm car in front of Fairfield's place any more than he did, but I kept my grumbling down and headed that way. As it was, I'd be scrambling to drive back to Albuquerque, take care of my office duties, and get out to the west side to escort Rachael to the barbeque. And I wasn't sure what I'd do with Rusty in the meantime, leave him to guard her house or take him home. We chatted about all this as I started the car and headed toward Cerrillos Road, leaving Santa Fe behind.

The hour-long drive to Albuquerque gave me time to think about the whole situation from a distance and it occurred to me that we weren't looking at the big picture here. There'd now been multiple notes. They'd escalated in tone, and killing the cat had taken the fear factor up a notch. But if someone truly wanted to kill Rachael they could have easily done it by now. They hadn't approached her, they hadn't caused physical harm—why?

If the goal is to frighten her, when would it stop? And why did a person set out to intimidate someone else? Control, power, to make them act in a certain way. No matter how much I mulled it over I kept coming back to her father. He'd used their dirty little secret to keep Rachael silent as a child. Maybe this was his only way to intimidate her now, as an adult.

Then again, Chuck clearly wanted to intimidate women; it was his entire modus operandi. But he had Nora now; he didn't seem to be after Rachael any more. Hank or Ryan? Thugs. Thugs love to intimidate. But was that good enough motive? They hardly knew her. Or could it be something to do with her world record, the only truly new event in her life right now? I chafed at the fragmentary clues, the scraps of knowledge that really didn't add up to anything. Nothing seemed to be fitting into place.

Bill Fairfield's apartment building looked exactly the same when I pulled into the lot. Ron had left fifteen minutes earlier and Fairfield's white Nissan sat in the same spot it had been on my first visit. I settled restlessly into my seat, scanning through the radio stations until I came to one with country music. Kenny Chesney's voice caught my attention and I relaxed a little.

After about an hour, during which I'd had all the songs about broken hearts I could handle and had switched to talk radio where my favorite guy was blasting the government for being crooked and incompetent, I noticed movement at Fairfield's window. The drapes, which had been closed, swished open. I glanced at my watch. A little after three. He was, perhaps, just getting up and ready to start his inverted daily schedule. I waited with a little more interest now that I knew I wasn't simply staring at a window with a sleeping body behind it.

My diligence was rewarded twenty minutes later when Fairfield came out. He was dressed again in khakis, a polo shirt, and light jacket with the zipper undone. He walked toward his car, glanced up and spotted mine, and changed directions. Uh oh.

I swear, my skills as a tail really must suck. Twice now, I'd been watching him, and twice he'd picked me out of the crowd. I opened my door and stepped out, keeping the door between me and the ex-con. At least I wanted the advantage of my five and a half feet, not that cowed feeling of sitting low in the car.

"We meet again," he greeted. "Still at it, I see." His tone was casual, almost friendly. Truthfully, I was having a hard time seeing him as a mad stalker out to kill his own daughter. But then, the events of twenty years ago didn't quite fit the present image either.

"Still here," I agreed.

"Is it productive use of your time?" He sent a crooked grin my way and I caught myself automatically smiling back. "I didn't see you out here the past couple of days."

"Let's just say I found a more productive use for my time. I went to Clovis."

"Ah." The look that flickered across his face certainly wasn't fear. Regret, maybe? Sadness?

"I hear you were there yourself within the last couple of weeks."

He nodded, shoving his hands into the pockets of his slacks. "Memories. When you're away…well, you know where I was all those years. When you're in a place like that you think about home a lot. When you go back, it's never the same. I'd actually thought I might kill a guy when I got there. But everything had changed."

His tone was so mild, his voice so soft that his words really didn't register immediately. I'd been gazing toward the mountains and by the time my focus snapped back to his face all I saw was a guy of about sixty who didn't remotely look like a killer.

"So, what did you learn in Clovis?" he asked.

I managed a little mental leap back to the previous day, wondering how much of it to discuss with him. Hell, I decided, just go for it.

"I learned that your wife's suicide probably wasn't. That seems awfully coincidental, doesn't it? Didn't the police question you about it at the time?"

He shifted his weight. "Sure they did. It was easy enough. I was already in jail. They asked me if Linda had been depressed, if there were 'extenuating circumstances' within the family." He shook his head and let out a laugh that came out as a bark. "What did they *think?* The woman believes her daughter has been molested, believes that her own husband did it, and sees her future with the country club set going down the toilet. Yeah, I'd say she was depressed."

"The medical examiner didn't find evidence of pills in her stomach."

"I heard that. I spent a lot of years thinking about that. Eventually, I figured it out. You would too, sooner or later. But I can save you a whole bunch of time. Want to take a ride with me?"

The request came so completely out of left field that I almost grabbed my purse and followed him. Reason prevailed. "Where to?"

"I want you to meet someone."

My puzzled expression told him that I hadn't a clue.

"Dean Patterson. I think you know who he is."

Dottie had told me that she thought her ex might be in Albuquerque.

"You've stayed friends with Dean Patterson?" I asked.

He shot me a condescending look. "Dean and I were never friends. Let's just say that I've finally begun to know him in the last few weeks."

With that cryptic message, he started to turn.

"Where would we be going?" I called out.

"Up on Montgomery. Ten, fifteen minutes away. I think you'd find it to be a revelation."

Getting into the car with him would be a really stupid move, I knew. "I'll follow you," I said.

"That's fine. You're good at it." He grinned widely this time and walked toward his car.

I turned my ignition and waited for his car to begin moving. Despite all I knew about him, I felt way too trusting of Bill Fairfield. Why? Was his political charm still alive and well? Was he simply getting back into his old mode where a smile and firm handshake got him anything he wanted? I reminded myself of his transgressions, repeating them like a mantra, as I followed him toward the unknown.

NINETEEN

WE FOLLOWED NEARLY the same route he'd taken the last time, but turned east this time on Montgomery. I stayed close and switched on my right turn signal when he did. Off a small side street, a left turn into a quiet cul de sac, and we came to a modern one-story building, stuccoed pale peach, surrounded by a fairly large parking lot full of cars. The sign near the entry sported large elaborate letters that said La Solana. I drew a blank.

Bill parked in the first open space he came to and I found one farther down the same row. We met near the entrance.

"What is this place?" I asked.

"A nursing home." He turned and activated the automatic door. It slid open with a faint whoosh and he stepped inside. I rushed to catch up.

Through an airlock, a second automatic door had already opened and I stepped through. A huge reception desk dominated the large lobby and I noticed hallways branching off from it. The main thing that caught my attention were the wheelchairs, probably ten or more, occupied by fragile, elderly people. A few of them looked up at us, hope in their eyes. Others stared at the walls or bobbed their heads as they chatted with unseen friends.

"Charlie?"

I snapped to attention and noticed that Bill was already standing at the opening to one of the branching corridors. I sidestepped around a tiny woman with a walker and joined him. The moment I caught up he began walking again.

"Dean Patterson works here?" I asked, surprised.

"Doesn't work, resides."

"What?" I tugged at his jacket sleeve to slow him down. "Wait a minute. Fill me in."

We paused at an alcove containing a single chair and end table with a telephone on it.

"I have to admit I'm confused," I said. "He lives here? He's not that old." I envisioned the mayoral candidate from the newspaper photos—tall, dark haired, beaming with confidence.

"He's got cancer. Terminal. A few months at best." Bill shrugged.

"But...family?"

"He's got no one. Dottie divorced him years ago and the son is busy with some high-power career in the Silicon Valley. I asked around in Clovis and found out where he was." He rubbed at a spot near his sideburn. "He's...well, you'll see. I think you'll find this interesting."

Leaving me with my mouth gaping, he stepped out of the alcove and continued down the long hall. I trotted along to keep up with his six-footer's stride. At the last door on the right, he paused. Tapping quietly on the frame, he called out to Patterson.

I stepped up in time to see a skinny old man tie the belt on his robe and lower himself into a waiting wheelchair. The two men exchanged greetings while I worked to recover my wits. The man in the chair was completely bald and so thin that I could have easily circled my fingers around his forearm. His sticklike legs were clad in flannel pajamas and he huddled into his velour robe for extra warmth. He'd shrunk so much in height that his shoulders barely cleared the edge of the chair's vinyl back. I would have never recognized him as Dean Patterson.

Bill lightly touched my shoulder as he spoke. "Dean, I want you to meet someone. Charlie's a, uh, a friend of Rachael's."

A flicker of uncertainty crossed Patterson's face as he nodded toward me.

"Can we find a spot to talk?" Bill asked.

"The dining room's usually got some coffee made," Dean said. His voice came out thin and wavery, but the spark in his eyes showed that he was very much with it.

I stepped aside as Bill took over and wheeled the chair into the hall. We passed through the lobby and started up one of the other halls. The dining room was the second door on the left. Tables with four chairs each dotted the room and I noticed a long counter at one end with coffee urns, iced tea, and soda dispensers. I offered to get drinks while Bill parked Dean's chair. As I went through the motions, I worked to clear my mind of the scatter of thoughts that rocketed through it. I had no idea where this was going.

"Dean and I have visited a couple of times since I've been back in town," Bill said as he sugared and stirred his coffee. He paused. "Hell, I don't know how to do this. Dean tires quickly, and I know Charlie's in a hurry. So let's just get to the point. Dean, would you tell Charlie the same story you told me the other day? About you and Linda."

Suddenly, things were beginning to make sense. My mind flashed back to the photos I'd taken from the newspaper in Clovis.

"I never thought I'd tell this to anyone," Dean began in his shaky voice. "Much less tell it twice in a week." His bony fingers worked at the padding on the arm of his chair. I chafed with impatience.

"You and Linda Fairfield had an affair years ago. Is that it?"

Both men stared at me.

"I'm not the completely incompetent investigator you thought," I aimed toward Bill. And to Dean: "Linda was obviously crazy about you at one point. But what happened?"

He fidgeted a bit more but noticed that my patience was wearing thin. "Oh, all right. We planned to get Bill out of the picture, then wait a discreet amount of time and be together. Dottie had already left me once. That little tidbit never made the papers, did it?"

I shook my head in acknowledgement.

"We came up with the plan to frame Bill for a crime so heinous that people in Clovis would never forgive him. What would work? Even in those little, sanctimonious Bible belt towns, they'll overlook the town drunk, the blatant extra-marital affair, oftentimes even murder. But they'd never forgive a man who molested his own daughter. Especially if she were the one to have him arrested and she tearfully testified in court."

I felt like I'd stepped onto the set of *The Twilight Zone*. "What…"

He waved me aside. "Let me finish." He sipped from the soft drink I'd brought him. "We staged the molestation. Whenever we knew Bill would be working late or be out of town, I'd slip over, put on some of his cologne, and tiptoe in to give the kid a feel-up."

He noticed my look of horror.

"Now, wait a minute. I never raped her. Never even took her clothes off. Not that I didn't get some ideas."

Bill stiffened in his chair and I felt like reaching out to strangle Dean, terminal illness or not. He merely stared us down. Finally, he continued with the story.

"Linda was supposed to plant the idea that Bill did it, make subtle remarks to the girl, that kind of thing."

"Supposed to?" I asked.

"She chickened out. After—mind you—after I'd already done…well, done those things. We started to argue more often. Pretty soon, having a mistress was worse than having a nagging wife."

"And what was going on with you all this time?" I asked Bill.

He stared at his coffee cup. "I didn't know what to think. I was getting these silent glares from Rachael, Linda was drunk half the time, the campaign was in full swing. It was all I could do to show up when and where I was supposed to and make my speeches."

"Rachael finally put a stop to all of it. She talked to her counselor at school and the counselor called the police," Dean said. "I remember the morning Bill was arrested. I'd heard the news and stopped by their house to 'console' Linda. Actually, I thought she'd finally taken charge of her daughter and forced her to call the police. When I got there, Linda was in a state. Ten in the morning and she'd already had at least a couple of drinks. She was raving about what a mistake she'd made. Now she'd lost her chance at being first lady and all her friends at the club would hate her. I calmed her down and left for a meeting.

"The next couple of weeks were sheer hell. With Bill out of the campaign, it looked like I would win easily and Dottie issued an ultimatum. We'd stay together, no arguments about it. There would be no scandal or she'd take me for everything I had. Ironically, she pointed to Rachael as the prime example of how a female could ruin a man's career with one well-placed phone call."

Bill got up to refill his coffee mug and I toyed with my soda glass, making patterns of wet rings on the table.

"The week before the election, Linda issued her own ultimatum. She demanded that I leave Dottie for her or she'd make the whole story public, about who really molested her daughter. Man, I was sweating it. I didn't think anyone would believe her, but I couldn't bet my whole career on that. We were in her bedroom that night. Rachael had gone to some school function and I knew I had to leave soon. Linda just kept taunting me. She'd kept it up since I'd arrived.

"I went into the bathroom and spotted her prescription sleeping pills, nearly a whole bottle. I started back into the bedroom. Was going to give her a lecture about mixing booze and pills—she was a suicide waiting to happen. Then it hit me that it could happen now, before she talked. I sent her to the kitchen to make me a sandwich and I broke the capsules open into her drink. Left the open bottle on her nightstand, wiped my prints off everything. When she came back with the sandwich I revved up the fight again and walked out. I knew she'd finish off the drink right away. And she did."

He rattled the ice cubes in his soda glass, finding it empty. "I'd like to lie down awhile," he said.

Bill took the handles of the chair and wheeled his former rival out the door. I drew in a deep breath and tried to assimilate the new information. What a complicated mess. I cleared our table and meandered toward the door, trying to formulate what I'd tell Rachael about all this.

"Charlie." Bill's soft voice caught my attention just before I reached the exit. "Now you see why I didn't need to kill him when I got to Clovis."

"Why do I have the feeling you wouldn't have anyway?"

"I'd like to reestablish contact with Rachael, somehow. Grayson's been trying to pave the way but she's very resentful of me. Rightly so. I was hard on her as a kid. Always wanted her to have that same level of ambition I had back then, the same drive that Grayson always showed. None of that helped, on top of the horrible things Linda and Dean made her believe."

"I'll see what I can do."

My dashboard clock told me it was nearly four. It would be a mad dash to get downtown to our office, process the paychecks, go home, and change clothes to get to the barbeque by six. Knowing Bill wasn't responsible for the threat notes alleviated one worry but opened up a bunch of others. Who *was* sending them? Now I felt like we had to be extra diligent.

I hit the auto-dial on my cell for Ron's number. He sounded harried.

"I haven't made it to the office yet," he said, "but I'll be there soon."

"I found out for certain that Bill isn't sending the threat notes. It's complicated and there's lots more but I'll tell you about it when we catch up with each other."

We ended the call as I pulled into the heavy traffic on Montgomery and made my way toward I-25. By the time I reached our quiet office neighborhood, I'd dodged three near accidents and was thoroughly fed up with society in general. I pulled into the parking area behind the office and headed inside.

"Where's Ron?" I asked.

"Don't know," Sally told me, looking up from her word processor. "He hasn't called in recently."

"I talked to him thirty minutes ago and he was planning to come in. See if you can track him down on his cell and make sure everything's okay. I better get started on the paychecks."

She gave me a grateful smile as she picked up her phone. I headed upstairs and switched on my computer. Five minutes later Sally buzzed me on the intercom.

"He's at Rachael's," she said. "Said he'll take her to the barbeque."

I shook my head in amazement. Was I going nuts, or was he? He'd clearly said....

"Oh." Sally paused. "He also said he'd leave Rusty at Rachael's tonight, if that's okay with you."

"Yeah, I guess." I pictured Rachael's expensive leather sofas, her impeccable furnishings. Rusty's not a purposely destructive dog at all, he's just big. Things sometimes get wagged off coffee tables. If someone tried to break in, claw marks might end up on the front door. Oh well. At that point claw marks would probably be the least of Rachael's problems. I turned to my work and put everything else out of my mind for the next half-hour. Once I'd seen Sally out the door and locked up everything else, I opted for the luxury of going home for a shower and change of clothes before heading back out to the balloon field. Not until I stood under the hot spray, taking extra time to enjoy my solitude, did the idea hit me. I thought I knew where we should be looking.

I dried quickly, pulled on clean jeans and a turtleneck and grabbed my leather jacket and purse, checking to be sure the Beretta was inside. The phone rang just as I reached for the doorknob. I dashed to the kitchen and picked it up distractedly. Drake.

"We're almost finished here," he said. "Another day, probably, at most."

I told him about the barbeque and that I was on my way out the door, and his cheery mood dropped a notch. "It'd be nice if we were doing some of this stuff together," he said.

"I know. I'd like that, too." I almost blurted my suspicions about the pregnancy, but this didn't seem like the best way to do it.

"Well, you sound busy and happy. Guess I better let you go."

"No rush. It'll start without me." I filled him in on the reason for my cheerful mood, that we'd ruled out Bill Fairfield and wouldn't have to continue our surveillance of him. We exchanged I-love-yous and clicked off.

It was only slightly after six when I reached Balloon Fiesta Park. I found the big tent with the party by following the lights and noise. For a crowd that often starts on their beer in the early morning, they're amazingly hearty in the evening. The upside, I figured, was that they all had to be up again by four, so this shindig couldn't possibly go very late tonight.

Ron stood by the bar, nursing his first beer of the evening. He's not a big drinker any time and rarely at all when working. I could tell by the expression on his face, though, that he was bored and ready for this gig to be over.

Well, poor baby. He'd spent the afternoon with an attractive woman and escorted her to a party. I approached and ordered a glass of merlot. From the first sip it didn't taste good to me. Oh, god, maybe I really was.... Rather than bringing Ron's attention to it, I opted to carry the wineglass around with me instead of immediately ordering something else.

He tipped his Stetson back and scratched at the skimpy hair above the hatband. "Food's over there," he said, indicating two long buffet tables at one end of the tent. Suddenly I felt a curious lightheadedness; I had to get something to eat. "Rachael's got a place in line, talking to the knockout blond," Ron said.

I left him at the bar and blatantly cut in with her. Liz Pierce greeted me with that look that meant she remembered my face but not my name.

"How was your day?" I asked Rachael.

"Heaven," she said. "I never did get around to paying those bills and organizing my desk. I picked up a book I'd been meaning to read for weeks and did nothing else all day."

"I've got some good news. About your dad."

She nodded politely but without lots of enthusiasm. "Later, okay?"

We moved forward and loaded plates with brisket, coleslaw, potato salad, and baked beans. The noise in the tent had risen to that level where the drunks try to out-shout the music and the musicians keep turning up the amps to hear themselves over the drunks. I had to get out of there.

Rachael moved to sit with a group of friends, smiling and appearing more relaxed than I'd seen her all week. Maybe she'd had a couple of glasses of wine; maybe she'd just decided that she couldn't live in fear all the time. I caught Ron's eye and he moved closer to her.

I stepped out of the tent, putting a small damper on the sound but not much. I set my plate on the hood of a car that afforded the only scrap of warmth in the chilly evening and proceeded to wolf down my meal. Ron followed a couple of minutes later, positioning himself so we could talk and he could keep an eye on Rachael through the open tent flap.

"Sorry I got snappish earlier," I said. I took another sip of the wine, which tasted better this time, and let the warm glow of the drink and solid comfort of food mellow me quickly.

"Me too." Ron stood awkwardly by the car, scuffing one booted toe in the dust.

I smiled and filled him in with the condensed version of what I'd learned in Clovis and this afternoon's surprising revelations by Dean Patterson. I also told him about Drake's call but didn't let on that I might actually be getting used to the idea of having a baby. I still needed to work through all the debris floating around in my mind.

He didn't seem to notice. His own muddled expression told me that he was still processing everything from the political rivalry, to the awful scheme Dean and Linda had come up with, to Linda's death. I dug into the barbequed meat with my plastic fork while he thought it over.

"What's our next step with Rachael, now that we know her father isn't involved?" I asked.

"So far, no one seems to have a very strong reason for wanting to take her out of the picture." He took a long pull on his beer.

"So, maybe we're dealing with a stranger? Some nut-case who wants to make a name for himself by harming a famous person?"

"It's not impossible," he admitted, "but it's usually the least likely scenario. Ninety percent of the time a victim knows her killer. And it's usually the most likely suspect all along, the spouse, the boyfriend. Murder is a crime of passion, Charlie."

I chewed down the last morsel of my Texas toast and followed it with one more sip of wine. I set the glass aside. I really shouldn't be drinking this stuff. "But we don't have a murder—yet. We have threats. We have words that talk about preventing Rachael from setting the record. We've assumed that the threats are real."

"We have to."

"Agreed. I'm not saying we shouldn't take them seriously. But maybe we can widen the scope of our search if we include people whose motive is to gain the spotlight for themselves."

"And that narrows our suspect list to what, a few million people?" He craned his neck to watch Rachael as she moved around inside the huge tent.

"Not necessarily." I posed the theory I'd had earlier. That someone within the ballooning community might not want to see Rachael succeed. He appeared to give that some serious thought and said he'd follow up on it.

"Drake's coming home tomorrow and I might be able to press him into service to help us with this. He's never been to Fiesta and he's eager to get in on it. For now, do you want me to stay at Rachael's again tonight?"

"Yeah, if you can. I better get back inside and hang close to her," he said. "She wants to fly tomorrow. Saturday and Sunday are the two biggest days for this gig. Mass ascensions, huge crowds. I can use your help."

Since taking the dog with us to the field would make life complicated in the morning, I told him I'd run out to Rachael's after the barbeque, get Rusty, and leave him in Elsa's care, and get back to Rachael's for the night. I could go out to the field with the crew in the morning. The logistics of it all reminded me that life would get infinitely more complicated with a child in the picture.

TWENTY

A MASS ASCENSION, despite its religious-sounding name, is simply a flight where all the balloons take off at once, ascending en masse to fill the sky with color. Albuquerque does this in a way that causes hearts to flutter, jaws to drop, and rolls of film to be shot with amazing rapidity. Of course, more than six hundred balloons can't literally take flight at exactly the same moment from an open field laid out in a grid where roughly one hundred can inflate and be ready at one time. The process is done in waves, with skilled launch directors giving the thumbs up to row after row of the huge craft, moving from the downwind edge of the field, allowing each successive row to take flight. By the time the first hundred are airborne the next wave have inflated and the process starts again. Within about an hour's time six hundred colored globes fill the blue October sky and create a scene most artists and all photographers live for. There's something so vivid, so ethereal about the sight…maybe it is a religious experience after all.

If there's something magical about standing on the ground and gazing at a sky full of color, there's an otherworldly feeling about being up there in the midst of it.

Against Grayson's strenuous protests, Rachael informed him that I would be her only passenger this morning. Although Grayson argued for a ride for his important client, Ron pointed out that if something happened during the flight,

Grayson wouldn't want to be liable for the man's safety. That settled that question.

I'd been able to keep my eyes on the crowd, watching for danger, trying to spot anyone who might show an overt interest in Rachael during the whole process of inflating the balloon and preparing for takeoff. I'd scanned the hoards of people as Rachael beckoned me to climb into the basket with her, and during the fleeting moment when we ceased to feel the ground under our feet, during that amazing moment I realized we were floating.

As the people below us began to fall away, transforming from upturned faces with open mouths to round blobs with dots for features, I have to admit that I couldn't help myself. I just had to take a minute to stare around me. Hundreds of inverted-teardrop shapes in every possible color combination hung in the air around us. Whooshing blasts from *Lady Liberty*'s burner occasionally interrupted the same sounds, fainter, from others.

By the time we'd climbed to a thousand feet or so above the ground, we began to move away from the launch field and I lost the details in people and objects below. This might be the most dangerous time in the flight—I wouldn't be able to spot hidden dangers, but a concealed sniper on the ground with a high-power rifle could easily sight in on Rachael.

She'd given me a quick overview of the burner controls and instruments and the theory behind flying the uncontrollable craft. If anything happened to her, I could theoretically take over but I was far from ready to put that to the test.

Rachael's radio crackled and Sam's voice came through.

"Rusty One, Rusty Chase now leaving the field."

Normally balloons and crews use the balloon's name to communicate on the busy frequencies that are shared by many. *Lady Liberty* would call out for Liberty Chase. But since announcing our every move could prove fatal in this case, we'd opted for the code word. I thought it funny that Rachael had taken to my loveable pooch so quickly that she'd picked his name.

"Rusty Chase, ten-four. Looks like we've got a box today."

"Saw that. You going with it?"

Rachael looked at me and we both shook our heads. "The box" is an Albuquerque phenomenon where wind currents often flow in exact opposite directions at different altitudes. From the ground up to about five hundred feet they'll be out of the north, taking the balloons due south; climb to one thousand feet and you'll head back due north; come down again to five hundred and you're going back south. It's not uncommon to take off, fly for an hour, and land near your starting point. Pilots and crowds both love it.

"Negative, Sam. Staying high's a better bet." She gave a few more blasts on the burner and we ascended to seventy-five hundred, about two thousand feet above the ground and well above most of the others in the crowded sky.

"Better," she announced, taking a deep breath and letting her arm drop from the overhead blast valve she'd been constantly attending since the flight began.

She pulled off one bulky glove and reached into her jacket pocket for a scrap of paper. On it she'd jotted down the winds aloft report from the pilot briefing this morning. "Looks like we can stay right about here, go north until we get nearly to Tramway, then drop down and find a good open spot," she said. She jammed the note back into her pocket and reached up to hit the blast valve again. "If we get too far north we'll end up having to deal with the Indians."

The Sandia Indians own the land north of Tramway Boulevard, where there are few roads and fewer gates. And you don't just fly in there casually; it takes a lot of time and some diplomatic talking to retrieve your balloon once you've crossed their fences. They've gotten easier to deal with in recent years, especially if you happen to land near their huge casino. That's one part of pueblo land they don't seem to mind sharing.

She radioed her intent to Sam. With our present course he wouldn't have to worry about crossing the Rio Grande, something that gets tricky with the few bridges that lead to the west side. We'd already tracked east of the balloon field and were about to cross Interstate 25. I spotted the truck as Sam maneuvered through traffic to follow Rachael's directions.

"Here, want to fly it for awhile?" Rachael asked me, taking my hand and raising it to the overhead blast valve.

I think my eyes grew bigger. My piloting experience is strictly limited to very, very controllable helicopters.

"C'mon, it's not hard," she said. "Until you get the feel for it, just watch your instruments." She pointed out the altimeter and rate of climb indicator. "You know these two guys, right? The only other thing to watch is the envelope temperature. If this little needle goes into the red zone we'll soon have crispy fabric up there." At the moment the needle was well below the red line.

I stared up into the vast cavern of empty space surrounded by thin nylon and I swallowed hard.

"Try it a few times," she said. "You'll get the feel of it."

I watched the rate of climb meter begin to drop slightly. I pulled tentatively on the burner control, a short blast. We began falling two hundred feet a minute, heading toward three hundred. I overcompensated with a long blast and felt the corresponding rise thirty seconds later. Rachael tapped my elbow, instructing me to quit burning. Before I knew it we were climbing three hundred feet a minute.

"It's not as easy as you make it look," I said.

"Stay with it," she said, "you'll get it soon." She coached

me with hand signals through a few more cycles, letting me know when to burn and when to let off. After ten or fifteen minutes I began to get the feel for it, although I still didn't dare take my eyes off the instruments.

"We're getting about to the limit of our northward travel," she said. "We better come down, track back south a bit, and find a spot." She watched me for a second to check my reaction.

"Landing?" I felt sweaty places forming under the parka that had felt so good at six in the predawn chill.

"I'll take over." She reached for the control, picking up the radio mike and announcing her intention to Rusty Chase.

I took off my jacket and stuffed it behind one of the fuel tanks. "That was fun," I said, hoping I sounded sincere. The lack of directional control still bothered me.

Rachael brought the balloon down to two hundred feet above the ground, her gradual descent a far cry from the hectic up and down movements I'd managed. She pointed out a dirt road about a quarter of a mile away in the middle of a patch of sage and chamisa. Housing developments framed the south and west sides of it and a row of power lines ran along the south edge of the houses. We were now only about fifty feet off the ground.

"Won't we…" I eyed the lines, knowing they were the single biggest danger to balloonists, but Rachael became intent on her task. I shut up and watched.

She guided the balloon with short bursts of heat and reached out with her free hand to grab the red line that led to the balloon's vent panel. I spotted our chase truck turning onto the road in front of us.

"Face forward," Rachael instructed, "grab the uprights with both hands, and hold on. Flex your knees slightly when we touch."

She shut off the blast valve and gave the red line a firm tug with both hands. The balloon settled perfectly on the dirt road. Sam had stopped the truck about ten yards away. The crew piled out and began walking toward us. I noticed Sam staring intently at the envelope above our heads.

"What's wrong, Sam?" Rachael called out.

He shook his head but pulled Ron aside and pointed upward. Ron squinted, shielding his eyes from the sun. They spoke a few words, but I couldn't keep up with it. Rachael had shut off the fuel and pulled the rip line, and the big red, white, and blue globe folded inward into a slack mass of fabric as it gave up the bubble of hot air that had held us in the sky. I became busy with trying to stay on my feet as the basket tipped over and we stepped onto terra firma.

I grabbed my jacket and remembered belatedly that I'd intended to take pictures with Drake's little digital camera, which hadn't left my pocket once after all.

Justin and the other crew members proceeded to pull the fabric taut, retrieve the envelope's storage bag, and ready the whole system to be stowed in the truck. I was in the process of checking the pockets of my jacket to be sure I'd not lost any of my belongings when Ron tapped me on the arm.

"We got problems," he murmured, pulling me away from the group.

"What?"

"Sam noticed them. Come take a look." He glanced back toward the crew, who were near the top of the balloon, setting the top deflation panel back in place. Rachael and Sam stood near the mouth of the balloon; he held a section of the fabric up for her to see. Ron nudged me closer to them.

Sam held up the fabric, emphasizing a hole about the diameter of his finger. "There are four of them," he said.

"What are they?" I asked.

"Bullet holes." His voice sounded grim.

I felt my knees go weak.

TWENTY-ONE

I LEANED AGAINST THE side of the wicker gondola. Rachael's face had gone white and Ron took her arm and hustled her to the truck, tucking her inside the cab and scanning the horizon in every direction.

"When did this happen?" Sam asked me.

"I...I...have no idea," I admitted. My mind whirred back over the past hour.

"Let's get moving," Ron ordered. "They probably watched her land and know exactly where we are."

"Guys! Double time," Sam shouted to the crew members.

Luckily, no one questioned. They knew their jobs and began stuffing the hundreds of yards of fabric into the bag. Within minutes, they'd disconnected the cables and shoved basket, bag, and inflator fan into the truck.

"Everyone stay low," Ron said. He positioned Rachael in the center of the backseat of the truck, as concealed as we could make her. I sat on one side of her, Danny the crew member on the other.

Sam drove and Ron rode with Justin in the back of the truck, inside the balloon gondola. Sam gunned the truck a little more than necessary, kicking up a cloud of dust on the road. He found a way into the nearby housing development and took a circuitous route down narrow residential streets.

"Where are we going?" Rachael asked, her voice sounding impatient and frightened at the same time.

"Not back to the balloon field," Sam said tersely. "First we're going to be sure we're not followed. Then we'll get you and the balloon hidden away."

Rachael started to open her mouth again, but I nudged her side. Clearly, Sam didn't want to discuss plans in front of the crew. From my position I could see his jaw working as he fought back anger. The young crew guys stayed quiet.

I glanced back at Ron. He'd pulled down the fluttering banner that identified *Lady Liberty* and tucked it discreetly away somewhere. As Sam picked up speed, Ron and Justin hunched into the basket, backs against the wind.

We wound through another residential neighborhood, without anyone apparently tailing us, until we emerged somehow onto Eubank. Sam headed due south, then got onto Interstate 40 and merged east, heading toward the mountains. I looked at Rachael, puzzled that we were apparently leaving town, but didn't say anything.

Sam changed lanes frequently, dodging between the big-rig truck traffic on the state's heavily traveled main east-west route. He exited fifteen minutes later at Tijeras and drove another twenty minutes, taking us deep into the mountains on Albuquerque's east side. Two more roads and a tiny dirt lane later, he eased into a narrow driveway bordered by scrub oak and cedar. Tall ponderosa pines grew thickly over the property. Two Rottweilers in a fenced run barked furiously, racing back and forth within the confined space. A hundred yards away, at the edge of a small meadow stood a barn. A dozen goats milled around inside a fenced enclosure.

Across the driveway from the dog run stood a house with redwood siding, a steeply pitched metal roof of sage green, and a wraparound porch. Barrels of brightly blooming impatiens bordered the steps leading to the front door and groupings of lawn furniture sat under the high branches of the pines.

Sam maneuvered the long pickup truck within a confined turnaround space and backed it up to a double garage door. He cut the engine and got out.

I turned to Rachael.

"This is Sam's house," she said. "Beautiful spot, huh?"

Everyone had piled out of the truck and Rachael and I followed suit.

Ron pulled me aside. "Didn't get a chance to tell you this before the flight," he said, "but we may have another suspect. I spoke with John O'Malley, the FAA designee who's going to be monitoring Rachael's record attempt." He dropped his voice. "He says that another woman has also filed the paperwork for a record attempt. It's something that has to be done months before the actual flight. Then the pilot has a three-month window in which to do the flight and have it confirmed. Rachael's at the beginning of her window—October, November, December. The other gal's window runs out the end of this month. Don't know if that means anything. She's not been in the news and I haven't had a chance to scout around with the ballooning crowd to see what her story is."

"Who is it?" I asked.

"Someone named Elizabeth Pierce."

"Liz Pierce! I met her. She's a friend of Rachael's." I tried to assimilate the information. What was going on here?

"Meeting," Sam announced, waving everyone over to him. He leaned against one of the huge pines while the group assembled. He cleared his throat for attention. "We had a closer call than I like this morning."

The young crew members who hadn't seen the bullet holes looked puzzled. Danny started to open his mouth, but settled back.

"No disrespect to our…" he started to say bodyguards but changed it quickly, "friends here. But this is how we're going to do things now."

Ron spluttered but I gripped his hand and dug my nails in. Sam clearly didn't want the entire crew to know the whole story. We should see how he wanted to handle it.

"We'll offload the balloon here and put it in the garage," Sam said. "Rachael, Ron, and Charlie will stay here while I drive the guys back to their cars. When I get back we'll discuss plans and decide how or *if* tomorrow will happen." Meaning the record attempt.

Rachael stirred but kept silent.

"I don't want anyone to say anything," he stared at each of the young crew members, "to anybody about this. Not a word about where we've put the balloon, where Rachael is, what's going on with the record attempt." He met each of our eyes.

"No partying tonight, guys."

A restless wave flowed through the group.

"I mean it. I need you fresh and alert in the morning." And not out socializing where you're likely to open your mouths. He didn't say it but they all got it. "We'll be in touch by phone once we finalize the plan."

He gave a little round-em-up signal and the boys began unloading equipment. Within five minutes everything had been stashed in one side of the double garage.

"Ron, on second thought, come with me. My car's still at the field and I'll need a second driver."

My brother, who's usually so much the runner-of-the-show, quietly climbed into the truck's shotgun seat.

"Charlie, you and Rachael stay inside until we get back. Keep everything locked." Sam stood beside the truck until Rachael and I went into the house. She made a show of locking the door and giving him an okay sign through the door's upper glass panes before he climbed into the driver's seat. We watched as the truck rolled down the narrow drive, then everything grew quiet.

"Rachael, did you know Liz Pierce had also filed for an altitude attempt?"

"What?" Clearly this news surprised her.

"Ron just told me. She must have done it months ago because her time-frame is almost up. She has to do it before the end of this month."

She got quiet and turned away from the door.

"Is there any chance she wants this record bad enough to try to scare you away from it?"

"Oh, surely not," she said. "I mean, anyone in the whole country could go for the same one. I could set it first and she could come along and beat me. Or vice versa."

She said it lightly enough that I felt somewhat reassured.

"Mind if I scout around?" I asked. Remote as the place might be, I wouldn't feel entirely at ease until I knew every window and door.

"Go ahead. I'm going to make a cup of tea, you want one?" I followed her down the narrow entry hall that opened into a large, sunny greatroom. A glance showed the kitchen on the left, a big sunroom on the right, French doors leading to a deck at the back.

Done in shades of Wedgwood blue and cream, the living room area featured a huge wraparound sectional sofa, rustic wood coffee table, oak entertainment center, and blue enameled woodburning stove. To the left, stairs led to a second story. Beyond them a well-equipped kitchen with deep blue tile floor and countertops that looked like a chef's dream. A wide counter opened into the dining room portion of the expanse. Oak high-backed stools at the counter provided an informal eating spot, while the dining table stretched the full length of that spacious room, easily seating eight. Rachael filled a large kettle at the kitchen sink and set it on a burner.

"Black or herbal?" she asked, opening the doors on a cleverly hidden pantry.

"Black," I said.

I circled through the kitchen and dining areas, back to the living room. Through the glass doors I saw a small, cozy deck furnished with a grouping of chairs and a neat little table-umbrella arrangement for eating outdoors. A large barbeque grill against the wall gave further testimony to the fact that Sam liked to cook.

I stepped out to the deck and walked its perimeter. At the far end, it looked into the dining room window; at the opposite end, near the French doors, an opening let out onto a gravel path that circled the house. I stood at the railing a moment and took a deep breath of pine and cedar. Except for the chirping of birds and the occasional skittering of a squirrel in the trees, silence enveloped the place.

A mere twenty feet from the back of the house the forest closed in tightly, I followed the gravel path to the right, rounding the corner of the sunroom. Inside, I could clearly see Rachael in the kitchen pulling mugs from a rack. A shiver of apprehension coursed over me. An old phrase about people in glass houses ran through my mind.

Beyond the sunroom, the wrap-around porch led to the front of the house. I took the two wooden steps up and faced another sliding glass door into a room I'd not seen yet. I tried the door and found it locked. Good.

Porch furniture of heavy wicker with cushioned seats stood invitingly at the wide corner where the ninety-degree angle cut back toward the front door where we'd first come in. Past that, the double garage doors stood solidly closed. I picked up the gravel path again on the far side of the garage and followed it past the kitchen and dining room windows, back to the French doors where I'd come out.

"Tea's ready," Rachael called as I came inside.

I took a mug and drifted through the living room. Double doors revealed that the small room I'd noticed from the outside was a study. I'd spotted one telephone in the kitchen. Another sat on the desk in here.

"What's upstairs?" I asked Rachael.

"Two bedrooms and two bathrooms. Take a look," she said.

I climbed carpeted stairs to a landing where a small bedroom, dressed in ruffles and lace, looked out over the driveway, toward the pen with the two Rottweilers. A bathroom on the same level featured a large window that extended from eye level to the ceiling, staring out into the trees.

Up another short flight of stairs, the master bedroom looked out over an open railing to the living room below. A doorway led to a small upper deck with a hot tub. A huge pine grew beside it and I briefly wondered whether it shed needles into the tub every time the cover stood open.

A second bath gave pretty much the same view as the first. Pastel wallpaper in shades of lavender and blue, along with framed prints of impressionistic girls in filmy white dresses gave the room a decidedly feminine tone. I nosed around in the bathroom for a moment but found only male products. Not so much as a pink toothbrush to indicate that Rachael ever spent the night here.

"Lots of feminine touches for a guy's house," I commented as I came back downstairs.

Rachael had taken a spot on the big, cushy sofa, her legs folded under her and her hands wrapped around her mug using it as a mini heater.

"Sam's wife," she said. "She died three years ago, but aside from giving away her clothes, he apparently hasn't changed a thing."

"Must feel kind of strange to you."

"Kinda. Guess it's the main reason we haven't moved in together. Living with a ghost in a cozy-country style house just isn't my thing. And Sam loves the mountains and his dairy goats. I can't imagine that he'd ever agree to move into the city."

I settled onto the sofa, stretching my legs along the opposite length of the big L from where she sat. "So, does that mean there's no future for you two? I get the feeling Sam really loves you."

"He does. I don't doubt that. It's just...I don't know." She drained the last of her tea and got up to pour another cup. "With everything this week, you know. I just can't think about it right now."

"Yeah." I had a lot of thinking to do after this week, too. I should have told Drake about my pregnancy suspicions when he called yesterday. I handed my mug over for a refill when she offered.

"Rachael, about your father..." Dean Patterson's revelations yesterday still preyed on my mind.

"I can't, Charlie. I can't even think about him right now."

"Even though we know he didn't send the—" I jumped when the phone rang.

"I tried your cell, but it says you're out of area," Ron said when Rachael handed the phone over to me. "Guess the mountains or the trees are interfering with the signal."

"So, what's the plan now?" I asked.

"Sam and I are going to run by the office. I had a couple more computer checks in the works and I want to see if the information has come in. We want to stay clear of the balloon field for a couple more hours anyway, then we'll get Sam's car and come back out there. After that, we'll see."

I walked out to the back deck, taking the conversation out of Rachael's earshot. "Are you guys planning for us all to spend the night out here?" I asked. "This house is isolated, sure, but if anyone finds out where we are, it's a security nightmare. There's not a drape or window shade in the place and even the second floor rooms are easily accessible."

He pondered that for a minute. "Guess we'll have to figure out something. Look, it's coming up on noon. I'll give you a call when we get ready to head back that direction. Scout around a little and see if you can map out an exit strategy."

Lucky me. I'm an accountant. What do I know about exit strategies? I carried the silent phone receiver back inside and locked the door behind me. Rachael had burrowed into the soft cushions on the big sectional and was dozing soundly.

I crossed quietly to the stairs and went up to the front bedroom, the ruffled one. Its large windows overlooked the driveway and dog run. The two Rottweilers paced along the fence between their water tub near the house and the front property line. By positioning myself at the left edge of the window I had a clear view down the driveway, nearly to the gate. Using this as a lookout point, we could easily know when anyone tried to approach the house—at least by the conventional method. I decided to walk down and see if Sam had closed the gate. Anyone who wanted to drive up to the house would manage to set off the dogs before they got close to us.

Rachael looked so peaceful on the sofa as I walked downstairs and let myself out. I wished I could relax enough to take a nap, too, but felt too keyed up at this point. I walked most of the two hundred yards to the gate before I realized that it was already closed. The two dogs trotted parallel to the drive, keeping wary eyes on me but seemingly accepting of the fact that I came here as an invited guest.

I examined the gate. It had only a standard latch, no chain or padlock. It certainly wasn't going to keep anyone out. The fence, except for the dog's enclosure, consisted of regular three-strand barbed wire, fine for keeping cows and horses in their rightful places, but useless against most anything else. Sam had said that the property was five acres. Knowing that a person could get through this fence at any point didn't do a lot to reassure me. I could only hope that our security lie in secrecy. No one had any reason to think they could find Rachael here. No one except her six crew members, anyone they might speak to, or god-only-knew how many people who knew where Sam lived. Yeah. Reassuring.

I trekked back to the house where I rechecked all the doors and windows before taking up a post in a rocking chair near the front window in the upstairs bedroom. The next thing I knew, I was pulling myself out of a groggy sleep. For precious minutes, I drifted between the uncertainty of my location and the leaden feeling that I couldn't drag myself up from the depths of sleep.

A stealthy sound of metal on metal came from somewhere within the house and I scrubbed at my eyelids with sandpapery fingertips to force them open. Sam's house. Clarity came in a flash. I stood up too fast and had to grip the arm of the rocker to keep my balance. After a minute I stepped out to the landing and scanned the lower floor. Rachael no longer lay on the sofa and I began to pick up the tiny sounds of someone puttering in the kitchen—pan against burner, the tinny clink of flatware in a drawer.

"Oh, there you are," she said as I walked into the kitchen. "Hungry?"

"What time is it?" I couldn't even begin to remember when I'd last eaten.

"Nearly four." She'd opened a can of soup and proceeded to pour it into a saucepan.

"I must have slept three hours!" Three hours in a chair, which no doubt accounted for the nagging crick in my neck. I rubbed at it as I watched her move about the kitchen.

Outside, the light had taken on a golden glow as the sun lowered in the sky. Bars of light scored the upper reaches of the living room walls and threw umber streaks across the pine tongue-and-groove ceiling. I strolled to the windows in the sunroom, noticing that the ground around the house was entirely in shadow.

"What's the word from the guys?" I asked. "They should be getting here any minute, shouldn't they?"

"They haven't called," she said. "I tried to call Sam's cell, but it didn't work. Oops—"

She dashed to the range top, where bubbling soup threatened to flow over the top of the pan. She grabbed the pan and switched off the burner in one deft move.

"I hope you like minestrone and I hope you like it hot," she said.

I took a seat on one of the oak bar stools where she'd laid out two place settings on the counter. "Sounds great to me."

She passed a plate of garlic bread she'd magically produced from somewhere. The smells of spicy soup and fragrant bread caused a rumble in my stomach and I didn't waste any time. Not another word passed between us for at least ten minutes.

"More?" she asked, carrying her bowl to the stove.

"No, thanks, I'm doing great." Now that my hunger pangs were subsiding I'd begun to wonder again about Ron and Sam. My brother isn't always the best at checking in with me, but he'd said he would call before they left town. On the other hand, he's notorious for getting into the middle of a computer search and losing all track of time. Maybe I better nudge him.

"You tried Sam's phone," I said, "maybe I should try Ron's." I picked up the cordless handset, punching the familiar numbers.

"That—"

"Hmm, not getting anything," I muttered.

She set her spoon down and wiped her mouth with a napkin. "That's what I started to tell you. It didn't work."

Trickles of dread edged up my forearms. "I thought you meant Sam's cell phone didn't work."

"No, this phone didn't work. The line seemed dead."

TWENTY-TWO

MY SOUP THREATENED a return visit. I dropped the telephone on the counter. "Rachael, why didn't you tell me this immediately?" My voice came out high and edgy.

"I didn't...I mean, do you think..." The color had gone out of her face.

I dashed up the stairs and posted myself at the edge of the front window. The shadowy driveway looked the same as before. One of the dogs was asleep at the door of their wooden doghouse. The other must be near the front of the property. My pulse slowed a tad. Surely they wouldn't be so completely unconcerned if a stranger had come anywhere near the house.

"Charlie?" Rachael stood tentatively at the bedroom door. I spun around at the sound of her voice.

"There doesn't seem to be anything out of place outside," I said.

"Look, I'm sorry. I didn't panic because the phones up here are always acting up. Electricity too. They're out for awhile then they come back on."

That knowledge reassured me somewhat. But I didn't like the feeling of being so cut off. No cell service, now no regular phone service either.

"Is it chilly in here?" I asked as we walked back down the stairs.

Outside the wide sunroom windows the shadows had deepened, giving the forest a dull gray old-black-and-white-movie feel. I considered what would happen when it truly became dark. The minute we switched on lights inside the house the outdoors would feel even darker, and we'd be as exposed as fish in an aquarium.

"I'll get some wood for a fire," Rachael said.

"Where is it?"

She gave me a funny look.

"The firewood, where is it kept?"

"There's a stack at the side of the driveway, near the dog run, and there's more in the garage."

"Get it from the garage." I watched her unlock the door in the kitchen that led down the steep flight of steps. "We better round up some flashlights," I said. "Where are they?"

"Hmm…let me think." Distracted from the garage mission, she turned to begin rummaging through kitchen drawers. "Here's one. And I think Sam has more on his workbench."

"Grab as many as you can find before you worry about the wood. Batteries, too."

I made the rounds of all doors and windows again, paranoidly rechecking locks. I couldn't imagine that I'd slept so soundly that I wouldn't have heard someone tampering with them, especially since the dogs would have surely barked. But I didn't place too much trust in the idea that the phone's being out of order was mere coincidence, either.

"Charlie! Charlie—quick!"

Rachael's voice came as a muted shout, far within the depths of the garage, as I'd just finished checking the lock on the upstairs balcony door leading to the hot tub. I raced through the master bedroom, down the two sets of stairs, and into the kitchen. She met me at the top of the garage stairs.

"You didn't go down there and do anything with the balloon, did you?" she said, her breath coming in bursts.

"No, what's happened?" I nearly shoved her down the stairs as we hurried back down.

At the far side of the garage stood the wicker gondola, the inflator fan, and box of accessories, just as the crew had left them. But the heavy canvas bag sat away from the other items, the top cinch-strap undone, spilling red, white, and blue fabric onto the floor.

"The crew didn't leave it like this," Rachael said. "I know they didn't."

"No…I'm sure you're right." I looked around the open bag, noticing scuffed footprints in the dust on the concrete floor. Then something gleamed in the glow of the overhead bulb. I knelt to check it out.

A knife.

My hand reached toward it but pulled back. Fingerprints. My automatic response kicked in.

"Rachael." I waved her over. "Recognize this?"

She knelt beside me and stared at the shiny blade. It looked like a hunting knife, perhaps, with a nicely carved wooden handle and a wickedly curving inch-wide blade that gleamed in its sharpness.

"No. I've never seen Sam carry anything like this," she said.

"We better leave it here until Ron can take a look. Maybe he can get prints off it."

"What's it doing here? Charlie, what's happening?" She'd unconsciously moved over to the balloon bag and began caressing the fabric of *Lady Liberty*.

"Looks to me like someone intended to damage the balloon to keep you from making your flight tomorrow," I said.

"But…" She didn't have to say it. We were both wondering who knew the balloon was here, in this garage. And how had they gotten in?

I tugged upward on each of the garage doors, testing, but they were both firmly in place. Then I noticed a small side door that must lead outdoors. I crossed to it quickly and tried the knob. The one door in the whole place I'd not checked and it was unlocked. Shit. I yanked it open and stepped out onto the pale gray gravel path. It stretched on my left to the driveway and to my right it passed the kitchen window and eventually wound around the back deck. Ahead of me a small clearing contained a tire swing and wooden picnic table, barely visible now in the fading light. Beyond that the forest had become thick and black.

"I don't see any damage," Rachael said, as I stepped back inside and carefully twisted both the deadbolt and the lock on the doorknob. She stood over the canvas bag and had pulled out several more yards of fabric. She was running her hands over the panels, one at a time.

Why, I wondered. If someone had gotten this far—standing over the balloon, knife in hand—it could only mean that we'd somehow interrupted them in the act. Perhaps with Rachael and me asleep they hadn't realized anyone was home. They could have fled when they heard clattering pans in the kitchen. But wouldn't they have made a few decisive cuts in the nylon before they ran? The thought that Rachael had frightened the intruder away just now, when she switched on the garage light to go for the firewood, was way too close for comfort. We better have a weapon, and I remembered with a sinking feeling that I'd left my gun with my things at Rachael's house. A fine bit of planning.

I found an old towel on Sam's workbench and tacked it over the half-panel window on the side door. We were now in the only place in the house where I didn't feel the eyes of the outside world could see us.

"We may have to spend the night here, in the garage," I told her, keeping my voice barely above a whisper. "Does Sam have any guns?"

"I don't…I'm not sure," she said, matching my tone.

I strode to the spot where the knife lie. Screw fingerprints. At this point we had to think about defending ourselves. I picked it up and looked it over. On closer inspection I saw that the blade could be folded into the handle. A small button released it. Another catch extended the blade, whipping it into working position with a suddenness that startled me. I practiced working the mechanism several times until I'd figured out the right way to hold it without danger of taking off three fingers as I did so. Folded, it didn't feel quite so deadly, and I slipped it into my jeans pocket.

"I think we can safely leave the garage light on," I told Rachael, "but nothing in the house, not even a night-light. Once it's completely dark outside, we can't afford it."

I figured that gave us about another thirty or forty-five minutes of half-light before we'd risk stumbling around and breaking our necks on some random piece of furniture.

"We better round up some food, warm clothes, and any weapons we can find."

"What's going on with Sam and Ron?" she asked. "Why aren't they back by now?"

Yeah, well, I wanted those answers, too. Especially since my loving brother had gone off, leaving the two of us miles from anywhere with no vehicle, no working telephone, no weapon, and not a hell of a lot of hope. I indulged in a short fantasy about wringing his neck before I roused Rachael into action.

"We better plan for this night on our own. If they get back, great. If not, well…we better be ready."

If there's anything I can't stand it's a helpless female who goes frantic in the face of danger. A hysterically screaming woman brings out in me the urge to slap. Fortunately, Rachael wasn't that woman and I gained a small measure of confidence when I watched her go into action.

"Okay, then," she said. "There are some sleeping bags on a shelf out here. We'll find them in a minute. I'll get extra blankets and pillows; I know where they are in the house." She caught my expression. "Well, we might as well be comfortable, right?"

"Where would I find winter jackets? Bedroom closets?"

"Probably."

"What about a gun?" I asked the question without much hope. She'd already become fuddled with that one. "Never mind, I'll look around. You gather some food—anything we won't have to cook."

"Got it."

We started up the garage steps cautiously. A spring closer had snapped the heavy door solidly closed when I came down, and I couldn't hear a thing on the other side. I pulled out the hunting knife and snapped it open. One couldn't be too careful. I drew the door open as quietly as possible and scanned the greatroom. Nothing looked out of place. Rachael followed me and we assessed the situation like a Special Forces team entering enemy territory. Once we'd ascertained that we were alone she took the kitchen and I headed upstairs.

Where does a guy hide a gun? Near his bedside, if I'd learned anything from my months of firearms discussions with Drake. I headed for the master bedroom and went for the side of the bed nearest the bathroom. That bit of reasoning doesn't need explanation for anyone, does it? The nightstand yielded nothing but a paperback book on top, a nailclipper, box of condoms, and two issues of *Playboy* in the drawer. Those and the pair of dirty socks in the open space beneath the drawer convinced me that Sam was 100 percent normal guy. So where did he keep the weapon?

Patting the carpet under the edge of the bed, at least as far as my forearm would go, netted one more pair of dirty socks and about forty-five dustballs, although I didn't stop to count them. The fact that I even took time to wonder about it was surely a sign that the tension was getting to me. I brushed my arm off on the bedspread—hey, it was Sam's fault I was having to do this anyway—and began a patdown of the pillows.

I had to give Sam credit in the vigilance department. The gun was under the pillow on the other side of the bed, positioned so he could merely stretch in his sleep and put his right hand on it. Unfortunately, I had to mark him down for lack of firepower. The pistol was a .22 revolver and of the six potential shots it offered, only three were left. He'd be lucky to kill a cat with those teeny bullets, much less a full-sized human being. But one never knows. If my life depended on it, at close range and with the right angle, I might use the thing. I stuck it into my waistband, berating myself again for not bringing my Beretta.

I'd hoped that the nightstand on the other side of the bed might offer up additional ammunition, but no such luck so I went on to the closet. I debated breaking the restriction about turning on lights, but a quick glance told me that at least four windows would expose me to anyone lurking outside. I pawed around the upper shelf in hopes that a box of .22 shells would fall into my hand, but that didn't work.

So, warm clothing. I knew Rachael pictured a cozy pajama party with our sleeping bags on the floor while we munched popcorn and cookies all night, but I had a feeling that the reality might involve more. I wanted a heavy coat and warm boots if I could find them. Mountain temperatures in the autumn could likely fall into the thirties, possibly even the twenties, not a place to be overnight in your street clothes.

My hands came across the reassuring feel of a sheepskin jacket and I pulled it off its hanger. If it came right down to it, I knew I'd offer Rachael the heavy coat, so I better find two of them. No other sheepskins offered themselves up but I did find another roomy parka whose fabric felt like that wind-proof all-weather stuff and the padding seemed adequate.

"Charlie?" Rachael's voice came tentatively up the stairs in the dark.

"In the main bedroom," I said. I heard her feeling her way up the remaining steps.

"I've put a bag full of snacks beside the garage door," she said, "and here are some gloves that I found on top of the fridge."

I showed her the two coats, which she inspected mostly by feel. I also told her about finding the pistol, but didn't elaborate on its inadequacies. We'd deal with that if the occasion arose. We edged our way back down the two short flights of stairs. The light at the windows now consisted of barely discernable gray rectangles. Another thing you never realize when you live in a city—just how dark absolute dark really is.

We'd left the light on in the garage, which I now realized was about to be a big liability. There would be that moment in time when we'd expose ourselves and our plan by opening it and heading down the stairs.

"Where is the switch to the garage light?" I asked.

"Top of the stairs. I think it's a foot or two away from the doorjamb."

"Okay, here's what we better do. Open the door as little as you can and still get your hand through. Reach through and switch off the light as fast as possible."

She followed instructions well, and I could only hope that whoever had come in once had either left the property entirely, or hadn't been near the back of the house where he'd easily observed our moves.

"Now, take the food sack with you and feel your way down three steps. That should give me room to get in." I edged the toes of my right foot over the step, then two more times, then pushed the heavy door closed. The light nearly blinded me when I hit the switch, but at least we didn't have to keep feeling our way down the steep stairs.

Rachael, in true pajama party fashion, proceeded to build us a cozy nest. She located some thick waterproof tarps and spread them out. Followed this with blankets—I had no idea where those came from—then the sleeping bags, pillows, and our sack of munchies. I half expected her to pull out fuzzy pink jammies with feet and begin changing into them.

"Can you work by flashlight? I'm not sure we should have the bright light on," I asked. I'd been in here less than ten minutes and was already anxious about what might be happening outside.

"Sure."

I switched off the overhead light and risked lifting one corner of the towel I'd tacked over the one window. The view showed me absolutely nothing. Pitch dark. I dropped the curtain and joined Rachael on the pile of bedding. Cold had begun to seep through my jeans, so I wrapped the insulated bulk of a sleeping bag over my lap.

"Cracker Jack?" she offered.

"One of my favorites." I rummaged through the provisions and also discovered two packages of cookies and a large airy bag of cheese popcorn. "Anything to drink with these?"

A blank look came over her face and I could see an uh-oh forming. "Oh, wait, there are sodas out here." She made her way over to the stairs, where cases of pop were stacked in an alcove. "Room temperature, but better than nothing." She brought each of us a canned Coke.

I surveyed my supplies, making sure I could locate things on a moment's notice. The cell phone in my purse still registered a "no signal," which didn't come as any surprise, and the portable phone from the house was still dead. I visualized Ron calling and getting no answer. He would know something was wrong, round up extra help, and be on his way here this very minute. Any time now, we'd hear vehicles pulling into the driveway and we'd all spend the rest of the evening laughing over this.

Except that Ron and Sam should have been back hours ago, the dogs should have raised a ruckus when someone entered the garage, and the feel of that folding knife still lay heavy in my pocket. Nothing about this whole situation felt right.

Another hour passed. No vehicles arrived and we'd run out of small talk. Rachael wandered over to the stack of equipment she'd accumulated for her altitude flight—parachute, oxygen tank and mask, super-thermal flight suit. She checked everything, I imagined for the hundredth time, then drifted back to the sleeping bags, pulled off her shoes, and burrowed into the downy cocoon. Despite the afternoon nap, I also felt my eyelids getting heavy. I allowed them to close for just a second.

The sound, when it came, was tiny. The merest scrape of something on gravel, the smallest metallic *chink* as the doorknob twisted. In my half-asleep state it could have been part of a dream. I roused slightly.

Every bit of sleep left me in the next second, though, as the door's glass panel crashed inward.

TWENTY-THREE

RACHAEL LET OUT A little shriek and sat up, pulling her covers tightly around her shoulders. A dozen thoughts flew through my mind, from defending ourselves with the three shots left in the .22, to close combat with the knife, to getting the hell out. The latter seemed like the best choice.

The flashlight beam swung wildly as I thrashed against my sleeping bag restraint.

"We gotta get out!" I rasped. "Grab the coats." I re-tucked the gun into my waistband and patted my pocket where the knife lay. "And your shoes!"

Something in the back of my mind told me we should be quiet, not let the intruder realize he'd nearly caught us, but the reality wasn't so easy to achieve. Rachael crashed into the paper bag of food as she lunged for the jackets and I nearly went headlong across the room when I stepped on the cylindrical metal flashlight and it rolled. Shadows rose and fell like malevolent spirits against the walls. A gloved hand came through the broken windowpane and patted the door frame in search of the knob.

"Quick! Up the stairs," I called to Rachael in a stage-whisper.

She bolted, arms full of sheepskin, her shoes dangling in her right hand. I followed right on her heels. The abandoned flashlight cast most of its light toward the workbench on the opposite wall, giving the stairwell only the slightest dim gray illumination.

"It's locked from the inside!" Her voice edged toward hysterics.

"What!" How had that happened?

I heard the knob downstairs rattle. No time to think. I ripped the pistol from my waistband and faced the door.

"Move over," I ordered.

Her eyes grew wide at the sight of the gun and she pressed herself against the wall. I aimed at the lock and pulled the trigger. Shreds of metal flew outward. I felt flecks of it hit my face.

A male voice cursed downstairs, closer now. I yanked the door open and shoved Rachael through.

"Go for the back door," I ordered.

She dashed through the dark house, fumbled momentarily with the lock on the door, and flung it open. I followed her tracks, doing my best not to stumble over furniture in the unfamiliar place. Behind me I heard heavy feet on the garage stairs. A second person pounded on the front door.

Rachael paused on the deck, waiting for me to catch up.

"Go! Go!" I shouted. "There's at least two of them."

She leaped the deck railing and bolted for the woods. The hillside climbed steeply. I barely managed to keep her in sight as I followed. At one point my foot dislodged a rock and I went down hard on one knee. Pain shot up my leg but the sounds of two men on the deck spurred me on.

Rachael raced over an unseen path. Thick layers of pine needles and brown oak leaves coated the ground and obscured all tracks. I followed faint white movements and realized she was running over the rocky ground in her socks. We covered a couple hundred feet before she slowed. I looked back and couldn't see the house at all.

"I've got to put shoes on," Rachel said, huffing to catch her breath. She sat down and brushed spiky needles from her socks. I kept watch below as she tugged her shoes on and quickly tied them. "Here, take a coat," she said. "I'll move faster if I'm not carrying them."

I reached for the parka. "Which direction are we heading?"

"Right now, basically east," she said. "Sam's land extends up here quite a ways. In fact, there's a gazebo on the highest point."

"But if we're going to get back to the city we need to go west, don't we?"

"Eventually. For now, maybe we can just get to the road that runs north and south. There's traffic there, and more houses."

A flashlight beam bobbed below. As much as I wished we had brought one, at this point it would be a liability. Too easy for the enemy to keep track.

Rachael spotted the light and took off again. It took all my concentration to keep up. Without her white socks leading me, my only guide was the pale brown collar of the sheepskin coat. I lost all sense of direction as we wound over the twisty trail. Five or ten minutes went by before she paused again, minutes of steep climbing that left my leg muscles throbbing.

"Breathe, Charlie," she said, watching me huff my way up the final three feet.

"Al…altitude," I croaked.

"Yeah, gets to you, huh?" With my blood pumping in noisy rushes through my eardrums and my breathing sounding like gusts of strong wind, I barely heard her. My body was warm in the heavy coat, but my hands felt like ice.

I felt better when I noticed that she, too, was breathing hard. We sat for a minute, scanning the hillside for light or movement. Nothing.

"I think we can head downhill now," Rachael said.

"Wait a sec—I think I heard…" I let my whisper trail away.

A twig snapped, closer than I liked. I clapped a hand over my mouth to hush my heavy breathing. Unfortunately, I couldn't silence my pounding heart.

"Did you…see which…way they went?" The male voice huffed roughly, his breath coming in ragged bursts.

"No." The second male puffed. "I think…we lost 'em."

"Shit!" Leaves crackled and pine branches swished in the air. Two heavy bodies settled onto the ground somewhere on the other side of a huge boulder, probably no more than twenty feet away.

"Gotta catch…my breath," one of them said.

I glanced uphill at Rachael and saw the whites of her wide eyes in the dark. I blinked twice at her and she blinked once in response. Five minutes of grunts and groans and shuffling dry ground matter followed.

"Shit, this ain't worth it," the first man said, once he could speak again. "My best knife gone, now I'm sitting out here in the middle of piss-off nowhere in the freezing-ass cold."

The other man grumbled something sympathetic sounding in response.

"I'm heading back," voice one said again. "You coming?"

A flashlight switched on and swung over the downhill terrain. I held my breath. One swing up the hill and we'd be spotted. Our luck held as the two men stood up and began following the beam back down the hill.

Once the beam was out of sight, Rachael reached over and squeezed my arm.

"Do we dare go back to the house?" she whispered.

"I don't think so. If that guy dropped his knife, he's still got intentions of damaging your balloon. We don't have any backup or sufficient weapons to take on two of them."

A pained look crossed her face at the mention of the balloon, but she saw the wisdom of letting it go in favor of staying alive.

"Can you find a way out of here that doesn't take us near the house?" I asked.

"Yeah, I'm pretty sure." She found an opening in the forest that headed downhill, and I followed. Sooner than I would have expected, we came to the barbed wire fence with the road on the other side. I held the upper strand for Rachael and she did the same for me once she'd crawled through.

"There are several houses along this road," she said. "Maybe we can find someone home and use a phone."

Wondering where our two pursuers had parked, I motioned Rachael to the edge of the dirt road. Out here, with a little more open space overhead, the glow from the city gave enough light to ease navigation.

"There's a house on the right—the Farnsworths'," Rachael said, "but I think Sam said they were out of town. We'll see. Otherwise, we may have to go another mile or so."

I didn't say anything but was secretly glad when lights appeared a few dozen yards away. My legs felt like mush spread with Jell-O. A small cabin sat in a clearing, lights shining in several of the windows, and a white pickup truck beside it. I felt tears prickle at my eyelids. A phone, a cup of hot cocoa, the familiar sound of Ron's voice… I began to visualize ahead to being able to sleep in my own bed, make love to my husband, and hug my dog. My legs picked up the pace.

Rachael and I nearly raced each other for the front door. She got there first and pounded on the door.

"Hello, Rachael."

We both spun to find ourselves facing the heavyset man who'd just come down from the mountainside.

"Kevin?" Rachael's face registered total confusion. "What…"

My brain tried to fix itself around the situation. Kevin Pierce.

"Come inside, ladies. I'm sure you're cold." He opened the cabin's door and politely pointed the way. Rachael stepped inside without question. I started to turn away but the second man stood right at my side. He smelled of sweat and his thinning black hair revealed dots of perspiration on the top of his shiny head. He gently took my elbow and spun me toward the door.

The place was much more rustic than Sam's, a cabin instead of a house. One main room served as living, dining, and kitchen, with a daybed along one wall. Two doors led away, probably to a bedroom and bath. A fireplace made of river stones dominated one of the short walls of the rectangular structure. I spotted a set of fireplace tools with a stack of newspapers beside them. A mantle contained several candles and an oil lamp, presumably of use during those frequent power outages Rachael had told me about. A yellow plaid sofa and two orange armchairs pretty well filled the place furniture-wise.

"Roger was just about to put some coffee on," Kevin said. "Weren't you?"

The man called Roger nodded but didn't move.

"Kevin, what are you doing here?" Rachael demanded. "The Farnsworths are on vacation, aren't they? Why are you in their house?"

He'd crossed the room to the sofa where two jackets lay in a pile. He didn't answer Rachael's question, but rummaged in a pocket for a pack of cigarettes and a lighter.

I piped up. "I think the more important question is, why were you at Sam's place a little while ago?"

Rachael gave a little gasp. "How did you find us there?" she demanded.

Rare is the criminal who can resist bragging a bit. "Liz told me. Didn't you notice *Beauty's Beast* flying near you today? She radioed me your landing spot, and a few minutes later told me that your guys were hustling to pack everything into the truck. I told her to fly higher and report, so she was able to tell me that Sam drove through a bunch of residential neighborhoods, then south on Eubank. By the time you turned onto I-40 it didn't take a rocket scientist to figure out that you'd head to Sam's place."

It hit me that Liz had mentioned their previous visit for a barbeque.

"And you're certainly no rocket scientist," Rachael said. "But why?"

Kevin's face hardened as he lit his cigarette.

"Dear ladies," he said. "It's too bad you've put this all together. My original goal was simply to scare you away from making your world record attempt, Rachael. The letters and shots at your balloon were supposed to make you hang it all up. But you didn't. You, with the best equipment, the money behind you, and that smart-ass Sam to help you cash in on it."

He focused on his friend. "Where's that coffee, Roger?" he demanded.

Roger finally left my side and headed for the small kitchen alcove. He pulled a coffeemaker from one corner of the countertop and began opening random cabinets in search of supplies.

I edged an inch closer to the door while Kevin's attention strayed.

"But no," he continued, "you couldn't just give up the record so my wife could take it. No, you had to keep up the brave face. All that publicity, all those reporters fawning over you."

"Liz wanted the record that much?" Rachael asked.

I edged another inch closer to the door.

"Do you honestly think she would've beaten you, with that crappy balloon of ours, with no oxygen equipment?"

"Well, sure," Rachael said tentatively. "Why not? I mean, I don't have any claim on it. Anyone can file the paperwork and make the attempt. Even if I do attempt it, there's no guarantee I'll actually get it."

I edged another inch closer to the door.

Unfortunately, this time Kevin noticed me. When I looked up he held a gun. A lot bigger gun than my measly .22.

"Let's get right to it," Kevin said. "You're not going out there tomorrow, Rachael. You didn't make the choice yourself, so I'm making it for you. Roger, skip the coffee. Find me a good place to stash these two."

Roger, good little gofer that he was, left the kitchen and began to explore the rest of the cabin. I realized, as he went around switching on lights, that the two of them must have only discovered the place minutes before Rachael and I arrived. They'd probably parked their truck in front of the dark cabin, rather than driving it all the way to Sam's. Then they'd gotten in somehow and turned on a few lights to make the truck seem like it belonged.

"Ladies, take off your coats," Kevin ordered. The gun convinced us to comply.

"Bathroom looks good," Roger reported. "No windows, not much way to get into trouble."

"Good. Secure that one first," Kevin said, giving a nod in my direction.

The shorter man pawed through a few kitchen drawers until he came up with a ball of twine. He twirled out a couple of feet of it and cut it with a kitchen knife. I felt my nose wrinkle as the stench of unwashed clothes and sweaty armpits came nearer. Before he could direct me to put my hands behind my back, I held them out in front. Any little advantage, I figured.

He doubled the twine and wound it tightly at my wrists.

No sailor, clearly, he yanked three granny knots into the rough string before turning to the second part of his assignment. I cringed as he raised my shirt to find the gun in my waistband.

"Nice view," Kevin commented. "But get on with it."

Roger patted my pockets, all of them, then thrust his hand into the one where I'd stashed the knife. "Look what I found," he said to Kevin as he slowly rubbed his palm against my thigh.

I came seriously close to kneeing him but realized that would only serve to remind him that he hadn't tied my feet. I gritted my teeth instead and actually looked forward to being locked in the bathroom.

"Ah, my knife," Kevin said. "You know, this thing's real dear to me. You woulda been in lots of trouble if I hadn't gotten it back."

Like we weren't already?

Roger, meanwhile, moved on to Rachael and gave her the same tying and frisking treatment. She came closer to actually kicking him, but he'd already given her a shove toward the open bathroom door and didn't notice.

Kevin waved the gun to show me that I better follow quietly, so I did.

The bathroom was pretty bare bones. Molded fiberglass tub-shower with plastic curtain, white porcelain toilet with a few chips in the lid, a similarly chipped white sink hanging from the wall. Decoration consisted of two blue towels and a walnut-framed mirror. Geez, where did these people keep their stuff? Doesn't everyone own toothbrushes, pill bottles, and general junk?

Roger gave each of us a ceremonial shove to assert his authority, but conveniently forgot to tie our legs. He only seemed to realize afterward that locking us in would prove tricky since the door opened inward and only locked from our side.

We heard him asking Kevin how he could rig the door to keep us in, but the conversation degenerated as they walked away. For good measure, I reached out and flipped the little button on the knob. A swift kick or a plastic card would easily get past it, but we'd made our statement.

I pressed my ear to the door and discerned that the men were back to the task of brewing coffee. My stomach growled as the smell of it began to come our way, but I told myself to get over it. Life was a little more complicated right now than what a cup of coffee would fix.

"What're we going to do?" Rachael whispered. She'd lowered the lid on the toilet, commandeering the best seat in the place.

I moved away from the door and perched on the edge of the tub. "Guess that depends on what they do. Maybe they only want to be sure you don't fly tomorrow. If we're lucky, they'll finish their coffee and go home. We can figure a way out of here once we know they aren't watching anymore."

"Should we start untying these things?" she asked, holding out her hands.

"Let's wait. Unless we can manage to yank that sink off the wall, we don't have much in the way of weapons in here." Of course, I could towel whip them. "Better let them think we're being submissive until we find out how far they're willing to go."

"That coffee's making me hungry. What time is it?"

I couldn't pull up my sleeve and angle my watch's face toward myself one-handed, so I held it out toward her.

"Nine? That's it?" she said. "It feels like three in the morning, doesn't it?"

The news heartened me somewhat. I kept holding out hope that Ron and Sam had merely met with some delay, or maybe they'd stopped for pizza at a place with incredibly slow service. They'd surely show up any time.

But where? There was no reason on earth to think they'd look for us in this cabin.

"So, what are our escape options?" I asked. "Give me some ideas."

"They fall asleep, we unlock the door, and walk out?"

"That'd be nice, but I wouldn't count on it."

"They leave, we unlock the door, and walk out?"

"Yeah, right. Roger's not the brightest bulb in the chandelier but even he's going to figure out that they have to barricade this door."

"We get our hands free and wait until we hear them starting to nail the door shut, or whatever they're going to do. Before they actually nail it, we open it from our side, kick 'em in the balls, and run for it."

"Well, I like that one a lot better." I had to smile at the image.

Rachael sniffed at the air. "Now I think I smell steak. You don't think they'll actually hang around and cook a great dinner, right here in front of us, do you?"

That truly was a depressing thought. I calculated that our shared can of soup must have been eaten five or six hours ago. And we'd not even made a dent in the cookies and other goodies that now lay scattered on the garage floor at Sam's. My stomach growled and Rachael looked at me with a grin.

A new noise came from the other side of the door, something scraping across the wooden floor. I closed my eyes to visualize what it could be. Furniture, maybe. Something large and heavy. The scrapes approached our door, becoming loud. They were planning to block us in with something, but I couldn't envision what would work. The sofa was big, but we'd simply climb out over it. The daybed, perhaps? I waited until I heard them move away and I twisted the little lock button and turned the knob slowly. Something large and wooden filled the doorway almost completely.

"What's that?" I whispered to Rachael.

She peeked and backed away. "Careful! Here they come."

I eased the door closed and relocked it.

"So? What do you think? I don't remember anything that big in the cabin," I said.

She sat again and thought. "The gun cabinet. I think Mr. Farnsworth had a gun cabinet in the bedroom."

I considered that. If the two men could push it into place, surely Rachael and I could push it away. Couldn't we? That's when I realized the steak Rachael smelled was really smoke.

TWENTY-FOUR

RACHAEL APPARENTLY REALIZED the implications about the same time I did. Her eyes grew wide and she began picking at the knots on her restraints with her teeth.

"Wait, that's not going to work," I said, realizing that wet twine would only form tighter knots. "Let's see if we can untie each other."

After a couple of fumbling minutes in which neither of us accomplished anything, I decided to hold still and merely let her work on my wrists. She picked at the knots with her short nails and slowly managed to loosen one small loop. At this rate it would take forever. I looked around the tiny room for an idea. Any sharp object would do. But the place was filled with nice, soft objects like towels and smooth ones like porcelain. Meanwhile, I could hear the two men moving another large object.

"Right...there," Kevin grunted. "Spread the stuff on the couch and let's get out of here."

The pungent odor of lighter fluid trickled under the closed door.

"We're never going to get untied," I said. "We better try to push our way through."

I opened the bathroom door again, in time to hear the front door of the cabin slam shut.

"They're gone. We've got to hurry."

We both crowded into the narrow doorway and put our

shoulders to the high, wooden cabinet. It shuddered but didn't move. Again. Same result. I stepped back to assess the situation. The door frame was only a couple of inches wider than the cabinet. No way to squeeze past it.

Through the crack, I spotted a touch of yellow. The men had pushed the sofa against the cabinet, effectively making an impenetrable barrier. Smoke began to drift around the edges of the door frame and a peek at the top of it told me that the ceiling of the main room was becoming murky. I pulled Rachael away from the door and slammed it.

"Wet those towels," I said. We were going to have to think of something else. As we stuffed the sopping material around the base of the door, wedging it as tightly closed as possible, I considered our options. There were none.

In an hour or so, someone would notice the flames and report the cabin fire. A volunteer fire department from somewhere miles away would find the place engulfed and do their best to keep the rest of the forest from going with it. If there was anything left of the two charred bodies, no one would know who they were because the cabin's owners were out of town. When Rachael and I never showed up again, Ron or Sam might think to investigate the chance that our dental work might match up. I felt despair wash over me. I hadn't seen Drake in nearly a week, he didn't even know that we might have made a baby. I didn't want it to end like this.

Drake. He'd never just sit by and wait to be burned up. He'd fight to the last second, with his last scrap of energy. I owed it to him to at least die trying.

Rachael sat on the floor with her head in her hands.

"This is bullshit," I screamed. "They're not getting us!" Burning anger replaced the lethargy that had nearly taken me.

She looked up.

"A woman's strength is in her hips and legs," I said. "We've been wasting our time trying to move that thing with our upper bodies. Grab a towel."

We pressed the wet towels to our faces and opened the door again. The smoke immediately rushed into the bathroom.

"Let's just try to budge one edge of it," I shouted through my soggy mask. "Lie down!"

We wedged our shoulders against the far wall, our feet against the stubborn cabinet. With both our strength, a concerted shove moved the object an inch.

"Yes! Do it again!" A count of three and another shove gave us two more inches. Twice more and we had a gap of a little over six inches to work with.

"How skinny can you make yourself?" Rachael asked.

"I think we can do it. Keep the towel over your face."

We jumped up. Rachael was shorter than me but slightly heavier in the hips. I pushed her forward to go first. She wriggled sideways, struggling to keep her bound hands in front of her face. One shoulder went through, one hip, no more.

"I'm stuck," she gasped.

"Get ready," I said. I pressed the middle of my back into the porcelain sink and used it for leverage as I threw both feet upward. There was just enough bend in my knees, and I shoved them out straight. The pressure in my back felt excruciating but the cabinet rocked and Rachael squeezed through. She stumbled into the smoky room but turned to peek at me through the open space.

"Can you make it?" she shouted.

"I think so." I better.

I raised the wet towel to my face again and edged into the crack as Rachael had done. My knuckles scraped against the corner of the cabinet and the belt loop on my jeans threatened to snag on the door frame, but I forced my way through.

"Run!" I screamed.

The yellow sofa was fully engulfed now, flames licking at the front of the gun cabinet and spreading across the floor. The backs of my hands felt singed as I dashed after Rachael, edging sideways past the burning couch and taking two big leaps through the section of burning floor. The soles of my sneakers threatened to stick but didn't.

Beyond the flaming area, smoke obscured everything. A pale glow indicated that the men had left the kitchen light on, but it was impossible to see details.

I dropped to my knees to get below the smoke. The outer door was straight ahead of me. I saw Rachael's legs, heading toward the glow.

"No!" I shouted. "Drop down! Go for the door!"

Somehow in the roar of fire and the craziness of our actions, she must have heard me. She fell to her knees and looked around dazedly. I dropped my towel just long enough to use my hands to point her toward the door. Snatching up the towel again, I inch-wormed my way after her.

Cold, clear air embraced us on the wooden front porch. We both hunched on our hands and knees, gasping, sucking in the cool elixir.

A crash sounded behind me and I spun, rolling to one shoulder. The rush of new oxygen had fed the fire, sending flames to the ceiling.

"We better get away from here," I panted. "This whole place is gonna go."

Without a plan, we stumbled to our feet and automatically headed up the road toward Sam's house. Somewhere in the hills, the sound of a siren wafted in and out.

TWENTY-FIVE

HEADLIGHTS CAME BOUNCING UP the road behind us. I stumbled and spun to face them. A pickup truck, not Kevin's surely. I ran for the side of the road, moving awkwardly with my hands still bound.

"Charlie! Charlie, wait!"

I came to a dead halt. Drake?

The truck pulled up beside us and he jammed the gearshift in Park. Nobody had ever looked so good to me as my husband at that moment.

He flung open the door and wrapped his arms around me. "What are you doing out here?" he asked as I began to shiver. "Where's your coat?"

"I…we…the fire…"

He sniffed, noticing my smoky odor, and held me at arm's length. He finally took in my sooty face, tangled hair, and the fact that my hands were tied. His eyes flitted to Rachael.

"Oh my god," he said. "Baby, what's happened here?"

He motioned Rachael over and put an arm around each of us, rubbing our backs briskly to warm us. As he murmured soothing words, I burrowed my head into his chest and let the tears spill.

"Come on, we've got to get you inside," he said, leading us toward the truck.

We pulled ourselves inside just as the flare of red strobes began to flash off the surrounding trees.

"Fire department. The cabin." I nodded toward the burning structure.

"Yeah, I noticed." His wry grin broke the awful evening's spell.

"Hey, we didn't start it," I protested.

"It's not Sam's place, is it?" he asked.

I gave him a look. Rachael assured him it wasn't and pointed the way. He put the truck in gear and we turned in at Sam's driveway just as the first fire truck topped the hill.

Twenty minutes later, after Drake had cut our bonds off and dressed our wounds (a few days of treatment with antibiotic salve and gauze would handle them), and Rachael had gone out to check on Sam's dogs (drugged but not dead, thank goodness), and I'd babbled out most of our story, we stood around the kitchen with mugs of hot chocolate. I had a million questions but fatigue caused them to swirl in my brain in a sludge of incoherency.

"Ron tried to call you for hours," he said.

"The phones aren't working." I'd already picked up the one in the study and found that it was still dead.

"We'll get back to town and report all this to the police," he said. "But there's something else. Before I tell you this next part, I want you to know that they're okay, so don't panic."

"What?" I gripped my warm mug. "There can't be more. Tell me there can't be more." I began pacing the length of the kitchen.

"You want to sit down? Hon, you're exhausted."

"Do I look like I could sit? What's going on?"

He glanced toward Rachael, who sat at the counter looking numb.

"Okay. The reason Ron and Sam didn't get back when they said they would is because they were in an accident on the freeway."

Rachael's head snapped up and I stopped in mid-track.

"They're at the hospital now. Ron's got a broken arm. Sam's...well, Sam's unconscious."

Rachael let out a tiny whimper. I set down my mug and went to her.

"They're doing tests," Drake said. "I don't know any more than that."

"We have to go," Rachael said.

I wanted nothing more than a hot shower and to fall into one of the beds for a few hours, but I knew she was right.

"How did you..." I turned to Drake.

"When Ron couldn't reach you he was nearly in a panic. He called me and I flew in. I called him when I landed and he told me you two were here alone. I wasn't even sure I could find the place but his directions were good."

I rushed around the house, retrieving my purse and hoping I hadn't forgotten anything important. Over the past few days my life had become so scattered, with possessions left at Rachael's, and here. I'd lived in such disarray that I couldn't remember much. I had the vague feeling that I'd left my heavy jacket in Sam's truck and I didn't hold out much hope for ever seeing it again.

Drake shepherded us out to his truck and turned up the heater. Once we'd bumped through a ditch to get around the fire trucks blocking most of the road, I must have succumbed to the warmth and motion. The next thing I knew Drake was gently shaking my shoulder and we were in the hospital parking lot. His dashboard clock said it was eleven thirty.

Rachael rushed ahead of us to the emergency entrance and vanished through the doors. Drake and I took time for a long embrace on the sidewalk before facing the bright lights indoors. The warmth of his familiar body made me suddenly wish we were at home at this hour, wrapped together under the covers, finding each other in the dark in one of those fun, spontaneous encounters. "Hon, there's—" I wasn't sure how to start. Maybe it was better to do the test before telling him about it.

He kissed the top of my head and pulled back. "You forgot to wash your face," he said, smiling. He wiped some black off the tip of my nose.

Like I had nothing else on my mind. I bristled for an instant.

"Drake! Thank god you found them." Ron stepped out the automatic doors. "Come in a second, it's freezing out here."

My eyes took a minute to adjust to the brilliant fluorescents of the emergency room. People filled the waiting area, whole families, some looking frantic, others numb and sitting in plastic chairs. Ron's shirt sleeve had been raggedly clipped off and his right arm sported a shiny white cast supported by a blue sling. His hair stood out in tufts on the sides, the thin top section mussed into a fuzzy nest. Aside from a few tiny cuts on his face, he looked okay.

"Sam's been in and out of consciousness, the doctors are saying. They've done some kind of scan on him. They actually let Rachael go back there," he told us. "It may be tomorrow before they have a prognosis."

I looked around at the crowded room. "Do you plan to stay with him?" I asked.

"I feel like I should," he said.

"I'm going to find a quiet spot and call the police," Drake murmured to me. He headed toward his truck.

Once again the fatigue washed over me. "Can we find someplace a little bit private?" I asked.

Ron and I stepped out to the airlock between two sets of automatic doors. As long as we stood to the side, we managed to keep the doors from standing open, but the nearly constant traffic of someone arriving or someone leaving interrupted every few minutes.

"I tried to reach you on the phone," he said. "I even left a message about the new information I'd gotten on Liz Pierce on your cell's voice mail."

I pulled the phone from my purse and looked. Yep, the tiny envelope icon told me I had a message waiting. "Well, we found out about Liz the hard way," I told him. I filled him in briefly on Kevin's breaking into Sam's garage, our escape through the woods, the capture, and the fire.

"So, I guess Rachael will want to stay by Sam until we know he's out of danger," Ron said. "We should probably stay with her, in case Pierce tries anything more."

"Well, it's not going to be me. I've had plenty of this whole situation, I'm pooped, and I'm going home. Kevin can get Rachael, for all I care, and Sam can...oh, god, I'm sorry. I—"

"What's with you, Charlie? You've been bitching at any and every thing for the last week. It's driving everyone nuts."

Drake walked in right then. I caught the same question in his eyes and wanted to reassure him. But at that moment a fierce pain gripped the middle of me. I doubled over and swayed. He reached out to catch me and someone shouted for a doctor.

TWENTY-SIX

I FADED BETWEEN DARKNESS and light. People stood around a gurney, pushing me down a corridor, wheels squeaking, lights overhead running past like the white lines on a highway. I rolled to my side, the worst cramps of my life gripping me in the middle.

"Drake," I gasped. "Where are you?"

His voice came from behind me, Ron's from somewhere near my feet. They both murmured reassuring things but I couldn't concentrate.

"BP's dropping," a female voice said.

My vision blurred and I faded out of the scene.

I woke up to find myself in a quiet room with dim lighting. Drake sat by my side. When he saw that my eyes had opened, he reached out and stroked my arm. I turned toward him and discovered that my left arm had tubes and needles taped to it. He settled for twining his fingers through mine on my right hand.

"It's okay, sweetie," he whispered.

I brought my left hand over to lay the palm on my stomach. "It's gone, isn't it?" I asked, looking at his face for the first time.

He nodded. His teeth clamped over his lower lip and I could tell his eyes were moist.

"I'm sorry I didn't tell you. I wanted to be sure."

"Shush, it's okay. This last week wouldn't have been the best time."

Scenes from the past few days flashed through my mind, too many things, too much to deal with. I closed my eyes and a tear slipped out.

"We can have another one," he said. "A lot more if you want them."

A little chuckle escaped me. "No, not lots. Promise me."

He squeezed my hand. "Okay, not lots."

"I...Drake?"

He stroked my face.

"I didn't even want this one," I said. "It's a terrible thing to say, but when I started to think it might be true I...I kept thinking no, it couldn't be. Then, for awhile, I started to get used to the idea and I thought it might be fun. But we shouldn't have a baby just because it might be fun. We should really, really want one and be ready for the responsibility. And I don't think I did. Do you think I could have wished for a miscarriage?"

"No," he murmured. "No, you could have never wished it. It just happened."

But I put myself in danger, I thought. The escape through the woods, the fire and smoke. I'd stressed my body more than I should have. But I didn't say it.

"We'll talk about all this later. We'll decide." He gave my hand a squeeze and stood up. "I'm going to get you some clothes. The doctor says you can go home in a few hours. They just want to watch your blood pressure for a little while."

For the first time I looked down and realized I was wearing one of those flimsy hospital gowns that hide nothing. My hair still smelled like smoke.

He caught my puzzled look. "They cut your clothes off and threw them away. It's okay, they were a mess anyway."

I could well imagine, with dirt, smoke, and blood. I turned my thoughts away from that.

"Can I have a shower?"

"Let's ask the nurse. Then I'll bring you something to wear and we'll pick up Rusty and we'll have our family back together again."

Ron appeared at the doorway. "Hey, kiddo," he said.

I gave him a grin that felt weak and waved him over to the bed. He took my hand and bent to kiss my cheek. "We may have to rename you Smokey the Detective," he joked. Drake blew me a kiss as he slipped out.

"I know, I know. I'm putting in for a shower right now." I leaned back against my pillows again. "How's Sam? And Rachael?"

"Things are still touch and go with him," he said. "She's at his side and not planning to budge until he wakes up."

It had been a rough night for all of us.

"I'll sit with you until Drake gets back," Ron said. He propped his sling on his leg to take the pressure off his neck and shoulder. "Then I guess I better get home and figure out what's next."

I couldn't let myself go there because one thought would lead to another and I wasn't ready to have to figure anything out yet. I must have dozed because I didn't remember anything else until I heard Drake talking to Ron. "Police said they have a warrant for Kevin Pierce," he was saying. By the time I pried my eyes open my brother had left and my husband was holding out a soft sweatsuit.

"Rusty's in the truck, eager to see you," he said. "The nurse said you're okay to go, so do you want your shower here or at home?"

I glanced down and saw that someone had unhooked the tubes from my arm.

"Home. Let's just get out of here." I'd already swung my legs over the edge of the bed and reached for the sweat pants.

Out in the parking lot, he unlocked the truck without a word and held my door open for me. Rusty nuzzled toward me from the backseat and I gave his ears a brisk rub. I climbed in and stared out the front as Drake started the engine. He reached for the gearshift but turned to me instead. I looked back at him.

He reached over and took my hand, kissing the palm. "Either way, I don't mind," he said.

That bothersome tingle came to my eyes again and I consciously pushed it away. This was not the night to begin dwelling on this subject. I would go home, sleep twelve hours, wake up. Soon, again, I'd have fabulous sex with my husband, and not leave the house for a week. So there.

I'd just begun to doze again when we reached our own driveway. The place looked so good to me that I'd climbed out of the truck and nearly made the front porch before Drake locked the truck. The sky was already beginning to lighten in the east.

If Rachael were flying today, the final Sunday of the Balloon Fiesta, we'd all be waking to our alarms right now. Thank goodness we weren't.

Drake and I moved automatically through the routine of getting ready for bed, neither of us saying much. I stripped out of the new sweatsuit, dumping it beside Drake's flight bag with his week's worth of dirty laundry, and stepped into the shower. The hot water felt good and I soaped and shampooed twice to get rid of the odor of smoke. Once I'd brushed my teeth and dried my hair, I felt nearly human.

We climbed into bed and snuggled close together. The scent of clean skin enveloped us and he nuzzled my neck. Then he yawned largely in mid-nuzzle and was asleep instantly. I wrapped his arm around myself and rolled onto my side.

But sleep didn't come. Tired as my poor body felt, the combination of too much stimulation and my groggy spells at the hospital just weren't going to let me find that deep well of concentrated darkness I craved. I lay there with my eyes wide open as the room went from black to gray to full color. At some point, Drake rolled over and began snoring softly. When the bedside clock said 8:14 I gave up. I edged out from under the covers and tiptoed past the sacked-out dog to grab my thick terry robe from the back of the bathroom door.

In the living room, I switched on the TV, tuning to one of the local stations that carried Balloon Fiesta coverage. With the volume low, I pulled an afghan over my legs and watched the hundreds of bright orbs against the backdrop of a perfect blue New Mexico sky. My interest quickened as I spotted Sara Haines, whom I'd met at the pilot party, flying *Early Morning Delight*. And there was *Scarlett's Dream*. I wanted to look for *Lady Liberty*, but knew she wouldn't be there. I wondered how long before Sam would get home, before the crew would assemble and tend to the bag of crumpled fabric that now lay on Sam's garage floor. I wondered whether Rachael was still at his side at the hospital, or if they'd given her enough positive news that she'd been able to go home yet.

"…competition for the women's world altitude record." The words riveted my attention.

"Yes, Sandy, that is big news," the male news commentator said. "All week we've been covering the events leading up to top lady balloonist Rachael Fairfield's attempt at this record. And now it appears someone else is going to do it."

"That's right, Dave. Rachael isn't even out here today. KQUE has been trying to reach her all morning to find out what's happened, but we've been unable to learn why the big change in plans."

"Why, indeed. Well, that's going to remain the question of

the day for now. Meanwhile, we've learned that the new contender is Liz Pierce, another New Mexico woman." He consulted his notes. "Liz originally comes from Texas, moved to Albuquerque three years ago, and quickly became active in the ballooning scene."

"Right, Dave. Since Albuquerque is known as the hot air ballooning capital of the world," Sandy emphasized these last words, as if every person in the audience didn't already know it, "many balloonists from around the country and indeed around the world move here for our nearly perfect flying conditions." I let them ramble on, blanking out much of it until I heard Kevin Pierce's name.

"…Max down on the field right now, talking live with Kevin Pierce, Liz Pierce's husband and crew chief for this flight. Max?"

Another talking head appeared, a dark haired guy with less than camera-perfect looks, who, like the others, was bundled into the latest in chic outdoor jacket, cap, and gloves.

"Thanks, Sandy, Dave. Yes, I've got the exclusive opportunity to speak with Kevin Pierce, Liz's husband, as they make final preparations here on the field for her attempt at this important world record." He turned and the camera angle widened to include the face of the guy who, at this point, probably thought he'd gotten rid of us last night. "Now, Kevin," Max continued, "your wife's attempt at this record comes as quite a surprise to most of our viewers, I'm sure."

"Well, Max, it's never been a real secret that there were two women going for this record. Liz has always been the more experienced pilot, the one most likely to actually accomplish the goal. The other lady's got an important brother, is all. He paid for lots of publicity. But Liz never let that intimidate her. She's got spunk, and she's gonna do this thing right."

I seethed over Kevin's gall. How dare he? I wanted to grab that stupid fuzzy caterpillar from his lower lip and rip it off.

"So," continued Max, the reporter, "we see that Liz Pierce is about to take off here from Balloon Fiesta Park."

The camera panned out to capture Kevin striding over to the gondola of *Beauty's Beast* and exchanging a long kiss with his wife. Liz grinned and waved to the camera, then pulled a long blast on her burner, and lifted off the ground.

"We'll be following with Liz's chase crew," Max said, "and bringing you the moment of touchdown when this historic flight concludes."

Historic, my ass, I thought. There are hundreds of aviation records. Even Rachael admitted that this was just one of many. News people—kings of hype. I watched the coverage switch back to the two anchors, then to shots of the entire sky now filled with color.

I couldn't sit still. I stomped to the kitchen and pulled out the phone directory, punching in Rachael's number as soon as I found it. Apparently she either wasn't home yet or had shut off her phone to ignore the press. I left a quick message on her machine. The Pierces' audacity in going for the record attempt when Kevin knew full well why Rachael was out of the competition ate at me. The bastard deserved to be in jail for about a dozen reasons.

Drake had reported this last night, but now I could pinpoint Kevin's location.

I paged through the phone directory and picked up the telephone again.

"Arson Investigation, Smith speaking." I couldn't conjure up a face to go with the bored-sounding voice, but that didn't matter.

"There was a cabin fire last night on Hummingbird Lane, off South 14. I know who started it. He locked two women inside, hoping to kill them."

"Yes."

I hurried on. "The man's name is Kevin Pierce." I spelled it in case the officer didn't get it the first time. "His wife is on TV right now, at the Balloon Fiesta. So is he. Bring him in for questioning, look for prints at the scene. He's your man. His white pickup truck was there last night. There's probably evidence in that, too."

"Ma'am, what is your name?"

I hung up. Took a deep breath. That felt good.

Rusty padded out of the bedroom and joined me. I filled his bowl with nuggets and let him out the back door. Nice, familiar routine things. As I tidied the kitchen, the wall calendar caught my eye. I flipped back to September, remembering where we'd been on which days. I'd only been ten days late. My mind grappled with the thought. What should I be thinking now, anyway? What's done is done, I told myself. A gray feeling settled over me but I blinked back the tears. It would take awhile to sort this all out, I realized.

I let the dog back in, made myself a cup of hot chocolate, and carried it back to the living room. With my afghan once again warming my legs, I took a few sips of the soothing beverage. Television coverage of Liz Pierce continued as a newsman who'd managed to snag a ride with her crew chattered. The camera aimed toward open sky, able to pick up the balloon as only a dark dot against stark blue. I felt my eyelids grow heavy and I burrowed into the cushions.

In the fitful sleep of early morning, I dreamed of being on the spot when police came for Kevin. I rode in the car with them to the police station, where the long institutional hallways suddenly turned into those of a hospital and a nurse was congratulating me on the birth of twins.

I woke with a jerk, clammy sweat covering my chest. I rubbed my face forcefully, digging sleep granules from the corners of my eyes. Rusty looked up at me from the rug, ears perked, questioning.

"Whoa, that was a nightmare," I said.

My cocoa had become tepid so I carried the mug to the kitchen and nuked it for a minute. Then, deciding that I really didn't want to fall back asleep, I dumped the old filter, found a new one, and started a fresh pot of coffee. While it brewed, I tiptoed into the bedroom where Drake had now nestled completely under the covers, and pulled fresh clothes from the closet. Doing my best to avoid the squeaky places in the wood floor I dressed in jeans and a sweater, brushed my teeth and hair, and swiped on a dash of lipstick. I felt nearly human.

Coffee and toast helped complete the illusion that I wasn't half-dead with exhaustion. I found myself pulled to the television once again.

"We'd like to let our audience know that we're extending our Balloon Fiesta coverage this morning to let all of you witness Liz Pierce's historic world altitude record live." Sandy, the too-perfect news anchor, turned to Dave, her much-too-perfect cohort.

"That's right, Sandy," he crooned. "Max and our cameraman, Ted, are on-scene with the crew of *Beauty's Beast*, as Liz Pierce is about to land somewhere near the foothills of the Sandias."

Max's face came on again and he filled about ten minutes with nothing more than we already knew, keeping a running commentary on Liz's great achievement that nearly made me ill. The camera guy managed to capture great video of the balloon drifting down to a picture perfect landing, while the crew dashed out to catch it and Kevin opened a bottle of champagne.

Liz pulled off her knit cap and fluffed her hair quickly before turning to face the reporter.

"How high did you actually go, Liz?" Max asked, shoving the microphone in front of Kevin's champagne bottle.

"Thirty-four hundred feet," she said, beaming.

"Woo-hoo!" Kevin shouted, sending a blast of feedback through the mike.

A chunky blond man wearing an FAA ballcap pushed his way to the gondola. "Sorry," he said to the camera, "formalities first."

Kevin stepped back to allow the FAA man to reach into the gondola and lift out a wooden box about a foot long and eight inches high. The barograph. It recorded the flight and would be sent to France to be certified before the record became official. But I had no doubt from the expression on Liz's face that she knew she'd done it. I felt a letdown for Rachael. All that work, now this.

I'd picked up the remote, ready to end the misery, when something caught my eye. As Max babbled on, interviewing Liz about the details of the flight, I saw a uniformed APD officer approach Kevin in the background. As the man spoke, Kevin's expression turned from joy to disbelief to horror.

TWENTY-SEVEN

THE COP PLAYED IT COOL and walked Kevin out of camera range. The news team, completely unaware of the real story, continued to chatter about Liz and the altitude record. I watched for a few more minutes until it became clear that they were winding down and hadn't picked up on the fact that Kevin was being questioned by the police.

I carried my plate and mug back to the kitchen, itching to be out there watching it all unfold. I'd love to see the expression on Kevin's face when he learned that Rachael and I had gotten away.

I imagined his shock when the police examined his truck and discovered particles of soot and ash. Surely they would still be there. Surely he hadn't taken the time to wash his clothes. I reached for the phone, wanting to tell the cops how to do their jobs. Before I touched it, it rang, startling me.

"Charlie, it's Rachael." Her voice sounded flat.

"How's Sam?"

"Better. He'll be okay. He woke up, it must have been right after you left, I don't know. The whole thing's pretty blurry. Anyway, the doctor wanted to keep him awake for a few hours. He took a pretty good bump to the head. So I sat with him and talked and kept him talking. He's got broken ribs and they aren't sure about other internal injuries yet. More tests today, I guess."

"Sounds positive, though?"

"Yes, much better than we'd expected. The cuts and puffy black eyes look pretty awful. I had a hard time getting past that and realizing those weren't the worst part. If there aren't internal injuries, he should be out in a few more days." She took a deep breath. "I guess you've heard about Liz?"

"It's been all over the TV and I figured reporters have probably been bugging you."

"Yeah, twenty-seven messages on my machine." She sighed. "I'm just too tired to say anything coherent right now. Yours is the only call I'm returning."

"Well, Liz's little victory is going to be short-lived," I said. "The police are talking to Kevin right now."

"About…"

"About last night. Drake reported him while we were at the hospital." I didn't mention my own hospital ordeal. She had enough on her plate right now. I filled her in on the scene I'd just watched on TV. "It's probably going to mean both of us testifying against him. Are you ready for that?"

"I'm not ready for anything except a bath and about twenty hours sleep right now," she said.

"Sorry. I know. I should have waited on this."

"No, no. I'm glad. You know, I always thought Liz was a friend. Kevin, too. I would have never imagined this."

I remembered the cozy little scene at the barbeque as Liz chatted with Rachael in the buffet line.

"Get your rest," I told her. "Everything else can come later."

The doorbell rang before I'd quite hung up the phone. I heard Rusty growl from the living room and I rushed to get the door before he could go into a complete fit and wake up Drake.

"Charlotte Parker?" The black man in the blue suit held up a badge.

Oh, god, now what?

"You phoned Arson Investigation this morning?"

"Uh, yeah. I did." Caller ID. I'd forgotten that most police calls gave them all they needed to know. That business about asking my name, totally unnecessary. "Come in," I said, stepping back.

He walked in the way cops do, scanning the room and getting the layout in his mind. Introduced himself as Detective Henson. "Actually, a Drake Langston reported the arson last night. Your call just confirmed it."

"My husband's asleep. We had a very late night. Do you mind if we talk in the kitchen?"

I led the way, filled two coffee mugs, and gave him the whole story. He scribbled notes and asked for one refill along the way. When I'd finished, he closed his notebook and asked whether Rachael could verify everything I'd told him.

"I'm sure she will," I said. "Just not today. She was at the hospital all night and just got home. This past month has been hell on her."

"Understand. We'll get with her in a day or so."

"So, what's going to happen to Kevin?"

"Evidence techs are out at the cabin now. We knew we had an arson by the time the fire crew got the flames under control. Furniture piled in front of a bathroom door, accelerant on the sofa. It was pretty clear. When I took your call this morning, I picked up on the fact that Pierce's white truck was at the scene." He grinned at me. "Yes, we do know how to match ash debris from the truck to that in the cabin. Don't worry, we'll get him."

He carried his mug to the sink and rinsed it. "The arson's going to be just one of Kevin Pierce's problems. Stalking and attempted murder earn even bigger points. I hope Ms. Fairfield's kept those notes."

"She has."

"And she'll testify?"

"We both will."

Henson stuffed his notebook and pen into an inside pocket and walked into the living room.

"What's going on?" Drake emerged from the bedroom wearing a pair of jeans and crookedly hanging polo shirt. His hair stuck out in little sleep twirls.

"Hon, this is Detective Henson from Arson Investigation." I briefed him quickly about the way Henson had found me.

"You have anything to add to this story?" Henson asked.

"I wasn't there." He told the detective how he'd gotten the call and came looking for us, only to find two stunned, smoky women with their hands tied, wandering up a mountain road. By the time he finished, Henson's jaw had begun to twitch and I had tears in my eyes.

"We'll get the sonofabitch," he assured us.

I SPENT THE NEXT couple of weeks in my office at RJP Investigations, doing the paperwork I'd planned to do during what I called "the week that went totally wrong." Drake had no out of town work, so we settled into a comfortable routine where he spent his days at the airport, catching up on maintenance on the helicopter, while I reveled in the mundane tasks of payroll, accounts payable and receivable, and going through the stacks of mail that awaited on my desk. Even the dog seemed pleased with the familiarity of our ordinary life as he lay flat out, belly up, on the floor of my office day after day.

A week later, Rachael called. "Sam's home now and we want to do a little something to thank the crew—and you and Drake and Ron, too, of course. How about a barbeque out at Sam's place on Saturday?"

I accepted for all of us.

Saturday dawned as one of those perfect October days, the

last of our Indian Summer. It wouldn't be long now until we began to feel the chill winds of winter, but this day would be just right for the gathering in the mountains. It felt strange to drive past the burned out shell of the neighboring cabin. Drake and I both got quiet as we approached. He squeezed my hand and I sent a little smile his way.

At Sam's the beer had begun to flow and the steaks were already smelling good. I left Drake and Ron beside the male gathering on the porch, while I went inside to offer Rachael a hand in the kitchen. I found her putting the finishing touches on a salad. Pots of baked beans and ears of corn boiled on the stovetop. She looked up and crossed the room to pull me into a warm embrace. We'd only spoken on the phone a couple of times since that climactic weekend, and I'd worried that things might be a little awkward between us.

"You doing okay?" she asked.

I knew she referred to the miscarriage and I nodded. "How about you?"

"My father's been trying to call but I haven't felt ready to talk to him yet," she said, shaking a bottle of salad dressing. "Do you think that's wrong?"

In the craziness of that last flight and the night at the cabin, I hadn't found the right time and place to tell Rachael the full story, only to tell her that I'd been convinced that her father was not the one sending the threats. Now, I pulled her aside to the big sectional sofa and filled her in on Dean Patterson's confession and his current condition. Her face drained of color as the story unfolded.

"My god," she whispered. "I sent him to prison for nothing."

"Patterson was very cunning," I said, deliberately staying away from her mother's role in the whole thing. "He purposely misdirected you. He wanted your father out of the mayoral race and out of your lives. And he accomplished that. You were wronged in so many ways, Rachael."

Tears welled in her eyes but didn't get the chance to overflow before Justin came striding into the room.

"Sam says he needs a platter for the steaks," he said.

Rachael ducked her head and I intercepted Justin. As she fled for the bathroom, I steered him to the kitchen and rummaged through cupboards until we came up with a couple of big plates. Once he'd left, Rachael reappeared, her face pale but composed. "I'll have to deal with this news later," she said. "Right now there are people to feed."

I started to offer to handle that part of it, but realized that she really wanted to buy some time. This was the kind of thing that would haunt her late at night, for more nights than she wanted to think about. For now, social interaction might stave off the demons.

We'd just finished putting the food on the table when the male hoard descended, bearing a pile of savory meat and the laughter of a carefree day. After everyone had taken seats, Sam called the group to attention.

"To life," he said, "to love, and to a terrific set of friends. You all hold special places in our hearts."

Rachael nodded agreement and glasses clinked around the table. I caught Ron's eye and realized he wanted to say something, but he held off until we'd all loaded our plates with food and the serious appetites became somewhat sated.

"I have some good news, too," he finally announced. "Kevin Pierce has been arrested on charges of arson, breaking and entering, malicious destruction of property, and attempted murder, two counts." He gave a triumphant smile.

"Malicious destruction of property?" I asked. I'd told Ron about the knife on the floor but that there'd been no damage to the balloon.

"The bullet holes. The jerk actually admitted to firing those shots but said he wasn't trying to kill anyone, just to harm the balloon and scare Rachael. Breaking and entering was for the incident here at Sam's garage. Even though Kevin got his knife back, his prints were all over the door frame and some of Rachael's other equipment in the garage. The investigators also got great sets of sooty prints off Kevin's truck. Kevin and the other guy, Roger Gibson, were neatly placed at the arson scene because of ashes in the truck that match those from the cabin."

"What about this Roger Gibson, who's he?" Rachael asked.

"A good candidate for America's Stupidest Criminals, I'd guess," he said. "Guy's got a sheet that goes back years, lots of petty smash and grab-type stuff. He gets arrested, does a few months, and comes back for more. Lived down the street from Kevin and they hooked up over beers at some bar in the south valley. Guess Roger talks more intelligently when he's had a few, 'cause he convinced Kevin he was the man for the job, vandalizing the balloon and putting another scare into Rachael."

"So, what's going to happen to them now?" I asked.

"Roger's pleaded to some stupid little count in return for telling all the juicy details. Kevin, he's got some hot lawyer. Guess they're selling their house to afford him, which leaves Liz living with her mother."

"Oh boy, I bet she's loving that."

"Yeah, well, the best part is that even the pricey lawyer hasn't managed to get Kevin out yet. The more he blabs, the less the attorney can do for him."

I pictured Kevin with his scroungy hair and that repulsive little beard-thing. Scraps of his braggadocios comments to Rachael and me, as he tied our hands and planned to kill us, came back to me. I hoped he kept up the bragging through his whole jail time and right into the state pen.

Rachael piped up. "The good news is that there wasn't any damage to the balloon. Thanks to my wonderful crew," she tilted her head toward their end of the table, "they've pulled the balloon out of the bag and we've examined every inch of it. The bullet holes still make me fighting mad, but she's structurally sound and ready for the flight. We checked over the other equipment, too, and wiped off the fingerprint dust the cops left behind."

"So, you're going for the record?" Ron asked.

"Oh, hell, yes." She laughed with more carefree warmth than I'd ever heard from her.

TWENTY-EIGHT

NOVEMBER 15. With little fanfare, no reporters, and a very subdued Grayson Fairfield on hand, we met at the Moriarty airport, a little town on the east side of the Sandias, away from Albuquerque's bustle and traffic.

Justin ably directed the crew members in the duties they already knew well. Ron, Sam, Drake, and I, along with Grayson, looked on. The FAA man was off to the side with Rachael, going over the use of the barograph, that sensitive instrument which would record her flight. We'd heard through the grapevine that Liz's record had been certified at 33,428 feet, a bit less than she'd claimed upon her triumphant landing. Rachael felt confident that she could beat it, but nothing's certain in this game.

Sam kept a watchful eye on the sky. Earlier, just before sunrise, a layer of high, thin clouds had moved over the mountains and they'd now scattered. That seemed worrisome to him, something about potentially high winds aloft.

"Once the guys get the envelope inflated and it's standing upright, he'll place the barograph inside," Sam said, nodding toward John O'Malley, the FAA designee.

Sam walked over to the back of Rachael's new truck and sorted through the equipment lying on the tailgate. She was already wearing her parachute, something she'd confided that she was terrified of using. "I'm going to float down with the balloon unless there's absolutely no other choice," she'd told me. Now,

Sam picked up the oxygen tank and hooked it into its bracket in the gondola. He hooked up the lines and checked them.

Rachael rechecked everything around the truck, making sure she hadn't left anything crucial behind. She climbed into the gondola and submitted to Sam's strapping the oxygen mask around her head and placing her warm knit cap over the straps. She pulled the mask aside just long enough to give him a kiss, then waited as the FAA man set the crucial wooden box in, next to her feet.

"Give it a little tap with your foot when you reach the top," he said, "just to make sure it registers."

"Radio check," said Sam. They went through a minute or so of verifying that the equipment worked.

The rest of us doled out hugs and squeezed her hands before backing away. Just as we did, a news van from Channel 6 roared up.

Sam's face hardened as he realized who it was. "Keep that guy out of the way," he shouted as the reporter and cameraman bailed from the van.

I turned to Ron who turned to Grayson.

The banker shrugged his shoulders. "Couldn't let the event go unrecorded," he said.

I wanted to slap him on Rachael's behalf, but restrained myself. Drake approached the newsmen and, with his usual diplomatic calm, assured them that they could get better shots by staying back. Before they could argue, Rachael blew a gloved-hand kiss to the crowd and hit the burner.

I watched in awe as the balloon climbed quickly. This was no leisurely drifting voyage over the crowded balloon field. Fuel consumption was everything here, the goal being to get as high as possible as fast as possible. Within seconds, Sam had the crew loading the inflator fan and other little items into the truck. Minutes later, the balloon had become a dot in the sky and we were on the road, four vehicles full of us. We stopped at the interstate, watching the dot grow smaller by the minute.

"No sense in heading out yet," Sam said. "Until she starts back down we won't know how far away she'll be."

The balloon faded from sight. A tiny contrail formed as the craft entered the frigid air above twenty thousand feet. I thought of Rachael's fear of having to use the parachute and sent up a silent prayer for her safety. Sam became very quiet, never taking his eyes off the little wisp of white vapor.

"She's probably switched to the second tank now," he murmured. "Time, someone?"

Justin, who'd set his watch to keep track of elapsed time, read it off for Sam. I could almost see the calculations run through his head. Rachael could use about three-fourths of her fuel going up, reserving one fourth for coming back down and landing. Sam, of course, knew all this in gallons and elapsed time but only the news reporter was brave enough to interrupt him to ask about it. For his trouble, the man got a curt, "Later."

Radio static came over Sam's CB and he asked her to say again. More static.

"Let's move!" Sam shouted.

He and the crew piled into the pickup truck. Drake and I, Ron and the FAA guy belted ourselves into my Jeep, Drake at the wheel. The reporter in the news van tried to push ahead but eventually made himself content with staying behind us, followed by Grayson alone in his Mercedes. The man had been a pain from the start, and I wondered whether Ron was truly getting the promised fantastic mortgage rate in return for putting up with him.

Drake ably managed to stay behind Sam along the interstate. We pulled over from time to time, as the crew watched the balloon once again become a dot, then a shape. "There she is," Drake said, breaking into my thoughts.

I looked out to see *Lady Liberty's* beautiful red, white, and blue design, as she floated ahead of us, about a half mile away. Somehow, when I hadn't been paying attention, we'd exited off the interstate and were now on a paved two-lane heading south. Sam roared along the road, not wanting to lose sight of her at this crucial juncture. Drake barreled forward, staying with him until Sam whipped to the side of the road and stopped. Luckily, the reporter was also on top of things. I glanced back nervously to see him slam on the brakes just in time. Grayson wasn't so lucky. He ended up roaring past and stopping in front of Sam.

Rachael and her airy craft floated about fifty feet off the ground, east of our position. I wanted to edge her to the right, to make the balloon land on the road ahead of us, but unfortunately they don't work that way.

Sam rolled forward again, edging around Grayson's car, and cruised until someone pointed out a farm road. He took it and one of the crew guys jumped out to open the gate. He closed it again after the four vehicles had pulled through. Sam waited for him, then raced off in a cloud of dust. The balloon was to our right and the wind had begun to pick up. She wouldn't be able to hold it inflated on the ground.

We lost sight of Sam momentarily in the swirling dust. Seconds later, though, we caught a glimpse of the truck and saw Rachael's crew running across the open field. Sage and prairie grass tore at our legs as we ran toward the downed balloon.

Rachael greeted us with a huge grin and tried to hug everyone at once.

"Over thirty-four, maybe closer to thirty-five," she said breathlessly. "I'm sure I got at least that high."

John pulled the barograph from the basket, looking it over and flipping a switch to deactivate it. The little instrument had done its job, now it was up to the Fédération to certify the results. He carried it to the Jeep and set it carefully on the back seat just as Grayson pulled up in the car that hadn't been able to keep up with everyone else.

He joined his sister and seemed genuinely happy about her success. Champagne appeared from a cooler and spurted brilliantly for the news camera. Rachael got the traditional christening from the first bottle and conducted an amazingly composed interview with bubbles of foam dripping from her face.

I stepped away from the hubbub for a minute. Kevin, in jail and probably facing serious time, all in the name of taking the spotlight, and that only for a short time. Liz, who'd held the world altitude record for only a month. I wondered if she felt it was all worth it. And me. Drake and I had talked about managing to be home together more.

Drake and Ron, both with cameras, snapped about a zillion pictures; the crew guys took swigs of champagne from the bottle; Sam, ever watchful, made sure the equipment was all put away before he let anyone have much to drink.

Rachael came over to me once the news team had gotten enough for their thirty-second spot. She hugged me tightly and whispered, "Thanks, Charlie. You know I wouldn't have been here today to do this, except for you."

I, of course, teared up and we held our embrace a moment before each of us could take a deep breath.

"I started out doing this," she said, "because it was a challenge, like climbing the Colorado fourteeners, something I thought I'd enjoy just for the pleasure of doing it. But you know, things changed along the way. Gray started that stupid publicity campaign and I began to hate the whole project.

Didn't even want to do it for awhile. Then the threats. Part of me wanted to quit—several times, in fact. But a big part of me knew that I couldn't give in. You can't let bullies call the shots and that's just what I would have been doing. They threaten me, I quit. Give them just what they wanted?"

"You'd never do that," I said. "Does it sound too corny to say that you have that all-American spirit?"

She chuckled. "I don't mind if it's corny."

A car pulled up just then. Grayson's Mercedes. None of us realized that he'd left. He stopped behind my Jeep and Bill Fairfield stepped out. Rachael tensed.

He walked over to us, his eyes steady on her.

"Shall I…" I began.

"No, stay," she whispered. "I'm not ready to be alone with him."

"Rachael, I can't expect everything to suddenly be all right between us," he said. His voice was surprisingly quiet. I think she'd expected a politician's bold oration. "I just wanted to come out and tell you how proud I am. I know I never gave you a fair shake as a kid. I didn't see you as ambitious enough, wanting to achieve enough. And I should have paid more attention to the things that were going on with your mother. Maybe I could have protected you."

She started to say something but he stepped in.

"I was wrong."

After "I love you" those are probably the most powerful words a person can say. Harder to say, in fact, than words of love. I turned away to give them a private moment but Rachael gripped my hand.

"Yes, Dad, you were. I never had your ambitions and I still don't. This wasn't something I did for the fame." She pointedly looked at her brother. "I did this for me. Just to know that I could."

Bill looked like he wanted to come closer, to hug his daughter, but he hesitated.

"I was wrong about a lot of other things, too. When you were a kid." He couldn't meet her eyes. "I only thought about my own goals and I've been so sorry I didn't see beyond them. I didn't treat anyone well, including your mother. It's largely my fault that she ended the way she did."

Rachael simply nodded. Grayson stood stock still, disbelief registering on his face. Much family history was being clarified in these moments and he clearly was having a hard time taking it all in. I felt decidedly out of place but Rachael kept her grip on my hand until Drake walked up.

"Trouble?" he asked.

Rachael smiled up at him with the grace of an angel. She took my hand and placed it in his. "No, no trouble. In fact a lot of old trouble has gotten better."

As Drake and I turned to walk away, I heard Rachael's voice. "Better, I said. Not gone, not perfect. But maybe we can work on that. I misjudged you in a lot of ways, too." I sneaked a peek backward to see that she'd placed her hand on her father's shoulder.

It had been a memorable month, in all ways.